Out at Home

Out at Home

GARY POMERANZ

HOUGHTON MIFFLIN COMPANY · BOSTON

1985

Copyright © 1985 by Gary Pomeranz

Library of Congress Cataloging in Publication Data

Pomeranz, Gary.
Out at home.

I. Title.
PS3566.O545O9   1985   813'.54   84–27760
ISBN 0–395–36980–0

Printed in the United States of America

P 10 9 8 7 6 5 4 3 2 1

The author is grateful for permission to quote
from the song "You Belong to Me" by Pee Wee
King, Redd Stewart, and Chilton Price.
Copyright © 1952 Ridgeway Music, Inc.
International copyright secured. All rights
reserved.

To Gloria Norris Pomeranz

AUTHOR'S NOTE

Out at Home seeks to re-create Chicago during the nineteen fifties, when the inelegance that has always been part of the city's style and enduring charm hadn't yet conceded anything to modern life. Husbands still took their wives to nightclubs. Guys still took their best gals dancing. Most ballplayers worked for peanuts and caroused every night. Though there was no Spieler, no Elmo, no Pelham or Bobby Wentworth, and certainly no Cub team that plotted anything, the sense of time and place and Weasel Arnie's story are what really matter. As they say these days, enjoy!

Part One

CHAPTER

1

NEAR THE END of my sophomore year, I was kicked out of the University of Illinois. They got me for making book on Big Ten basketball games. "Weasel" Arnie Barzov was in plenty hot water, way over my five-foot, four inches. Doing time wasn't exactly your everyday thing for a Jewish kid from a good home on Lincoln Park West, but the definite possibility was facing me. All the same, I figured my grandfather would somehow get me out of it.

Max sent down a sharp La Salle Street lawyer to represent me. The sharpie got the school officials to back off going to the local district attorney. The way he put it to them was that there were certain things that might lead people to believe I hadn't limited my operation to students on the Champaign-Urbana campus and was doing business with gamblers all over the country, might've even approached certain key Illini players to shave points. *This* could open a can of worms that would stink even louder and longer than the great City College scandal a while back that stayed in the headlines all over the country for a long time. Much better for everyone concerned, he suggested, for the story to stop right now. If *they* would keep their mouths shut, *I* would keep mine. It was a shrewd

move and it cut the deal. I would drop out of school because I was homesick and no mention of gambling activi-
ties would go on my record. The sharpie had really saved
my ass, and no question I was grateful. The funny thing,
though, was that I didn't *feel* all that relieved. It was like
getting saved didn't have all that much to do with the reasons I started gambling in the first place.

I was thinking about what I was going to tell people as
I drove back to Chicago, particularly Myrna and Max.
Should I try to explain to my gorgeous nutty mother, my
Abbe Lane look-alike? I could see her in one of her figure-
clinging party dresses, with her dark brown hair freshly
waved at the beauty parlor. Just maybe, if I got home
early enough, she'd have a little time to talk to me before
she went out with Eagle-Nose or whatever asshole she was
going out with tonight. Very likely she'd sit next to me on
the sofa and hold my hands in hers and look at me with
those big brown eyes filled with concern. Her Chanel No. 5
would hit me like a breeze off Lake Michigan and distract
me from listening and I'd look into those beautiful eyes
and be hypnotized and wonder again, for maybe the mil-
lionth time, why it was that my brother Dan got to look
more like her and I got to look more like Zach. And then
I'd pick up her babble (she didn't *sound* like Abbe Lane):
"Oh Arnold, I just know somebody has been having a terrible influence on you. What kind of people have you been
keeping company with down there? I just don't know
what gets into you sometimes. You act as though you
don't have every advantage in life and that I don't care
about you. Why do you want to make it seem as though I
don't love you? Tell me what made you do such a thing?"

It would stop me cold. Should I try, one more time, to
get through to her? Should I take a chance and say,
"*Myrna,* if you close your eyes and make two fists and
concentrate on what I'm going to say, I'll do my best to

explain"? But the thought of her confusing the issue one more time — always making it seem like the only important thing was that *I* was failing her — was too much for me. I wasn't going to be suckered into letting her do it again, I couldn't bear being made a fool of this time. This was serious stuff I wanted to unload, about everyone's relationship to everyone in our family. But every time a discussion with Myrna about our family got serious, the quicker she'd fade away. God forbid she should ever have to hear anything that might make *her* responsible for anything! Those brown eyes would go blank and she'd get up and look in the mirror and start smoothing her perfect hair. She'd say something like, "But now that it's over, Arnold, you can start doing all the right things again. I think you should call Jules tomorrow. He says he's got a job for you managing one of his awning outlets. Remember, you've still got the rest of your life to make us all proud of you." And then she'd probably snap on the idiot box and watch a game show or read a movie magazine until her date showed up. I wouldn't even bother to tell her that I didn't want Eagle-Nose's lousy job.

Then there was Max, my millionaire grandfather, to deal with. He was such a hypocrite! He'd like you to believe all his years of hard work and his brains had paid off in his success. Ha! The truth of the matter was that Max was just plain lucky to be in the right place at the right time to fall into big bucks. At the start of World War Two he was a smalltime horse-and-buggy scrap dealer who happened to hold an option on a special kind of metal that was needed to build firing pins in artillery guns and *this* was how he made it! He may have been chairman of the board of Belson Metal Supplies, but he was still a stingy grasping pushcart dealer who could squeeze your feelings the same way he squeezed a nickel and made you feel obligated for everything he gave. He'd be mystified by what

I'd done, since he was always telling me *he* could give me all the money I'd ever need.

How could I explain that the reason I booked downstate had nothing to do with money? No one I knew would understand. Not Max. Not Zach who called regularly from out of the west to find out if I needed anything extra to get through school. Not my big-deal writer brother who did the same from out of the east. They all knew my other grandfather, when he died, left me enough to pay my way through school. They all knew I'd made enough in card games in high school to pay my own way. So screw it. I wasn't going to try to explain my feelings. It was too frustrating, other people wanting me to say and do things that only pleased them and didn't do one single thing for me. When was someone going to try to understand me?

I was driving through the corn fields south of Chicago when I did a strange thing. I pulled over to the side of the road and got out of my car and crossed the highway. It was getting dark and the sun was setting over this perfectly flat land, as far as I could see. I felt the darkness steal over me and a sense of being all alone in the world rose in my heart. In the beginning it felt good to be all alone, it was so peaceful not wanting to explain anything to anyone. But after a while all the peace got disturbing, then frightening, and I heard myself cry out to the all-at-once blazing sky: *"Why did you guys run out on us? You'd think Myrna and me were the strong ones, that you were the ones that needed help the most. Well, we're not the strong ones. You were too concerned with yourselves, you didn't want to bother with how screwed up we were. I can't play the violin and I can't write books and I'm short and I look like a weasel and I can't be someone that other people want me to be if I can't be someone to me. I can't give Myrna back what you guys took away from her. You screwed her head up real good, made it impossible for me to reach her. And she hasn't got the guts to reach out to me. Couldn't you've figured it would happen when you pulled out on her, left me holding the bag? But okay, you got out. Good luck and God bless you. Who needs your phone calls? Who needs your money? The both of you can stick it as far as I'm concerned. Screw the both of you. I'll figure out the answers for myself."*

I went back to my car and drove fast back to Chicago. Earlier in the day, I'd talked to Pigeon-Face Pinsky, Eagle-Nose's son, and I knew there was a poker game tonight at Pigeon-Face's place. Now I called him from the first gas station and said to hold a spot for me. I'd skip having to deal with Myrna before her date and be instead with guys who would respect me and be in awe of what I'd done. My answer to these guys, when they asked me why I did it, would be to say casually, without making a big deal of it, as the cards were dealt around the table, that I liked the action, the thrill of doing something exciting and outside the law and getting away with it. Then I'd coolly cut it off with a funny wrap-up, like telling them my reason for leaving school was being homesick. That one was pretty funny.

I'd get home when the dawn was breaking and miss Myrna, who'd already be asleep. I'd set the alarm for noon and still miss her, 'cause she'd still be sleeping. I'd have brunch at Maury's Delicatessen on Diversey and have time to study the pitchers for all the ballgames being played tomorrow and call my bookie. By one-thirty I'd be in a box seat at Wrigley Field to watch the Cubs–Cards game. The Cubs were showing signs of being pennant contenders this year and that would be enough for a while to help me forget what happened downstate.

2

A MONTH WENT BY. Between card games and ballgames and the track, I was doing okay, had made more than five grand since I'd come back to Chicago. It was funny to think I was doing much better than a lot of the old men of a lot of my friends were doing in their regular jobs and businesses. These were guys who were doing real well by the standards of the money-conscious crowd I grew up with, but it didn't please me a bit.

Around two A.M., I was sitting in Candido's, a bright, busy restaurant on Rush Street. It was filled with night people: customers and workers and entertainers and musicians from all the hotels and nightclubs and bars in the area; cops and crooks and sports and studs; all kinds of hard- and soft-faced pretty boys and girls; shadowy high- and low-life figures that inhabited the neighborhood. This was a world of gold and glitter and sleaze. The great wealth of the great houses and apartments of the streets between Dearborn Parkway and the Outer Drive rubbed shoulders with the low-class drifters' world around Clark Street. I was watching the people come and go, was thinking about the Cubs, who were hanging in in what was shaping up as an exciting four-team race. They were in fourth place but only four games behind the leader.

The Cubs hadn't won a pennant since '45, with a war-time ballclub, when the best major-league players were still in service. The best Cub players then were Phil Cavaretta and Bill Nicholson and Stan Hack and Andy Pafko. In a Series that one Chicago sports writer predicted neither team could win, the Cubs lost in seven games to the Detroit Tigers. I only dimly remembered that time.

It was after the war, I was around ten, when I began to follow the Cubs. It was also the time when a great lumber fortune replaced a great chewing-gum fortune when Pelham Wentworth bought the Cubs from Phillip Wrigley. It always seemed to me just like the two of them got together in the locker room of their exclusive country club and Wrigley sold Wentworth his old golf bag with all his old clubs in it, and Wentworth went right out and started to play with them and didn't improve his game a bit.

To his credit, Wentworth was a guy willing to spend his money to improve the team, but keeping the same dumb Cub management that Wrigley had stayed with for years did him in from the start. The Cubs spent a lot on a farm system and tried to make smart deals, but nothing ever seemed to work out. Cavaretta and Nicholson and Hack and Pafko stayed around for years and the parade of other faces included Don Johnson and Lenny Merrullo and Peanuts Lowery and Dom Dallesandro and Emil Verban and Bob Rush and Johnny Schmitz and Roy Smalley and Ransom Jackson and Bill Serena and Hal Jeffcoat and Eddie Miksis, and they were really lousy teams. After '46, when they finished third, I spent all the years till I was eighteen rooting for a club that never once made it to the first division, was dead last more times than I like to remember. Probably the most exciting thing that happened was when Eddie Waitkus, the Cubs' ex-first sacker, who'd been traded to the Phillies, was shot at the Edgewater Beach Hotel by a woman who said he jilted her.

It was hard for me like it must've been hard for every other diehard Cub fan ever to imagine the team as a winner. The saving thing was that you could never doubt that old Pel Wentworth always kept trying. He'd take full-page ads in the sports pages to apologize for the team's failures. His disappointment was clear to see in the interviews he gave on radio and television and the comments he made in the papers. Every Cub fan shared his sense of failure. He never let us feel too comfortable with losing as a way of life, that it was all totally hopeless. He was an inspiration to keep praying and paying our way in to Wrigley Field.

But it wasn't that way with his son. When Pelham Wentworth died a few years ago, and his second wife soon after him, control of the team passed to A. Robert Wentworth, his son by his first wife, and Bobby was as tight as a virgin's crotch in running the team. He didn't give a damn about the Cubs and regularly said things in the papers that showed he was ashamed of inheriting something so raunchy as a baseball team. He freely admitted he'd never attended a Cub game in his life. Polo playing and breeding horses and drinking martinis at garden parties that were photographed for the *Tribune* society page were more his speed. He would've sold the team the day he got it if the conditions of old-man Wentworth's will didn't prevent him without the total consent of his younger stepbrother and stepsister. They shared in the ownership and loved the team as much as old Wentworth and his second wife, their mother, had. His philosophy was, as long as the fans were still coming out, it was their problem; he'd continue to run the team on a shoestring. But the Cubs went quickly from bad to worse, attendance sank to an all-time low, and something big had to be done to keep the Wentworth family from finally losing a lot of money. That's why last year Bobby consented to hire Seymour "the Spieler" La Chance.

It shocked the town at first that he would ever hire a flashy guy like Spieler. All the Cubs managers for the last twenty years had been long-time Cub ballplayers who'd stayed on in the organization. But Spieler had a well-earned reputation as a fast-talking, high-living, publicity-grabbing, two-fisted, controversial figure. He was a sporter of beautiful women, a crony of movie stars and entertainers and hoodlums and gamblers and other professional jocks and society types who were always getting their names in gossip columns. He was so much like Bobby himself in a different-class way that you'd think Bobby wouldn't want him around to upstage his act. All the same, just like the rest of us, Bobby hoped that Spieler's colorful style would give the Cubs a jolt. Especially since it was rumored that the three-year contract Spieler had extracted from him was worth a pretty penny and made Spieler the best-paid manager in the majors.

Spieler had good reason to demand top dollar. He'd managed in the majors for eleven years with the Cards and the Braves and won a pennant with each of them. He had a reputation as a winner. Eight times his teams had finished in the first division and there was something about him when it really counted in the heat of a pennant race that brought out the best in his players, got them to play over their heads as a team. Both of his pennants had been with clubs that didn't have great talent, but it was still surprising when suddenly, during the middle of last season, his Cub team, seemingly doomed to the second division, jelled and got hot and rose from last to third in July and August. It wasn't his fault that the team just didn't have the guns during the September run — Cub fans were just grateful for the unknown thrill of winning — and everyone was saying, Wait till *next* year! During the off-season, the Cubs made a couple of trades and the team really seemed like a contender. Add to it that Spieler, since he'd come to Chicago, was more or less on his best behavior — no paternity suits or brawls in bars or feuds with players or reporters like he'd had in the past — and he said the reason was, in an interview with columnist Mike Ginsburg in the *Sun-Times*, that recently turning fifty had mellowed him and made him rethink his values. So everything seemed right for the coming season.

But as any baseball fan knows for sure, the game is full of surprises and the team got off to a bad start this year through no fault of Spieler's. The problem was that Bobby Wentworth went off and got himself into a Spieler-like jam. It came out in the papers — even the staid *Tribune* couldn't resist making it a front-page story — that Bobby's skeet-shooting wife was suing him for divorce for carrying on with a trashy dancer, a Chez Paree Adorable no less. Bobby hardly had time to shit before he found out that she'd hired a couple of matrimonial vultures to really take him to the cleaners.

All this happened over the winter while a lot of Cub players were trying to negotiate for decent raises on account of the good seasons they'd had. The most determined player of all was the great center-fielder, Elmo Speakes, who'd been magnificent. After playing a decade in the Negro leagues, Elmo had finally broken into the majors in the late forties, after Jackie Robinson and Larry Doby, and seeing his best years and all their earning power taken away from him had made him bitter and outspoken about it. He was determined to hold out all season if he didn't get the dough he wanted. Bobby Wentworth, on the other hand, was equally determined not to let go of a nickel if he could help it because his old man's will had stipulated that the basic business — Wentworth Lumber — could never be sued for Bobby's personal problems. Everything he coughed up to his wife would have to come from Cub coffers.

True to their code of never revealing the inside dirt of

professional sports in the city, the Chicago papers didn't tell how Bobby eventually stemmed the tide. There were rumors and stories in bars on the near north side that Bobby had called in Spieler and asked him to play a strong hand in quelling the revolt and, before spring training was over, all but one of the Cub players had backed down from their demands and accepted what management offered them. It was Elmo Speakes who held out the longest, to the end of May, and the Cubs got off to a terrible start largely because of his absence. But once he returned, and was slugging again despite his bitterness, the team perked up and returned to its winning ways. Spieler's magic was working again. No other manager could've turned a team around so quickly.

Could the Cubs win the pennant? Could Spieler keep pulling rabbits out of his hat with his never-say-die confidence and enthusiasm? Maybe. But then any fool knew that you couldn't count on Spieler to do it all. He was, after all, no better than his players. And like his past pennant winners, this Cub team wasn't loaded with stars. With the exception of Elmo and Elijah St. John, the great right-hander from the Dominican Republic, the other Cub players were going to have to have, all together, their best seasons in the majors. Whatever the odds, I wanted to believe that Spieler and the Cubs could pull it off, that Spieler would finally get what he himself said over and over again in the papers was the only thing he still wanted from baseball, to win the World Series. Whatever the odds, win or lose, right down to the wire when every pitch counted, I would've bet my bottom dollar that they could do it.

A beautiful Oriental girl came into Candido's. She was in her early twenties, taller than most Orientals, and she had straight silky hair turned under at her shoulders. Her eyes fascinated me. They were almond-shaped and came right out of her sharp high cheekbones at a down-turned angle. She had perfect ivory-yellow skin. Her name was Kim and I'd seen her in here at least a dozen times and not once had she ever smiled. A constant scowl was on her face. I knew her name because I'd heard some guys talking to her once, in a booth next to mine. I'd gotten the impression from that conversation that Kim was a high-priced hooker. It was just an impression, nothing more, I had no proof or anything, but something about the way she handled herself, a certain been-around air, her shiny expensive dress under her trench coat, the scorn in her eyes as she coolly brushed off the jerks, all these things added to it. The fact that she might be a hooker both attracted and disturbed me. The fact was, I was infatuated with Kim, came to Candido's every night to look for her and talk to her, but didn't have the nerve to introduce myself. What could this tall never-smiling been-around beauty possibly say to little Weasel Arnie?

Tonight, though, I was determined to make a break-through. I'd had a great day betting, had won on all eight games in both leagues, and psyched myself up to approach her. What I planned to do was to go up to her booth and say something like: "Say, we've been seeing each other around a lot lately. You're a very attractive lady and I'd like to know you better. My name is Arnie Barzov and how about having something to eat with me." My smooth manner and my expensive Baskin's suit would impress her that I was someone she ought to know. After I'd slipped into her booth and we were chatting easily, I'd suggest we should have dinner tonight at a fine restaurant, like the Buttery at the Ambassador West. This way she'd catch on fast that I was a big spender. And while she found that out, maybe she'd also catch on that I was a nice guy.

Luck was with me as she sat down in the booth right in

front of me. She glanced at me and her nostrils flared with anger. Her look went right through me, as though I wasn't there. My confidence melted to my toes and I stared down at my morning *Sun-Times*.

It was open to the sports pages and I tried to concentrate on today's games and the starting pitchers. It was another full schedule, with hot teams and good pitchers going against one another — Robin Roberts against Warren Spahn, Whitey Ford against Billy Pierce, Ewell Blackwell against Sal Maglie — and it wasn't going to be easy to make a buck today. But it was no use. Every few seconds I kept looking up at Kim's beautiful face in profile, kept seeing that angry look that both saw and didn't see me.

I noticed the kid sitting in the booth across from me. He'd come in a few seconds after Kim, was about my age, maybe a little older, an obvious hayseed judging by his frayed paperboard suitcase and old worn suit that didn't fit right. He was real tall and gawky, all arms and legs and elbows and knees, and he leaned back and sprawled out at an angle under the table, rested his head on the cushioned top of the booth and stared wearily at the fancy chandelier above him, as though its odd design of metal birds reminded him of his problem. He was just one more bird from the sticks himself come to try his hand in Chicago and finding out it was a lot of trouble. Suddenly he sat up and stared at Kim.

I heard myself say, with a smirk, "Would you like me to introduce you?"

The kid turned his head and looked at me, as though he was trying to decide if I was kidding him. He said, in a thick southern drawl, "I'd be mighty obliged if you'd do that for me. I got something pretty important to ask her."

"Sure thing," I said. "What's your name, so I can introduce you."

"James Lee Jackson. But people call me Jamey. Tell her I don't mean her no harm. I just wanna ask her about someone. I got an idea she may know a friend of mine."

Now I realized what I'd done. I started sweating inside my clothes. And Kim was scowling at both of us. She'd overheard us and was wondering if I had the nerve to go through with it, so I had no choice but to go through with it.

"Hi...," I said, smiling nervously, sliding out of my seat and going up to her. "My, uh, friend here...Jamey Lee Jackson...would like to talk to you for a minute, if you don't mind...He's, uh, got a few questions he'd like to ask you...uh, about...a lost friend of his...or something like that."

Kim's glare moved from me to the hayseed. Her mouth got tighter. "You the guy who calling me before?" she demanded.

Jamey's Adam's apple bobbed up and down; he bravely nodded.

"Now you follow me too."

"No, no, you shouldn't think that. That's not really what I'm doing."

"I tell you all I know. What else you want from me?"

"I just want to ask you a few more things, please. You didn't give me much time on the phone. It's real important to me."

I had to admit there was something appealing about the hayseed. He made you feel for him. He wasn't a bad-looking guy either. Regular features. Deep-set intense eyes in a thin sincere face. Cowlicks in his hair. Anyway, Kim didn't shoot him down. Instead, she stared hard at him. "Hokay," she said irritably, "make it snappy."

I wasn't about to miss this. As Jamey slid in on one side of her circular booth, I slid in on the other. He took a white envelope from inside his suit jacket and removed a photograph from it. He placed it in front of Kim.

It was a picture of a pretty girl in her twenties with long wild ringletted hair. She was sitting on the top rail of a wood fence, playing a guitar. The fence ran around the front lawn of an old single-story frame house. Beyond the house, you could see hills with lots of tall piny trees.

"You gotta remember," Jamey said, "the picture was taken a few years ago. She probably don't look so much like that now."

Kim nodded. "Yeah, she could be one I met," she said, her eyes screwing up in thought. "But like I told you, it only once, maybe eight, nine month ago. I never see her again."

"Are you *sure* she didn't tell you where she moved to? Any little thing could be so important. You're my only lead right now. If you can't help me, I've got to check out one hundred twenty-three names in the Chicago phone book that could be her, and I've got no idea where to begin. I'm not even sure if she's using the same name anymore. So I'd surely be obliged if you'd think on it."

Kim pursed her lips even tighter. In spite of her reluctance, she was thinking. "What her name right now?"

"It's either Angie Bishop or Angie Jackson. She had a bad marriage as a teen-ager to a guy named Bishop. She's been divorced for years, but she kept his name 'cause she started singing with it. Then I heard from her she was using Jackson in Chicago. Then I heard from her she was back to Bishop. So I don't know for sure."

Kim looked at the photograph again. "You mean she sing this hillybilly stuff?" Kim's mouth curled with disapproval of the guitar.

"No, I don't believe Angie wanted to do that. She wants to sing in nightclubs, like the Blue Room of the Roosevelt Hotel in New Orleans. She used to listen to that all the time on the radio. She likes singers like June Christy and Peggy Lee, you ever heard of them? But who knows what she's had to do for a living."

"Yeah," Kim said, "who know?" She fell into thought for maybe thirty seconds, then looked at Jamey. "I think maybe I remember something. That one time she came back to pick up luggage. Maybe she tell me something about going with airline pilot. It seem like his name Harry and he got wife, kids in Kansas City but living with Angie out near airport somewhere. I don't know if she was singing. I think that maybe all she tell me." Kim thought hard a few moments longer. "Yeah, that all I know."

"Well, my goodness, it's a lot more than I knew before I met you. I really don't know how to thank you, Miss —"

Kim nodded once, abruptly cutting Jamey off and not giving her name. "Eight, nine month is long time in Chicago. Lot things happen. You better no waste time. Better start looking right away."

Jamey's brow knitted. "Yeah," he sighed, his enthusiasm dampened. "Now that you put it that way, I'm still not sure how to begin."

"You go out to the airport and check all the people at all the flight counters. You start asking them about a pilot named Harry, with a wife and kids in Kansas City, who may or may not still be living out near the airport. That's what you do for a starter." It was me talking.

"And where's the airport?" asked Jamey.

"It's a pretty good distance. 4800 West, 5500 South. You can drive there in about an hour."

"I don't have a car. I just got to Chicago last night. You won't believe how many times I got lost going all over today."

The last thing I wanted was to go on a wild goose chase with this hayseed looking for his girl friend. It didn't seem likely he'd find her. At the same time, he did need some help...

"You sure this girl *want* you to find her?" Kim asked, suddenly curious.

"I'm not sure at all," Jamey said honestly. "But she's not my girl friend. She's my sister. We used to be real close and I gotta find out if we still are. I gotta know what I mean to her."

A strange silence fell over the three of us.

Kim angrily broke the silence. "So why the fuck you no offer to drive him?" She glared fiercely at me.

"I was just going to," I said, embarrassed.

"You better." Scowling, she got up and left.

"My goodness but she's a strange one," Jamey said. "Didn't even want to be thanked."

I had to agree that Kim was awful strange.

CHAPTER

3

MAYBE I'D AGREED to drive Jamey to the airport, but I'd be damned if I was going to miss the Cubs–Pirates game in the afternoon, back on the north side. For that reason — also that he had less than a hundred bucks and nowhere to spend the night — I asked him to stay with me. I'd moved into an apartment on North State Parkway, just a few blocks away from Candido's. This way we could get started early. I told him if we got any leads at Midway, we'd check them out right after the game. He keyed in to me perfectly. "I'm a big baseball fan myself," he said agreeably. "If we don't find out somethin' bad, maybe I'll go with you. It'd be my first major-league game."

Jamey fell into a sound sleep on the sofa right away. The next morning, after I'd made some phone calls, we went to a delicatessen, got sweet rolls and coffee, and ate as we drove west on Division, through the industrial section near the Chicago River. Jamey didn't have much to say this morning, like the neighborhood was kind of grim. He was probably thinking about his sister and the long trip he'd made to find her. He'd told me he was from Alcoma, Mississippi, population 73, about 100 miles south of Memphis, Tennessee, but he'd been to Memphis no more than twenty times in his life. And compared to Chicago, Memphis was like Alcoma. I was curious to find out something about his sister and why she'd run away, but figured this wasn't the time. Anyway, Jamey began to look around in awe at all the sights as I turned onto Ogden Avenue and headed southwest through the heart of the city.

I didn't mind that he was quiet. I wanted to think some more about how weird it was that Kim could so easily command me to help this kid. And when I stopped thinking about that, like Jamey, I started to look around at the sights. More times than I could count since my high school days, whenever the other members of my family were squabbling and I had to get away from them, or just the times when I was blue and didn't want to be with anyone, I would get in my car and drive all over Chicago.

The big main street we were on, Ogden Avenue, was one of my favorites. It cut diagonally through the basic north-south, east-west grid of the city and the impressions you got were spread out and striking, it was like looking through a kaleidoscope where the same things are endlessly repeated in different ways. Neighborhoods rolled past with their busy shopping areas and endless residential streets with rows of identical houses stretching for blocks and blocks. So would big green city parks with their statues of Polish heroes. So would dozens of different kinds of churches with wildly designed tall towers and turrets and spires reaching up into the sky. So would constant traffic and throngs of people of every race and color. As I was enjoying all this one more time, it came back to me that my brother, Dan, who had studied to be a painter at the Art Institute, also liked to drive around and look at the city, and this killed my pleasure. It made me angrier the more I thought about it, to be like him in any way. I tried to get it out of my head, and asked Jamey who his favorite team was.

"The St. Louis Cardinals. I pick up all their games on

short-wave radio down in Missippi. I believe they're gonna take the pennant."

"*I* don't think so!"

"Sure. You think the Cubs will win."

"Damn right! I *know* they'll win."

Jamey shrugged and smiled out his window.

"What makes you so sure the Cards will win?"

"Arnie, you're being such a help, I don't want to argue about who's going to win the pennant."

"I'm *not* looking to argue with you."

"Well, you're sure acting like it."

"Well, you're *wrong!* I make money betting on baseball games. I want to hear your reasons. Just maybe," I chided him, "you'll tell me something I don't know."

Jamey was surprised. "You mean that's why you were studying the schedule in the paper last night? And that's why you were talking about the games over the phone this morning?"

"You got it, friend. I was placing bets with my bookie."

"I'll be. I don't know if I'm gonna like everything that goes on in this city."

"What's wrong with betting on baseball games? Or football games or boxing? A lot of people do."

"I guess it just doesn't seem right to me. I can't explain exactly. It's like ... something special is taken away from the game ... something special that you can't get from anything else but the game. Baseball gets like every other thing in the world. You know what I mean?"

"I know what you mean. And I think you're a jerk if you look on sports as having some kind of magic about them. I'm telling you because I happen to know a little bit about the way it is. Money and betting are part of sports. You're being soft in the head if you think different."

Jamey got depressed. "You mean you never get soft in the head when you're betting?"

I thought about it. "Well, sometimes, I guess. Only where the Cubs are concerned, to tell the truth. I bet on them because I *want* them to win. But nothing else, I assure you."

Jamey grinned. "So you see," he said, "you really have some of the same feelings as me. You think about the Cubs as something special, something that's different from the rest of life. If they win the pennant, it's gonna give you a pleasure you can't get from anything else."

This guy was pretty annoying with his know-it-all smile and his cocksure answers, but I couldn't deny that he was right. I didn't say anything. Looked straight ahead for a few minutes. Then I let him have it. If he was so damn smart about baseball, which was the impression he gave, I wanted to know what he thought about the bets I'd made this morning.

It turned out Jamey *was* pretty smart. He agreed with my reasons for seven of my eight choices and actually got me to thinking about changing my bet on the Boston–Kansas City game. I asked him again why he thought the Cards were a better team than the Cubs this year.

Suddenly Jamey wasn't shy at all in talking about baseball. Now he was glad to say a lot of things. Though the Cubs' first three starting pitchers were probably better than the Cards', he said with total conviction, the Cards had more depth in starters and their relief pitchers were better than the Cubs'. "Jimmy Weatherford is the only relief pitcher the Cubs can rely on, but he's going to be worn out pretty soon at the rate he's going. Been out of the bullpen five straight times in five days, in case you haven't noticed. And there's not a soul to back him up."

"What about Randy Dodds?" I shot back. "He had a good year with the Cubs last year and a lot of great ones with the Cards. You should remember that."

"Randy Dodds' best days are behind him."

"What makes you say that? He and Jimmy Weatherford were one of the best relief teams in the majors last year."

"Until Randy started getting bombed in the stretch drive in September. Same thing so far this season. And you know why it's happened? Because Randy's thirty-six years old, that's why. Face it, Arnie. He's finished. That's the reason Spieler La Chance only uses him to mop up these days."

I didn't want to admit it, but Jamey was right. Randy Dodds was one of my favorite players, a never-give-up competitor who'd come in time after time last season in the middle innings and held the other team in check until the Cubs rallied and won and Jimmy Weatherford finished up. The funny thing about Randy was that on the mound he was as mean-looking as anyone you'd want to see, with the lanky raw-boned look of a cowboy; but in person there was something sweet and sad about him. I went to the opening of a shoe store he was appearing at and asked him what it was like being in the major leagues. He thought about it and said, "Well, I'll tell ya, kid. Life in the majors is like a train ride on the Twentieth Century Limited. You never want to reach the stop where you have to get off."

"It's just a slump," I insisted. "He's had them before and come out of them better than ever."

Jamey shook his head.

"Spieler will find a way to jack him up," I said.

"I wouldn't count on Spieler and his tricks too much this year."

"I guess you don't think much of him either."

Jamey grinned with tight lips, as though he knew something about Spieler that no one else knew.

"I'm asking you what you think is wrong with Spieler."

Jamey fidgeted before answering. "Well, don't blame me if you don't like what you hear. I think Spieler La

Chance is a showoff and a glory hog. He wants to take all the credit for the success of a team. I remember when he was managing the Cards a few years ago. The year after they won the pennant, the team fell apart. Spieler got into a lot of squabbles with different players. He started quarreling with the general manager. He started going with some woman and lost interest in the team. He didn't even show up for a couple of ballgames and it was later found out he was at the racetrack."

I grinned at Spieler's escapades. I really regretted that he wasn't still carrying on in Chicago. I said to Jamey, "I don't think you like Spieler because he's his own man, because he breaks all the rules you want to believe in."

"Maybe you're right, Arnie. I don't like Spieler because guys like him give baseball a bad name."

"Well. I don't agree with you. As a matter of fact, I wish you'd just shut up about him. I admire him very much."

Jamey shook his head, as though he felt sorry for me.

We were both silent as I drove. Jamey had upset me. I didn't want to admit there could be a lot of truth to the things he said.

I turned south on Cicero Avenue and told Jamey we were getting close to the airport. His face got tense and I decided it still wasn't the time to ask him about his sister. Instead, I told him we should be just as determined in questioning the flight clerks as he was in finding Kim. I didn't think we had much chance of finding Angie, but I didn't want to tell him that.

We got lucky, though. At our second flight desk, a TWA clerk named Walter called over a hostess named Marie and asked him if a pilot named Harry Wardlaw hadn't been going a while back with a singer with reddish-brown hair who seemed to resemble Angie in the picture that Jamey showed him.

He passed the picture to Marie and she agreed that the

person going with Harry Wardlaw could be the woman in the picture, but she and Harry had broken up sometime last year. And she knew for a fact that Harry wasn't making any runs through Chicago anymore.

I asked her if there was any way we could find out where he lived. Marie said that as far as she could recall, when Harry was in Chicago, he rented a house somewhere not far from the airport. She thought a moment, then her face brightened and she said that the thing we ought to do was go over to the TWA administration office — she pointed the way — and ask if they still had his Chicago address on file. Even if Harry hadn't lived here for a while, they sometimes took their time about bringing things up to date.

And it worked! In his file, Harry Wardlaw's old address was listed at a street only a couple of miles from the airport.

Jamey and I dashed through the terminal and out to the parking lot to my car. We got there in ten minutes. It was five after twelve when we parked at the end of the block. Small one-story frame bungalows with poor paint jobs and a run-down look lined the block on both sides. The lawns had bare spots and were overgrown with weeds. A few weak elms were here and there. The whole block had a transient air, as though pilots and stewardesses might be the only renters.

Harry Wardlaw's place was in the middle of the block. We looked through the gauzy curtains in the front windows to see if anyone was home. A woman was pacing back and forth across the living room.

"I can't quite make out her face," Jamey said. "There's a piano against the wall."

We moved to the small front porch at the side of the house. Jamey looked at me before ringing the bell. "Arnie ... do you mind standing back a little ... so I can talk to her alone?"

"No problem."

Jamey pressed the buzzer. There was no answer for maybe thirty seconds. He pressed the buzzer again, longer ... It was still silent. A third firm ring. After which a voice called out: "Is that you, Johnny?" It was a strangely bold and fearful tone.

"It's not Johnny, Angie. It's Jamey. I come to be with you."

Another silence. Jamey was about to call out again when we heard the chain lock being removed and the door opened. Jamey's sister stood there staring at him.

She was an awfully striking girl, had Jamey's deep-set eyes and strong features and swirls of reddish-brown hair and a redhead's fair complexion. She was wearing a matching skirt and jacket and seemed like she was getting ready to go somewhere.

Her face showed different feelings about seeing Jamey. She was surprised. She was glad. She wasn't glad. Her eyes got sad and her mouth got firm.

"Aren't you happy to see me, Angie? I didn't come to be no trouble. I didn't come to stay a long time."

Angie couldn't help but look tearful. She put out her arms and drew Jamey down toward her and he had to bend awkwardly to be in her embrace. Over his shoulder, though, her eyes nearly closed and her look got pained, as though it was her bad luck that her brother should drop into her life at exactly the wrong time. But she wouldn't tell him. "Oh Jamey," she said, reassuring him, "of course I'm happy to see you. This is a wonderful surprise." As she held him, her eyes scanned the street nervously.

She saw me. Was startled and drew back from Jamey. "Who's he?" she wanted to know.

"He's my friend, Arnie. Don't be afraid of him. I would've never found you without him."

She forced a smile. "Well, both of you come in," she said with phony cheerfulness.

Angie locked the door and bolted the chain again. She still had that forced smile as she turned to us. "Sit down," she ordered, pointing at a couch.

Jamey and I sat down side by side on thin foam cushions covered with cheap orange chintz. The place was a mess. At our knees was a brown Formica coffee table with three tall stacks of teetering sheet music on it. To our right, along the wall, was a battered-looking upright piano with stacks of teetering sheet music on top of it. Across the living room, next to the entrance to the kitchen, was a dining table also stacked with sheet music and spilled with lots of other things: clothes, hair curlers, stockings, phonograph records, shoes, brassieres, slips. Things were also strewn on the floor and other chairs and side tables.

"Now, Jamey, the last thing I want is for you to think you're unwelcome. You've got to understand that now, 'cause I don't want you to misunderstand what I'm going to say next, which is that even you've got to admit you really caught me off guard. You should of let me know a little in advance before you came up here. Life isn't so simple as it is down in Alcoma."

"But how could I let you know when I didn't even know where you lived?"

Angie winced. She shook her head and ran the back of her hand across her eyes. "I'm sorry, Jamey. So much going on, I got confused for a minute. It just seemed like I'd sent you that letter I'd written. I did write one to you recently ... telling you I planned to have you up real soon ... only I never got around to finishing it. It's in this mess somewhere," her eyes roved helplessly around the room, "and I'll show it to you soon as I get the chance."

"You don't have to show me anything. I believe you. Only you shoulda written more often."

Angie looked pained again. She drew the corners of her mouth in and nodded guiltily. "Please, Jamey, don't make me feel bad right now," she said. "I don't need to feel bad right now. I've got enough to handle."

"I'm sorry, Angie. You know I didn't mean to upset you. The only reason I'm up here is to maybe help you get whatever you want."

Angie's face melted. The tears welled again in her eyes. She closed them and shook her head and clenched her fist in anger at herself. She opened her eyes. "I'm sorry, Jamey, I didn't mean to say what I did. But you got to understand that things are kind of frantic now. I've got to ask you to do something that you're not going to understand, but I want you to do it, anyway. Okay, Jamey?"

Jamey stared fearfully at Angie. "What is it?"

"I want you and your friend Arnie to go away right now. I want you to give me your number where you're staying and I promise to get in touch just as quick as I can — probably no later than this afternoon." Her look asked us to go quickly and not give her any trouble.

"But I just got here, Angie... It's been three years since I've seen you. Why can't I just —"

"Jamey, this is something I just can't help. Someone's coming over to see me. He should be here any minute. There are things I've got to talk to him about alone. It won't help anything if you and your friend are here. Please go now and I promise I'll call you as soon as I can. Just as soon as I take care of this business." Her look was firm.

"I still don't understand why I can't be here, Angie. I won't get in the way or nothin'." Jamey looked desperately around the room, as though one of the things strewn about might somehow solve the problem.

"Because I won't allow it! This isn't anything I want you to hear. It's better for me to tell you la —"

The doorbell rang!

Angie whirled and stared at the front door. "Dammit to

hell," she swore. "All I needed was another five minutes."

The doorbell rang again, twice, impatiently.

"I'm coming, Johnny, I'm coming. Hold your horses," she called out. She looked hurriedly around the room, whispered quickly: "Listen to me. There's no time to quarrel. "You've got to do exactly as I say. The two of you get in the bedroom and stay out of sight. You're going to hear things you're not going to like or understand, but you've got to stay behind that door and not show yourself for any reason. You hear me, Jamey? Now go on, get in there."

We did as we were told. The bedroom was behind the dining table across the room. The buzzer was one long grinding sound. Jamey stood next to the door so he could peek through it. I sat down on the messy bed in the messy room and shook my head in disgust. How the hell had I gotten into this?

"I'm coming, goddammit, I *said* I was coming." She opened the door.

A coarse Chicago-style voice said, "Are yuh okay, Angie? I thought maybe you was sick or somethin'."

"I'm okay, Johnny."

"Then let's get moving. The session is set for two and it's a long way to the Loop. You know how independent these recording guys are. Screw up their schedule by two minutes and they can lose all enthusiasm for you."

"I know it, Johnny, and I appreciate your concern. But I've been doing a lot of thinking about this session and there's something I want to say to you. I wish you'd sit down a minute."

"Hey, doncha hear me, Angie — we're late! I know you got lots of butterflies about it, but there ain't nothin' we can't talk about in the car. Get your stuff and let's go. You're on your way to becoming a big recording star."

"I don't think so, Johnny."

There was a dead silence in the other room. When

Johnny spoke again, the enthusiasm had gone out of him. "What do you mean," he said, scarcely able to hold his anger down, "when you say *you don't think so!* This is a helluva time for you to say somethin' like that!"

"That's why I'd like you to sit down for a few minutes, so I can explain it to you."

"Explain *what?* Since when did you decide that you're gonna do the thinking for us? Let's get something straight right now! *I* do the thinking. *You* do the singing. I don't give a shit what you think. You've got no right to think. Understand me?"

"I'm not going to do it, Johnny. I'm grateful for the time and trouble you've taken, but I can't do it. Recording Italian love songs is not the best thing for my career."

You didn't have to see Johnny to know how furious he was. That heavy silence said it all. His anger spewed out: "*You dumb bitch!* You've got the nerve to pull this shit on me, after all I've done for you. What were you when I found you, an over-the-hill Gaslight girl reduced to checking coats. If you were a horse, they would've turned you into manure by now. I took you out of the garbage and dolled you up and got you started as a singer and *this* is how you repay me. I ought to break your face."

"You've got the right to be mad, Johnny. But I think I'm doing us both a favor by pulling out now. It won't work. I'm no good at what you want me to do. You'd be disappointed with me."

"What does it take to make you understand, stupid? I'm going to *make* you a star. It's in the bag. You know Uncle Pietro controls all the juke boxes in Cook County. You know his contacts in New York and Vegas. You're gonna be another Rosey Clooney."

"But that's just the point. I'm *not* another Rosemary Clooney. And I'm not Patti Page or Teresa Brewer or Doris Day or Dinah Shore. I'm me, Angie Bishop, a nightclub and jazz singer, a ballad and blues singer, nothing else. Just because Uncle Pietro controls all the juke boxes doesn't mean he can make me a star. He can force all the juke box owners in the world to stock my Italian songs, but no one is going to pay a nickel for them. It's been tried before with other singers and it hasn't worked, and Uncle Pietro, if he knows the business, knows what I'm talking about. Please tell him I'm doing him a favor by getting out now."

Another fuming silence. Then Johnny spoke with a threatening hiss: "No, if anyone is gonna do any explaining to Uncle Pietro, it's gonna be you, baby. I put my reputation on the line with him. I told him I got a winner. Where do you think I got the bread to stake you? You think your arrangements and rehearsal sessions were cheap? Uncle Pietro loaned me five grand on your account, which he expects back in the form of a hit song. So if you think you can pull out now, you got another think coming. You're going to this session if I have to drag you there."

"You never told me the money wasn't your own, but I swear I'll pay you back every penny of it. I intended to anyway. Just don't make a scene, Johnny."

"Don't make a scene, huh? Are you coming?"

"I'm not going, Johnny. You can break every bone in my body and I won't do it. Stay away from me."

"You bitch, I'll punch your throat."

Jamey jumped out of the bedroom.

"Keep your hands off her, mister, I'm warning you." I wasn't quite so brave, only moved to the door to peek out and see what was going on.

Johnny was amazed. "Who the hell are you, kid?"

Jamey was standing in front of Angie. "You better get out of here this minute."

"Who *is* this kid, Angie? What kind of kinky stuff have you been pulling on me?"

"My name is Jamey Jackson and it's my sister you're insulting, and I promise you I'll kill you if you don't get out of here."

All the time I only heard him, Johnny sounded like a punk. Now that I saw him, it was no surprise that he also looked like a punk. He was about thirty, had the soft handsome face of a stud, weak and selfish, with a black greasy pompadour. I would've laid odds that he wouldn't have the guts to take on Jamey, and he didn't. Thank God, he wasn't packing a gun.

At the same time, punk that he was, he had connections to dangerous crooks. It was no fun getting tangled up with Uncle Pietro Celli. I admired Angie for not wanting to get us involved in this. Only a hayseed like Jamey would plunge in the way he did. I hoped Johnny would take off now. I didn't want any part of this.

Johnny said, "Hey, Angie, maybe you better explain to your brother what kind of trouble he's asking for. You better tell him to get his butt out of here. I know guys who'll break his legs and dump him in the Chicago River. You, too, if you don't come with me."

Jamey was a strong kid. With one hand, he raised a chair by its leg to shoulder height and took a step toward Johnny. "I think you've said enough, mister. You better get out of here now." He started toward Johnny.

"*Don't, Jamey!*" Angie and I said it nearly together. I stepped out of the bedroom.

Johnny was astonished. "What, another brother? Holy shit, who else you got in there?"

"I'm not her brother," I said boldly. "I'm a guy with contacts better than yours to Uncle Pietro. All Uncle Pietro has to find out is what an asshole you've been, and I guarantee you, you'll be making pizzas the rest of your life."

I figured that would make Johnny think twice. He

didn't say anything, just eyed me suspiciously, wondering if I was telling the truth. "You talk awful big for a little turd. If you know someone with ins to Pietro, you better say his name. He better be good or you're going to be in the river with your friends here."

Johnny was right! I'd better be good! He'd never know how scared I was as I smiled coolly at him for a few seconds. "You ever heard of Eagle-Nose Pinsky?" I asked smoothly.

Johnny's face clouded. I could tell Eagle-Nose's name was familiar to him, but he wasn't sure how important he was, and he didn't want to let on that he wasn't sure. And he was still suspicious. "How come a little turd like you has connections to Pinsky?"

"Why don't you ask Eagle-Nose and find out?"

"You still ain't said your connection to him."

"Tell you what you do, Johnny. You pick up that phone and call Uncle Pietro. Ask him to get in touch with Eagle-Nose Pinsky. Tell him to ask Eagle-Nose if he ever heard of Arnie Barzov. Okay, Johnny? You show us what a big man you are with Uncle Pietro and make the call."

Johnny stared at me. He stared at the phone. I'd called his bluff. He didn't have the guts to make the call.

"I'll check you out in my own way," he bullshitted, "and I'll tell you somethin', turd. You better be right or the three of you are in the river. Nobody makes a fool of Johnny Salerno and gets away with it. You got me, turd?"

"I got you, punk. Now take a walk."

"You ain't seen the last of me, turd."

"I'm sure I haven't, punk. Take a walk."

Johnny left. Angie and Jamey collapsed, holding each other on the sofa. I sank into an armchair and stared blindly. The loudest sound was our hearts thumping.

"That was wonderful what you boys did just now," Angie said. "I'm sure glad you showed up when you did."

"Don't thank me yet," I said. "I may not have any thanks coming."

"What do you mean?"

"I mean that I had to say something to get him out of here. I was just taking a chance that Eagle-Nose has got the clout to save us."

"You mean he may not have the clout?" Angie asked.

I nodded unhappily at her and Jamey.

"Who *is* this Eagle-Nose?" Jamey asked.

"Eagle-Nose Pinsky is the guy my mother is going with. He's got the reputation as a guy with all kinds of important connections in the city. But that might not cut ice with Uncle Pietro, who's one of the biggest crooks in the country. He controls dozens of things, you name it. Eagle-Nose Pinsky is way out of his league. And when Uncle Pietro finds out he's out five grand on account of you, Angie, he might not be so pleased about it."

"So what are we going to do?" Jamey asked.

"At this moment, I don't know," I said. "I gotta think about it."

CHAPTER

4

ONE THING I didn't have to think too hard about was that the three of us better get out of here right away! Just because Johnny Salerno didn't have the guts to call Uncle Pietro on the spot didn't mean he wouldn't come back and cause more trouble to make up for it.

I told Angie to pack a suitcase with whatever she needed for a few days, that it would be best to stay away from her place for a while. She didn't need coaxing, grabbed a suitcase and started throwing things in it. Three problems, though. Where were she and Jamey going to stay? She had less than fifty dollars to her name and wouldn't be paid by the club she was working at for a few days. I told her not to worry about it, I'd help her out with what she needed. The second problem was that her car was at a garage being repaired and she would need some way to get to it. I told her I'd help her out with that too. The third problem — the biggest of all and the most pressing — was what about her club date tonight. An important agent was coming to see her and Johnny didn't know about it and what if he showed up and caused a scene. "We'll handle him somehow," I heard myself say.

Fifteen minutes later, we were driving back to the north

side on Ogden Avenue again. As Jamey sat next to me and talked to Angie in the back, I was furious with myself. What a jerk I was, getting all tangled up with this hayseed kid and his bad-news sister with her punk boyfriend. Just my luck to have to show myself to the punk and save their asses and now we were all in it together! On the other hand, I couldn't forget what Angie said. If I hadn't driven Jamey out today, and he hadn't saved Angie, and I hadn't saved them, Angie would've been stomped on by Salerno. I'd heard how punks like him were with women. And Angie was one brave lady who didn't deserve that kind of treatment. So maybe I *had* done the right thing. Who knew? What I had to think about right now was, could I find a way out for us without bringing Eagle-Nose in on it? He'd go out of his skull if he knew how I'd used his name. And could I find a way to take care of Angie and Jamey and get them and their problems out of my life as soon as possible? I still didn't have any ready answers and so I listened to them talk.

Jamey was telling Angie about his experiences in the day and a half he'd been in Chicago. He'd taken a twelve-hour train ride from north Mississippi and arrived after midnight at the Illinois Central Station. A porter had directed him to a YMCA in the Loop, in a seedy section under the El tracks on Van Buren. Despite the hour, after checking into his room, he'd immediately gone back down to the lobby and started looking up all the Angela Bishops in the phone book. There were eight of them, and as he wrote their numbers on a pad, he checked to see if one matched his only clue, written at the top of the pad: Angie's telephone number from more than a year and a half ago. None did. So he got a roll of nickels from the desk clerk and made his first call, Angie's old number. There was no answer. Then he called the other eight numbers and for his trouble got three no answers, three people who told him they didn't know a white female singer from Mississippi, and two Negro women who one after the other cursed his ear off for waking them up. He also called Angie's old number again and there was still no answer. He wasn't fazed. He took the telephone book up to his room and, before he fell asleep, made up that list of 123 names, including all the listings of her maiden name, A. Jackson and Angie Jackson, that she might be using.

He started checking them out as soon as he waked. His first call was to the old number, but still no answer. Then he tried the three no answers on his Angela Bishop list. When *they* didn't answer, he decided to trek out to the three different addresses, which turned out to be in three different sections of the city, far apart from each other: in the Hyde Park section on the south side, in the Rogers Park section on the north side, on the northwest side not far from the suburb of Park Ridge. He had to take Els and buses to get to each place, got lost each time. He never dreamed how big Chicago was, and by the time I saw him at Candido's that night, he couldn't help but be exhausted from his long useless rides.

Fortunately, at different times during the day, he'd stopped and made calls on his A. Bishop list and to Angie's old number. It was on the latter that he finally made contact with Kim in the late afternoon. She was in a hurry and about to leave her apartment, but the little bit of information she hastily gave him, with an Oriental accent — "Yeah, yeah, I think maybe woman who live here before me name Angie. She came back to apartment once to get some things, but she no tell me where she go. And I never see her again" — made him determined to find Kim right away and find out whatever more he could. But first he had to find out where she lived. The way to find out was so obvious, it didn't occur to him for fifteen or twenty minutes, while sitting on a park bench. Of course! The operator would give him the address to match the number! She lived in the Rush Street area, on Superior, that honky-tonk world west of Clark, and an hour later he was checking the mailboxes of her apartment building for Oriental names. There were none. The girl he'd talked to apparently didn't have an Oriental name. He found a phone booth in a drugstore on the corner and dialed her number again. There was no answer. He went back to the building and found the janitor's apartment and rang his bell and found out that, yes, an Oriental girl named Kim Moreau did live in the building, on the top floor, in apartment 4A, and she came and went at different hours, he didn't know where she worked. The janitor said she probably was a model or showgirl or something like that, and them kind of girls worked those kind of hours. Anyway, she was tall and striking, a real looker, and Jamey would know her when he saw her.

Jamey decided to wait for her on the steps of the apartment building across the street. He got very lucky because she returned within an hour. She went past in a hurry with a scowl on her face and he decided he'd better not ring her bell just yet, he'd phone her in a little while when he hoped she'd be in a better mood. But as the minutes passed, he didn't exactly feel confident about calling and getting her to talk to him. Better to wait for her to come down again and check her mood. A few hours later — it was close to two A.M. — just as he was about to call it a night and wait till the morning to contact her, she came down again, still scowling and still in a hurry, and he followed her to Candido's, where, he explained to Angie, he met her and me, and Kim persuaded me to drive him to the airport.

Angie was deeply moved by Jamey's story. "Words can't say how grateful I am, to both of you. You guys came in the nick of time, saved my life, I'm sure of it. And Jamey honey, I've got to say this right out, the way you acted for me this morning only makes me feel worse about the way I've neglected you these past few years."

"I only came up because Gram-mom passed away."

Angie looked stricken. "Oh, Jamey, why didn't you say so?"

"No one to stay with now, with both Gram-mom and Grand-pa passed away."

Angie took Jamey in her arms. "Oh, Jamey, how could I be so thoughtless... I'm sorry... I'm so sorry." She started to cry.

"It was one of the things I came up here to tell ya. Would've called or wrote if I knew how to find you. I'm sorry to tell you now, seeing the situation you got, but I figured you'd want to know about Gram-mom..."

Angie continued to cry. She hugged Jamey closer.

"I want you to know, Angie, you shouldn't feel you got to take care of me. Did you ever figure I could take care of you?"

She looked tenderly at him. "But it shouldn't *be* for you to take care of me. Your job should be to take care of yourself. You've got your whole life ahead of you — love and marriage and kids and finding out what you want to do — without your having to worry about me."

"I can do all them other things too."

"But you have no idea what life up here is like. It's a big adjustment to make."

"You made it. Lots of other people have too. I don't see any reason why I can't do it."

Angie couldn't answer that. I could see the mixed feelings in her eyes in the rearview mirror, could see that Jamey's dropping into her life right now was going to cause her a lot of problems. But she didn't complain about it. Instead, those eyes became part of a warm smile. "Despite the fact that I haven't been such a great sister,

Jamey," she said affectionately, "I want you to know that I love you. Always have. Whatever happens, you can always believe that."

"It's what I came to Chicago to hear, Angie. Whatever happens, you just made the whole trip worthwhile."

The more I heard, the more I liked these people. I knew I was kidding myself if I thought I was going to be able to protect Angie and Jamey and then drop out of their lives. What could I do, send them back to Mississippi? That was no answer. Angie needed to be in Chicago for her singing career, and Jamey needed to be with her. I knew what I had to do.

I pulled into a drive-in burger joint near Ogden and Western. I told them to order lunch on me while I made a call from a gas station across the way.

Much as I didn't want to get involved with Eagle-Nose, a certain part of me enjoyed laying this on him. He was a bigger punk than Johnny Salerno, more full of crap. He was always mouthing off about his connections with mobsters and politicians and business big shots and was just bullshitting most of the time. "It's not what you know, it's who you know," I'd heard him say a hundred times, his big black cigar sticking out of his beardy face at a cocky angle. "Okay, Eagle, old boy," I said as I dialed, "you better be in with Uncle Pietro or your ass is in trouble too."

But he wasn't at his main store, and his manager said he'd gone out for lunch and hadn't come back; he didn't know if or when he'd return.

This meant I had to make another call I didn't want to. I had to call Myrna because she more than anyone might know where Eagle-Nose was, or at least where I could find him tonight. I looked at my watch: one-fifteen. She *should* be up by now. I could see her padding around in one of her big frilly Mae West robes, rubbing expensive creams under her eyes or reading movie magazines with her coffee.

That same certain part of me didn't mind laying this on Myrna either.

"Hello."

"It's your youngest son, Arnie, Myrna. Remember me?"

"Remember you? Sure I remember you. You're the son that got thrown out of college for doing God knows what."

"Not God knows what, Myrna. Taking bets on Big Ten games. That makes me a gambler just like Eagle-Nose, that loudmouth jerk you're going with."

"At least Jules doesn't get caught."

" 'At least Jules doesn't get caught.' Pretty good, Myrn. Pretty good comeback indeed! 'At least Jules doesn't get caught.' Nice, Myrn. Very nice. I gotta hand it to ya."

"*You* aren't being very nice. I hope you didn't call just to insult Jules Pinsky."

"No, as a matter of fact, I want to talk to him."

"It's about time you accepted his job."

"I still don't want his lousy job."

"That's why you want to talk to him? To tell him you still don't want his job? Arnold, will you ever realize how ungrateful you are? Jules is concerned about you like I'm concerned about you. We discussed you at great length last night at Fritzel's. Frankly, we both don't understand why you act —"

"Myrn! *Please* listen close. I don't want to tell Eagle-Nose I don't want his job. I need to talk to him about something else. It's very important."

"So why call me, then?"

"Because I tried to reach him just now and his manager doesn't know where he is. Since you're his best girl, I thought you might know where he is."

"You know something about you, Arnold? You're more than not nice. You're nasty. Why do you make fun of my relationship with Jules? Why do you insist on calling me his best girl? You make it seem like there's something wrong going on. I don't deserve to be insulted that way by my son."

"Aw, Myrn, c'mon now. I didn't mean to hurt your feelings. I'm sorry. Do you know where I can get in touch with Eagle-Nose?"

"Sorry! I bet you're sorry. You don't know the pain you cause when you say things like that. Do you think my situation with Jules is easy? Do you think I like being the woman he loves while he's married to someone else? Do you think I like holding the key to his happiness and not being able to do anything about it? Answer that, you selfish boy, always thinking of your own problems."

Here we went again, off and running on the same old track. Myrna had a positive genius for always turning it around and making it seem every time like I was failing her. The fact of the matter was that I didn't hold anything against her because she was going with a married man. In the strangest way, I was kinda proud of her for that, for doing something daring that no one in her crowd would ever dream of doing. My gripe was that she was going with a schmuck like Eagle-Nose. If she wanted to go with a married guy, at least let her go with one worth going with! Nutty as she was, Myrna had a lot of good things going for her. She was one terrific-looking woman, movie-star stunning, great gams. She dressed in the best of fashion, elegant, subtle shades, not like her girl friends in loud clashing colors and overloaded with jewelry and makeup.

Her apartment was elegant too, in good taste, not like the gaudy Miami Beach hotel lobbies of her friends. When she wasn't batty, she could be charming and funny and really make a man feel good about being with her. But ever since Zach had run away, she'd stuck with crumbs like Eagle-Nose who couldn't hold a candle to her. She should have more pride, and I tried to tell her every chance I got, but I couldn't get through to her about it any more than I could about anything else. At any rate, it was really the pot calling the kettle black, her calling me selfish. She never even asked me what my problem was. "Myrn," I said in my nicest, cut-the-crap way, "how's about your best guess where you think Eagle-Nose is. I really need to talk to him."

"He's probably at the track or the baseball game. At least, that's where he told me last night he might be today. If you don't catch up with him this afternoon, he's going to be here tonight. He asked me to host his monthly poker game with his friends. It starts around seven-thirty."

It was enough to make me vomit, Myrn hosting Eagle-Nose's poker game, but what choice did I have? "Tell Eagle-Nose I'll see him tonight at your place. I'll get there as early as I can, maybe even before the game starts."

"As long as you're on the line, Arnold, there's one thing I want to say to you. You've been disappointing me about a lot of things lately and this is one thing I don't want you to disappoint me on."

"I'm listening."

"Though this is only the end of June, I'm reminding you early that I'm expecting you to go to Cousin Selma's son Alvin's bar mitzvah in Lake Geneva on Labor Day weekend. I'm telling you now, it's going to be a big deal and I don't want you to embarrass me by not showing up like you did for Aunt Mollie's son Ronnie's wedding last year. You might even enjoy it if you let yourself. They're negotiating for Nat "King" Cole or Tony Martin to entertain. And definitely Vaughn Monroe and his band will be there. So make a place in your memory. I think you can do this one thing for me."

Another great thing about Myrna was her gift for irrelevance. "I'm glad you told me, Myrn," I said. "I'll put it right on my social calendar. Don't let Vaughn Monroe let you forget about reminding Eagle-Nose that I need to see him." I hung up.

The ballgame! Until Myrna mentioned it, I'd completely forgotten. I looked at my watch. It was after one-thirty, the game had already started. Two things struck me. Eagle-Nose might be there in his regular box. Even if he wasn't, I had to do something with Angie and Jamey until I could talk to him tonight, and Wrigley Field seemed as good a place as any to keep them out of trouble.

I returned to the car and told them I'd arranged to see Eagle-Nose tonight. I explained to Angie we had time to kill and suggested we go to the game, which was what Jamey and I were going to do if we hadn't found her. Angie said it was all right with her so long as I got her back to her club date on the southwest side by ten o'clock. I told her I would.

"Then I don't mind going to the ballgame at all," she said. "Maybe I can even get to see a player I know."

I turned my head and nearly hit a car in the next lane. Jamey also looked at Angie in surprise. "You know a player on the Cubs?" we both said.

"Yes, indeed. His name is Randy Dodds."

"You know Randy Dodds?" Jamey said, impressed.

I was impressed too. "Funny you should know him," I said to Angie. "Jamey and I were just talking about him on the drive to your place, weren't we, Jamey?" I grinned at his uncomfortable expression.

"How did you meet Randy Dodds?" Jamey asked, wriggling out of the ticklish situation.

"Oh, I've known him for a couple of months now, ever since the baseball season started. Randy stopped in at the club one night and we started talking. We've gone out maybe half a dozen times. He's been a big help to me. He's the one who helped convince me that I shouldn't cut those Italian love songs. He said I should stick to what I do best. He gave me the confidence to tell Johnny I didn't want to do it. I hope Johnny never finds out how helpful Randy was. He'd be threatening Randy too, if he knew. I hope I get a chance to see Randy and tell him what happened."

"We'll try," I said, and got the game on the radio. Bert Wilson, the voice of the Cubs, told us that the Cubs were already down 3–0 in the first inning. We were 2400 west and 1300 south at that point. Half an hour and two innings later we were 1000 west and 3600 north, parking in the ballpark lot, with the sand-colored walls of Wrigley Field rising over us. The Cubs were still down 3–0.

I got us box seats down the third-base line, near the railing and a little beyond the Cubs' dugout. The bleachers above the green ivy-covered wall that circled the outfield were packed; the great number of white shirts sparkled in the sun and created the illusion from left field around to right of a long white banner furling in the breeze. The box seats around us and the grandstand above were also packed. There was an electric excitement in the crowd on account of the Cubs' success.

But it was going to be a tough game for them. The Pirates had their ace pitcher, Bob Friend, going and he was mowing the Cubs down. The big black scoreboard that rose up behind the bleachers in center field indicated that he hadn't given up a hit yet.

Spieler La Chance himself was coaching third base. A wiry little guy, he was all motion in his baggy pants and peaked cap, giving signs and vulgar gestures, clapping, leading his team with what Mike Ginsburg, in one of his columns, called his "loquacious barrage." He had a habit of doing dance steps in the coaches' box, going back to his early days, when he was a professional ballroom dancer and had even danced in the chorus of a Broadway musical. Because of his dancing background, Ginsburg had also described his facial features as a combination of Rudolph

Valentino and George Raft and Fred Astaire. It was true. Spieler had Raft's coiled eyes and Valentino's handsome profile dropping down into Astaire's V-shaped chin with his thin mouth and sly grin. In his relations with women, he was known to be romantic and dapper like the three of them. He wasn't romantic and dapper with the Pirate players, could almost flay their skin off with his vicious razzing.

Despite the excitement of the morning, from the moment he sat down, Jamey's eyes were glued to the action of the first big-league game he'd ever seen. Angie watched in a distracted worried way that showed she was also thinking about this morning and tonight. I pointed out to her where Randy Dodds was sitting in the Cubs' bullpen down the left-field line and every so often she stared in his direction. Unfortunately, he was at the far end of the bench, hidden behind other players. "Do you think he'll get in the game?" she asked once.

Jamey, concentrating on the action, automatically popping popcorn into his mouth, said the wrong thing: "Well, I hope not, for Arnie's sake."

Two vertical furrows in Angie's brow deepened as she eyed her brother. "Why not?" she asked, defending Randy. "Isn't he a good player?"

Jamey realized what he'd done and looked reassuringly at Angie. "No, I didn't mean that at all, believe me."

"Well, what *do* you mean, boy? Speak up now."

As Jamey squirmed silently, I tried to help him out. "He means that he hopes it isn't necessary for the Cubs to use him. He knows that I've got a bet on the Cubs and that if the Cubs' starting pitcher can go the distance, it's more likely the Cubs will win. The Cubs' relief pitchers have been used a lot lately, and it will be a big help to the team if they don't have to pitch today. You follow what I mean?"

She reluctantly nodded. I had a feeling that, like me,

she knew that Randy hadn't been very good lately and wanted to be told that the problem wasn't as bad as it seemed.

In the fifth inning, the Cubs stopped the no-hitter and scored a run. In the sixth they got another run and the score was 3–2. The Pirates put two men on base with one out in the seventh and Spieler brought in Jimmy Weatherford, the Cubs' number-one reliever. He got the side out without the Pirates scoring.

Angie forced the issue. "Why didn't the manager bring in Randy?" she asked, looking at Jamey.

Jamey looked innocently at her and shook his head.

She looked at me. "Beats me," I said. "You'll have to ask Spieler that one."

In the bottom of the seventh, Wally Koslowski, the Cubs' huge first-sacker, hit a tremendous two-run homer into Sheffield Avenue. It hit a building across the street. The Cubs led 4–3. The crowd roared for five minutes. Could Jimmy Weatherford hold the Pirates in the eighth and ninth? They had their best hitters up.

"How much money did you bet on the game?" Angie asked me.

"A lot. Five hundred dollars."

"Well, Randy still may have a chance to help you win it. He's warming up in the bullpen." She had this defiant look.

So he was. Now *I* had an uncomfortable expression. Jamey was grinning at me with this hope-he-isn't-needed-for-your-sake expression. I felt guilty because I hoped so, too.

Jimmy Weatherford got the first Pirate on a fly ball. He got the second on a pop-up. The third batter worked the count to three-and-two and walked.

Spieler and the catcher, Ironhead Sykes, and Wally Koslowski and Joey de Angelo gathered on the mound to give encouragement to Jimmy Weatherford. As Spieler walked back to the dugout, he motioned to the bullpen for Randy Dodds to start throwing harder. If the Pirates tied the score or went ahead, Spieler would have to use a pinch-hitter for Jimmy Weatherford in the bottom of the eighth.

The next batter sent a screamer back at Weatherford. It hit him flush on the wrist of his pitching hand and sent him writhing to the ground in pain. The ball rolled slowly to the shortstop, who was playing deep, and the batter beat it out. There were runners on first and second, and the game had to be delayed as Jimmy Weatherford, howling in pain, was removed and Randy Dodds came in to replace him.

The crowd held its breath like one person as Randy warmed up. Jamey smiled tightly at me. I smiled nervously back at him. Angie called out, "C'mon, Randy. You can do it," then bit her lower lip.

He was wild and walked the first batter on four pitches. Now the bases were loaded. He threw a strike and then four straight balls to the next batter and the score was tied. Another pitcher was warming up quickly as Spieler went to the mound. His body facing Spieler, his hands on his hips, but his face looking toward the plate, Randy had a faraway expression, like he was worried about a lot more than the ballgame. On his tiptoes, Spieler was cooing softly into Randy's ear, trying to bring him back to the game. Finally, Randy nodded grimly, and Spieler wheeled like General Patton and strode back to the dugout.

The count went to two-and-nothing on the next hitter. Randy came in with a fastball and it was driven hard through the diamond into center field — almost! Joey de Angelo, the little shortstop, gloved the ball going into center field, whirled in midair like a ballet dancer and got the ball to the second baseman an instant before the sliding runner hit the bag. The Cubs were out of the inning with a tie score. Jamey and Angie and I and all the other 23,371 Cub fans sighed together.

The Cubs didn't score in the last of the eighth.

Randy Dodds started the ninth by giving up a double off the wall. He walked the next batter. The third batter sacrificed the runners to second and third. The next batter was intentionally walked to fill the bases and create a play at any base. The next batter went to three-and-two, fouled off five pitches, and then popped up. The next batter struck out on three pitches. Somewhere in the midst of all the trouble, Randy had found his groove and was pitching beautifully.

The Pirate relief pitcher was pitching beautifully too. The Cubs didn't score in their half of the ninth.

In the tenth, Randy's hard sinker was beaten harmlessly into the ground three times and the Pirates were easy outs. But how long could he go?

In the last of the tenth, with two outs, the Cub batter doubled down the left-field line. Randy Dodds was the next batter, and he wasn't a good hitter, and it seemed right for Spieler to pinch-hit for him. But for some reason Spieler didn't, and Randy came out of the dugout to hit, and the crowd — not a soul had left — murmured in surprise.

Randy swung twice and missed. The next pitch he looped feebly into the outfield. No one could get it and it fell for a hit and the winning run scored. The crowd went wild!

What a sensational victory! To a man, the Cubs swarmed out of the dugout to congratulate Randy. The crowd was on its feet cheering, cheering for things to come.

Angie had her fist in the air and she called out to Randy as he headed into the dugout. He heard her and looked up and came over to the railing. "Hey, what a terrific surprise, Angie! Am I glad to see you. Hey, this makes the whole day perfect!"

"You were wonderful, Randy. I'm so proud of you."

Randy took Angie in his arms and brought her over the railing onto the field. "I don't know what brought you here," he said happily, "but I'm sure glad y'are."

Angie said she would explain everything to him after he showered. The only thing she wanted to do at the moment was introduce him to her brother. She pointed to Jamey.

Randy motioned for Jamey to come down on the field. I went right with him. Randy and Jamey shook hands and Randy said he'd heard from his sister that Jamey was real interested in baseball. Jamey introduced me to Randy, and I reminded him that we'd met a couple of years ago at Abrams Department Store, on Devon and Artesian. The funny thing was, Randy remembered meeting me.

Randy suggested that the three of us wait for him at his car in the Cubs' parking lot. He would join us real quick. But a grainy voice behind me said he wouldn't hear of such a thing.

Spieler, happy as a boy, had come over to see who the people were with Randy. Not even waiting to be introduced to us, he insisted that we all come along to the clubhouse and wait for Randy there. Randy, he explained, was the star of the game, and the reporters wanted to talk to him. With a gleam in his eye, he looked at Angie and said this lovely lady could wait in his office so she wouldn't have to undergo the remarks of any of the players. "You kids can protect her if any of my guys try to make out with her." He laughed heartily and moved us all along into the clubhouse.

It was the most unforgettable day of my life. Along with everything else that happened, there I was in the Cubs' locker room with my favorite ballplayers all around me as they happily undressed and showered. There was Spieler

La Chance confidently telling the reporters around him why he let Randy Dodds bat for himself: "Because when I went out to see him in the eighth, when the bases were jammed, I told him that I already knew Weatherford had a broken hand and was going to be out at least a couple of months, and he was my man in the bullpen come hell or high water. I sink or swim with you. If I had pinch-hit for him in the tenth, that woulda made a liar out of me and you guys all know Spieler La Chance, he cannot tell a lie." Spieler winked and laughed and did a little dance step.

A reporter turned to Randy and asked him what he thought of the Cubs' chances to take the pennant. Randy rubbed his chin a moment before he answered. "I think Spieler La Chance is taking us all the way," he said modestly. "I sure as hell hope so," he added, more enthusiastically. And all around, the players raised their bottles of beer and cheered. Not everyone in the room liked Spieler — some players openly disliked him — but all of them were saying that like him or not, Spieler was going to play an important role in getting them into the World Series.

The only person not impressed by the scene was Elmo Speakes. The great center-fielder was sitting nearby in front of his locker and watching the reporters around Spieler and Randy with his usual sour expression. He started to mimic Spieler's grainy voice. "All the way with Spieler," he said without enthusiasm. "Spieler La Chance, he cannot tell a lie. She-it, man."

CHAPTER

5

I'D LOOKED FOR EAGLE-NOSE in his regular box between innings of the game but was glad he wasn't there.
I'd be better off dealing with him at the poker game tonight. It was also fine with me that Randy Dodds wanted
to take Angie and Jamey out for dinner. He wanted to
take me too, but I begged off. Angie needed to tell Randy
whatever she wanted to tell him about what happened at
her place, and I needed the time alone to think. I told
Angie and Jamey to meet me at Myrna's place no later
than eight-thirty sharp. After I talked to Eagle-Nose, this
would give me time enough to take Angie to her club for
her first set at ten.

I drove to Myrna's from Wrigley Field. Her apartment
was on Lincoln Park West, 2200 north near the lake. It
was on the top floor of a fifteen-story building, with a
great view overlooking the park and the Outer Drive and
Lake Michigan. I kept a key to the place and took the
elevator up and let myself in. Fortunately, she wasn't
there and I didn't have to waste any energy jawing with
her about anything. I went to the kitchen and got a couple
of bottles of beer and started toward my room. To get
there, I had to go through the dining room and the living

room and past Myrna's and Dan's bedrooms down a long L-shaped hallway. My room was right where the two directions met. Zach's study was around the corner, the last room in the big apartment.

In the doorway between the dining room and the living room I stopped and looked around, took in both stylishly furnished rooms at the same time, and remembered the way things used to be. I saw the high ceilings and the tall windows and the simple but elegant charm of the thin molding framing each light cream-colored wall; saw the scroll-like design of the lintels and cornices; saw the comfortable furniture with pretty patterns that blended perfectly with the dark wood of the tables and buffets and cabinets and piano; saw the handsome lamps with their pastel silk shades and the Oriental and Persian rugs on the shining parquet floor.

We'd moved into this apartment in early 1949. I think that Zach and Myrna somehow hoped to make a new happy start here. I was in high school and my brother Dan was about to finish his second year in a combined program of the Art Institute and the University of Chicago. But my brother never did spend much time here. He lived with a girl on the south side near the university during his junior year, and she gave him a bad time and left him in the spring of '50, and it wasn't too long before he married someone else and then left his pregnant wife and joined the army and served in Korea. When he got back in '52, he still lived near the university and wrote a novel and got divorced and wrote another novel, which made him rich and famous and too good for Chicago, so he moved to New York with his second wife and second kid. In all that time I never saw him more than three or four times in the apartment. I never saw him anywhere more than six or eight times, including his two weddings; he never knew I existed. And then, not too long after he took off for New

York, Zach decided to do the same, only he went west to Oregon, leaving Myrna and me in shock to stagger around the place the best we could. There certainly hadn't been much happiness here.

As I stood there, I remembered the beautiful throbbing sounds of Zach's violin, which he played in his den at the back of the apartment. Like wind, the music would sweep around the corner and travel up the long hallway and brush the lonely furniture and fill up every inch of space. Many times Myrna and I would be seated on opposite sides of the living room, reading or being still or whatever, and we could feel the sadness as clearly as we could see the morning sunlight slanting across the parquet floor.

I did something I hadn't done in a long time. Zach had left all his violin records behind. I went to his den and took some from a case. Then I went to my room and stacked them on my record player, turned it on. As the grand sounds of the Brahms Violin Concerto came on, I took off my suit and hung it over a chair. In my underwear, I sat on my bed and sipped my beer and listened for the introduction of the solo violin, listened until the beautiful first movement ended. Then I took a shower and shaved and put on fresh underwear. I lay on my bed and started my second beer. Myrna had said the game would start at seven-thirty and it was already nearly seven, so there wasn't long to wait. I got up and lifted the Brahms off the turntable and played it again from the start. Propped against the headboard I listened very closely.

Why did I need this syrupy stuff, this romantic goop that my old man loved like his life depended on it? He had studied the violin as a kid, and shortly after he married Myrna, in 1929, Zach was good enough to audition for a second-violinist spot with the Chicago Symphony. Though he didn't make it, the conductor, Frederick Stock, was so impressed he offered to recommend my father to

other symphony orchestras in smaller cities. Zach and
Myrna thought hard about it — it would've made my old
man very happy — but in the end they decided not to.
Myrna had just found out she was pregnant with Dan.
That was the year, of course, when the bottom dropped
out of everything, the Great Crash happened and the De-
pression was getting started, the cushion that Zach's old
man Charlie would've given him was taken away when
Charlie lost a bundle in land and stocks he'd bought on
margin and had to cut back on his men's clothing business. He closed one of his stores and let a couple of men
go at the other and brought Zach in to help him. All the
same, Zach never let playing the fiddle get too far away
from him. He worked with various bands in the area,
sometimes did pit jobs at the Chicago Theatre or the Oriental in the Loop, did weddings and bar mitzvahs and private parties, and gave violin lessons in the evening.

As the thirties moved on, he took on more and more
students, worked more band jobs, and worked less and
less with his father; not because he was necessarily making more money, but because he liked making music more.
He also played himself every chance he could. One of my
earliest childhood memories was of him playing the violin
every Sunday afternoon in the living room of our apartment. Two of the few luxuries he allowed himself in those
days were an expensive violin and records made of all the
great violin concertos without the violin part. He himself
would play the solo part with the orchestra.

Imagine a little guy like me with sweet weasel features
and a pencil mustache and longish flowing musician's hair
with his eyes closed, a white handkerchief folded between
his chin and the violin, his bow running back and forth
over the strings, producing beautiful sounds and lost in a
wonderful world of his own. Though he never said so when
I got to know him better, shortly before he left, I got the

feeling he always regretted never going off in '29 and being a second violinist in a symphony orchestra somewhere.

But if listening to violin music produced mixed feelings in me, thinking about Eagle-Nose and the poker game didn't. The nerve of the son of a bitch holding the game in our apartment! Whatever things I held against my father, Eagle-Nose couldn't hold a candle to him in any way. The three of them, Zach and Myrna and Eagle-Nose, were in the same class in high school. Eagle-Nose had always been hot for Myrna and they went together for a couple of years, until Myrna shafted him and started going with Zach. Eagle-Nose never got over it, not for twenty-five years, right through his marriage to the human fireplug, five-one Esther Goldenson with her forty-one-inch cannons, and the growing up of their three gross children, Pigeon-Face, Beaver-Teeth, and Goose-Lips.

The fact that it was little weasel-faced Zachary Barzov, the unpopular outsider who played the violin, who aced him out for Myrna Keeshin, the prettiest and most popular girl in their class, must've made him wake up in a fury and gnash his teeth all through the years. You had to know that he always cared because, though he and Myrna never saw each other socially after high school, as soon as word got out on the Chicago grapevine that Zach had run away and gone out west, the first person that Myrna heard from, offering sympathy and a shoulder to cry on and the desire to provide whatever need she might have, was Eagle-Nose. Unfortunately, Myrna's need, as it turned out, was to humiliate herself by going out with him.

When that crap started up, I called her on it hard. No matter how bad she felt about her busted marriage, there was no reason for her to be seen with such a vulgar putz. The only reason he had the nerve to get in touch with her was because he'd struck it rich in the siding business and

paid p.r. guys to keep his name in Kup's Column and get
him mentioned by Jack Eigen on his radio show from the
Chez Paree and make it seem like he had all kinds of connections in high places. He was all of a sudden a big deal
because there were houses lined up one after another for
blocks and blocks in Polish neighborhoods with his ugly
green-and-white aluminum awnings! He was all of a sudden a big deal because he sponsored a softball team at
Thillens Stadium!

"The guy doesn't deserve to wear Zach's dirty underwear," I screamed at her. "He doesn't deserve to use your
dirty toilet paper," I said even louder. Myrna's eyes
blinked with agreement when I hit her with that, and her
eyes glazed with tears. But she wasn't about to concede a
thing. "You realize, of course," she said reproachfully,
"the person you're speaking so highly of is the person who
walked out on us."

"Believe me, Myrn, it tears me up just like it tears you
up. But Zach had his reasons. You've got to admit that
much."

She wouldn't. "You're too hard on Jules. *He* would
never run out on me."

"No, he'd crawl away like a lizard if only you would tell
him to get lost."

"You don't understand. You don't understand," she
shot back, getting hysterical. "Jules Pinsky is right for me
because of who he is."

"Because he's an asshole?"

Again she blinked in agreement. "I'm going to pretend
I didn't hear you say that."

"Then how about the fact that he's also a married
man?"

"That is no problem. I would *never* allow Jules to leave
his wife."

This was too much for me. I didn't object to her going

out with a married man, but there was no way I could understand her reason for doing it! I tried something else. "But don't you see what he's doing? He's putting you on display for his old high school buddies. He's showing you off like a prize. It's like he's still back at Marshall High with you. It's disgusting."

Again I'd scored. Myrna stared at me, her lips pursed. Her hair bouncing, she turned away from me with her pretty nose raised. "So he's showing me off. So what? Maybe I want to be shown off by Jules Pinsky. Maybe that's all I deserve."

I heard the sounds of people in the living room. Evidently Myrna had come in at the same time as some of the guys, was getting things ready for them. I turned the sound up louder on the record player to get rid of the noise. "The nerve of that son of a bitch!" I said again. I knew I'd better calm down before I went out there.

Eagle-Nose's poker club was made up of guys he'd graduated high school with and who kept up with one another through this monthly get-together. Though not all the members were as successful as Eagle-Nose (he preferred it that way), they thought the same way he did about money. Individually, some of the guys I liked, some I thought were finks, but the idea of them being together like this was disgusting. There was such a cloud of sadness that hung over them when they were all together. The more successful they were, the better things were going for them — the loudmouths like Eagle-Nose would always let you know about the new gold handles on their toilets or the five grand they were shelling out for their kid's bar mitzvah at the Conrad Hilton or the dough they were laying out for a couple of weeks at the mud baths in Hot Springs — the darker the cloud of sadness that hung over them. It was like they were all lost and not sure who they were or what was happening to them, and when they got together like this, it was to protect themselves from a kind of terror that they couldn't even communicate to one another, like the terror, maybe, I'd felt on the road back to Chicago. They couldn't find a way to talk to one another — could only desperately bullshit about how well they were doing — about their sense of life being all downhill since they'd left high school, married, started businesses, had kids, gone to war, and thrived.

Lately, the thing that turned my stomach even more was that the sons of these guys were starting to sit in on the games. These were guys around my own age, some I'd known in high school, like Pigeon-Face Pinsky, and all of a sudden, without putting in the twenty-five years like their old men had, they were acting the same age as them, with the same terror hanging over them. It was like the fathers, in letting their sons sit in, were vampires drawing blood out of them to keep themselves young, and turning them into vampires like themselves. Because all of them, old and young alike, were clinging to their high school days, as though life never could or would seem so alive and exciting again. And the worst guy of all, leading the way, was Eagle-Nose, big cheese, showing off Myrna as his high school sweetheart come back to him, trying to make life now seem like it was then. I really dreaded going into that room full of guys.

But I had to. It was seven-thirty. I quickly put on my suit and knotted my tie and started down the hallway. Fortunately, I overheard snatches of conversation that made me realize it wasn't going to be as bad as I expected. The talk was all about the Cubs' great win today and could they take the pennant. They were also reminiscing about the great Cub teams of the thirties, when they made it to the World Series three times. Someone was recalling when Babe Ruth, in the Series of '32 at Wrigley Field, was supposed to have pointed to the bleachers with his bat and then hit a home run off Charlie Root in that very direction. Someone else remembered '35, when the Cubs had a twenty-one-game streak in September to edge the Cards. Someone else thought of '38, the last game of the season, when Gabby Hartnett hit a home run in the twilight off Mace Brown of the Pirates to win the pennant. I stood there and listened for a minute before entering the room. It was amazing the way the Cubs' chances were lifting the spirits of the guys.

My appearance also gave them a rise.

"Hey, hey, look who's here. Weasel Arnie in sharp threads. To what do we owe the pleasure?"

The whole bunch was genuinely glad to see me. I nodded at Solly Fink in shower curtains and Harvey Ganz in shoes and the rest seated around the oval dinner table with the green baize and leather pads laid over it for card playing. Across the way, in one of her pretty party dresses, Myrna was checking out a ton of catered deli food on the buffet table.

Eagle-Nose, in splendid profile, chomping on his black cigar, was studying his cards, slowly spreading them with his thumb. At the same time, his eyes sized up the cards on the table. "Howarya, Arnie baby," he said in that flat, smug way, not looking up but insinuating he already knew how I was.

"I've got to talk to you, Jules," I said.

He continued to study his cards, not saying anything. "I know you do, Arnie," he said finally, looking at me, with his five-o'clock-shadow jaws and dark little bird eyes forming into a knowing smirk. "Your mother said it was pretty important. Raise fifty," he said, as the bet came to him. "I'm glad you know who to come to for important stuff." He gave me that smug grin.

"It is pretty important, Jules. It's also pretty urgent. Can you talk to me in my room?"

"I will, Arnie," he said casually, "just as soon as I take

this hand. My brilliant son Irwin here thinks he can take his old man." The other players had folded and Pigeon-Face was staring grimly at his father. "On the other hand," Eagle-Nose said slyly, "maybe we ought to discuss it right here in front of Irwin. Irwin thinks he's too good for his father these days. He's carrying on some kind of rebellion. He doesn't seem to appreciate the split-level ranch-house roof over his head or the Olds Eighty-eight he got for his graduation or the gas he charges on his old man's credit card or the ten g's a year he shells out for him to live in style at Ohio State. Maybe he should find out from you, Arnie, who's found it out firsthand, that people listen when Jules Pinsky's name comes up, and that when Jules says that his son shouldn't study theater arts, he knows what he's talking about. Maybe you should tell him that I can buy him a goddamn Balaban and Katz movie house to practice his drama in. Would you please enlighten him on this score, Arnie?"

I couldn't care less that Pigeon-Face was rebelling against his father. Or that Eagle-Nose was diddling him. They were both schmucks as far as I was concerned. And Pigeon-Face was one of the world's worst poker players, a real mark. No, what I didn't understand was why Eagle-Nose was diddling me. Could it be he really knew something about what I wanted to tell him? "The game will get along without you for fifteen minutes, Jules," I said. "It's better that we talk alone."

"As you wish, Arnie. Maybe it's best like you say. I got a few things to say to you too. Show you a side of me you never knew." He snorted contemptuously at Pigeon-Face and the twenty-dollar bet he'd just made. "See your double saw," he said gleefully, "and raise you a hundred, Ir-win. You think you can play with your old man, huh?"

Myrna had moved close to us to hear our conversation. With her hands on her hips, she was looking at me sternly.

"And while you're talking to my stubborn son, Jules," she said sharply, as though it were the only thing in the world that was of any importance — the Russians could be dropping bombs on Chicago and she wouldn't care — "I wish you would speak to the young man and remind him of his responsibility to me to go to Cousin Selma's son Alvin's bar mitzvah in September. I myself have tried to tell him, but he doesn't ever seem to want to do what his mother wants. You'd think what I was asking was impossible."

Maybe Eagle-Nose thought he was being super cool with me. But Myrna's *ack-ack* made him wince. Apparently she'd been drilling him pretty good — "bar mitzvah, bar mitzvah" — about my going to Lake Geneva.

"Yeah, I'll remind him of that," Eagle-Nose said wearily, straining a smile up at Myrna and patting her behind to get her to shut up already. Then he looked across at Pigeon-Face and shook his head in disgust. Pigeon-Face, after pondering for several minutes, had just raised Eagle-Nose by another hundred bucks and was clean out of chips. He was working out his rebellion as a cabbie and had probably been cleaned out of a month's wages. With contempt, Eagle-Nose threw another hundred bucks into the pot and called Pigeon-Face. The latter turned over a pair of fives. "Stupid schmuck," Eagle-Nose screamed at him, turning over his own full house. "You shouldn't be playing this game if you don't know how to. You should've folded three cards ago, you putzhole." He was offended that Pigeon-Face was such a lousy player.

"And you're a putzhole, too, Dad," Pigeon-Face said sullenly.

Eagle-Nose nodded in solemn agreement. "I *am* a putz ... for conceiving such a dumkopf son. A dog could play a better hand of poker than you!" Having destroyed Pigeon-Face, whose head and shoulders sagged and face flushed with shame, he sat back and smiled with satisfaction at the guys around the table. "But who am I to complain?" he said, spreading his hands. "If the kid wants me to take his money, why should I care? Hey, dumkopf, you've got your hack parked out front. Go pick up a few fares and come back when you've got the cash to ante up again. Never let it be said that Jules Pinsky never gave a sucker a second chance to be a sucker again." He guffawed heartily.

"Well, now you've got to excuse me, fellas. Me and Arnie got some private business to discuss. But Siding King will be back, never fear. Too much bread in the bakery for him to stay away too long." He rose and followed me through the living room and down the hall to my room.

I sat on my bed. Eagle-Nose turned down the volume on the Beethoven Violin Concerto so it couldn't be heard, then sat down on a straight chair. I got up and raised the sound so it was soft background. I paced around.

Eagle-Nose said, lighting his cigar, "So what's it gonna hurt to please your mother by going to the bar mitzvah? Answer me that."

"I think you've got enough problems with Irwin," I said sharply, "without butting into my affairs, which are none of your business. Besides, it's not why I want to talk to you."

Eagle-Nose had in injured look. "Arnie, Arnie, why don't you ever give me a chance? What is it I always do so wrong to always get you so pissed at me? Your mother cares for me. I care for her. Why hold that against me?"

"Myrna doesn't know who she cares for. Your being around only makes her more confused. So don't think you're such a godsend. Now, do you want to listen to me or keep listening to yourself? Something happened today I think you ought to know about."

Jules grinned. "I *know* something happened today, Arnie. I know all about it, and I want *you* to know it's already all taken care of. No fuss, no sweat when Jules Pinsky, the Siding King, takes care of things. Maybe you'll learn from this I'm not such a bad guy."

I was wary. If Eagle-Nose knew everything that happened, he sure was acting strange. Could it be that he really did have the clout to get me off the hook? "Tell me what you know, Jules," I said. "Who clued you in?"

He was really pleased with himself. He leaned back in his chair so that the front legs were off the ground, took a long draw on his cigar, and exhaled slowly. "Sometimes I get the idea you don't exactly have the greatest confidence in me, Arnie," he said, grinning with fake disappointment, "and that kinda gets me right here." He rapped his cigar hand several times against his heart. "The name Johnny Salerno mean anything to you?" he asked, sticking it in.

"So Salerno did get in touch with you. What did the punk say?"

"What do punks usually say? He tried to tell me how you messed up his deal with his broad. I sure gotta hand it to you," Eagle-Nose chuckled, "you sure pulled off a ballsy caper. I'm really impressed. Shows that when it comes to ballsy capers, you're almost in the Jules Pinsky league."

"So you backed me up with Salerno?"

"Can you doubt it, Arnie? I told Salerno you were like my own son to me. I told the crumb where to get off for doubting you in the first place. I cut him off and told him, far as I was concerned, the matter was over, kaput. You kicked his ass and I'm proud of the way you did it. Now, doesn't that tell you something about me?"

"And he took it? I mean he just swallowed your line whole? He didn't mention anyone else?"

"He was scared shitless after I let him know who he was talking to. It only goes to show, Arnie, what I've been telling you all along, it's not *what* you know, it's *who* you know, and you gotta admit, you're pretty lucky to know me."

"He never mentioned Uncle Pietro?"

Eagle-Nose's face darkened. "Uncle Pietro Celli? What's he got to do with this?"

It was like I figured. Salerno *had* pussyfooted with Eagle-Nose. He didn't have the guts to tell him the whole story after Eagle-Nose turned him off. He left it up to me to tell him.

"Salerno borrowed five grand from Uncle Pietro to promote the career of the singer. He had a deal to share the profits on a hit song with Pietro. Not only is he not going to have the hit song, he doesn't have the five grand to repay him."

"Yeah, but what does all this have to do with me?"

"The way I got Salerno to back off going to Pietro and telling him that the singer had backed out of the deal, and I was part of it, was to tell him that I knew someone big who wouldn't be afraid to tell Pietro how it was Salerno himself who queered the deal by being such a schmuck. That someone was you. I told him you'd get Pietro to kick his ass Pietro-style if he started shooting off his mouth to Pietro. So far it's held him off. Now you've scared him some more. The only problem, no matter how you cut it, is that Salerno still owes Pietro the five grand, and sooner or later, when Pietro asks him about it, he's going to have to tell him."

Eagle-Nose was turning white as I explained. His face twisted in pain. He could barely stutter: "How . . . how . . . how could you say something like that . . . without knowing what you're talking about?"

"Well, didn't you just get done telling me about your connections? Aren't you known as the Jewish guy in Chicago with the biggest in to the mob? I've heard you say so over a hundred times."

The veins in Eagle-Nose's head were swelling. He was turning beet red. I thought he might hemorrhage at any second. "You little putz. How could you say something like that? Don't you realize there are things you say that you mean and other things that you don't mean so much — it's more for show. I was never *serious* when I said I had the kind of connections *you're* talking about. Oh, shit, Uncle Pietro..." Eagle-Nose clapped his hand to his suddenly sweating forehead.

"You mean you were bullshitting all along? You don't really have any connections with Uncle Pietro? You don't have Mayor Daley and Jake Arvey and the city council and Adlai Stevenson and President Eisenhower and John Foster Dulles in your hip pocket like you like to tell everyone at Fritzel's? You mean you were really full of shit all the time?"

Eagle-Nose spread his hands in hopeless explanation. "I know him... I don't know him... It's not like I can go up to Pietro and explain to him why this broad is costing him five grand and he shouldn't do anything about it on account of I can vouch for the kid that squashed the deal. No, no, Arnie, I can't do anything like that. Incidentally" — Eagle-Nose's face darkened again as new thought hit him — "what *about* the five grand? Pietro's going to expect *someone* to pay it. He may expect that someone to be me. Oh, shit, Arnie, you've really done it this time."

"You don't have to worry about the five grand, Jules. The five grand is not your problem. I'll probably find out more about it tonight."

"Tonight? What's happening tonight?"

Before I could explain, though, I heard a voice singing in the hallway, coming toward my room. It was strangely familiar, I'd heard it only recently...

" 'See the Pyramids *along* the Nile... / Watch the sun rise... on a tropic isle... / Just remember... all the *while*... / You belong... to *me*.' "

There was a knock at the door. I said come in. It was none other than Spieler La Chance. With a boozy glow, he opened the door and bent into the room, his alert, bright eyes taking us in. He was dressed like Adolph Menjou, in a beautiful double-breasted pin-striped suit. "I hope I'm not interrupting a deep session," he said cheerfully.

"Mr. La Chance, what are you —"

"*Shhhh.*" Spieler put his finger against his lips and cocked his ear toward the record player. "What a gorgeous piece," he said, and went over to the record player and bent toward the speaker to hear the piano, violin and cello playing together in soaring melody. "Do you mind?" he said to me, indicating he wanted to turn the volume up.

"Be my guest."

Spieler did it. He stood up and raised his head and closed his eyes, let the stirring romantic music flow through him. He hummed along. "Bum-*bum*-bum-bum-bum-bum. Bum-*bum*-bum-bumbum-bum. Ah, wonderful," he sighed, "just gorgeous. The name of this piece is on the tip of my tongue. Who's it by, Arnie?"

I'd heard it before, too. It was a favorite of Zach's. But I couldn't think of the composer either. The record had been misplaced in a Bach record jacket, so there was no help there. I told Spieler I would stop the record player to look at the record.

"No, don't bother. Sometimes it's a pleasure not knowing something for a while. I'll get it. And speaking of remembering, I'm supposed to remind you you're supposed to drive Angie out to the Villa Georgio. They're all waiting in the living room for you. Are you in pain?" he asked Eagle-Nose who'd been sitting there with this stupefied look on his sweaty face.

"Uncle Pietro ... Oh, Christ ... ," he muttered.

I looked at my watch. Time to get going. I told Spieler I'd join him and the others in two minutes. He left me alone with Eagle-Nose. I took a last look at him. He was too far gone for any more discussion. I joined the others in the dining room.

All the guys, old and young alike, had this amazed look on their faces as Spieler and Randy kibitzed with them. It was like the two baseball heroes had magically dropped from the sky, like gods, to put in an appearance here. Not only had the Cubs' success gotten the guys off their usual boasting bullshit, but the real live presence of the guys responsible for that success made them beside themselves with pleasure. It was like a lightning flash of happiness they might never know again.

Angie and Jamey stood by, and Jamey came over and explained that Spieler had invited Randy and Angie and Jamey to join him and his date, Vicki, for dinner, and Spieler had picked up the tab. At the restaurant, Angie had revealed that a top agent was coming to hear her perform tonight and Spieler said, if she was that good, then everyone ought to go to the nightclub with her and cheer her performance. Everyone at the table agreed. I was going to ask Jamey if Angie had had a chance to tell Randy what happened this morning, but from the warning look that Angie shot me, I knew she hadn't. As Spieler and Randy continued to jaw, she came over to me and tried to get in a word. But Myrna, good hostess that she always was, carried over a tray of chopped-liver finger sandwiches on little round pieces of rye bread and pressed them on Angie as we tried to talk. "You'll need energy for your performance," she insisted. "Take a few in these napkins."

For me she played a different but familiar tune. "Yes, you'll go to nightclubs and God knows where else all over the city, but to Cousin Selma's bar mitzvah for Alvin you won't go for my sake, you uncaring child."

I turned and glared at her. "Enough already with that bar mitzvah crap, Myrn. Cut it out, you hear?"

I'd nailed her for once. She stood there blinking, looking sorry that she'd said it. But then in her loony way, she was right back trying to make me feel guilty about something else. "Did you ever think that your mother would like to go to the nightclub with you?"

What could I say to that? "Tell Eagle-Nose you and him are welcome to come."

Now Spieler was at Myrna's side. He saw the chopped-liver finger sandwiches and took a bite from one. "Ah, delish," he said, "almost as tasty-looking as the pretty ladies in this room. This one's an emerald," he said, taking Angie's cheek between his thumb and forefinger, "and this one's a ruby," doing the same with his other hand to Myrna. Gently he drew each lady toward him until their lips were against each cheek and they planted giggling kisses on him. "Ah, women," he sighed, "sometimes you are *so* wonderful and sometimes you are *so* bad. Either way, Seymour the Spieler is your slave forever. Shall we go on to the nightclub, everyone?"

My car was parked nearby and we all piled in and, within a few minutes, for the second time that day, I was driving on Ogden Avenue, headed back to the southwest side. There wasn't much traffic now and the sights of the city rolled past like a negative exposure of everything we'd seen earlier. I'd put the top down and there were hundreds of stars in the broad dark sky. Angie was between Spieler and me in front. Spieler's date Vicki — a flaming readhead with enormous jugs — was between Randy and Jamey in back. Randy was pulling on a half-pint of bourbon and telling Jamey funny stories about his minor-league experiences with the Memphis Chicks of the Southern Association. The Chicks were Jamey's favorite minor-league team, and when we stopped for a light, I looked back and saw that he had that same amazed look as the guys at the poker game.

Spieler had drifted into a world of his own. Head back on top of the seat, he gazed up at all those stars. "Ah, Chicago," he said gratefully. "I'm so glad you're a big-league town. The town that Spieler La Chance could not close down. Thank God I'm not managing in Cincinnati." Then he took a pull of his own half-pint and drifted away again, with a distant gleam in his eye. Once he came out with a grainy refrain: " 'See the market place in *old* ... Al-giers ... / Send me photographs and sou-ve-nirs ... / Just remember when a dream ap-*pears* ... / You belong ... to *me*.' "

He hummed right after: "*Bum*-bum-bum-bumbum-bum. *Bum*-bum-bum-bumbum-bum."

Angie whispered to me: "Did you talk to Eagle-Nose Pinsky?"

"Um-huhm."

"So, what's up?"

"So, it's tricky. Salerno got in touch with Eagle-Nose. Eagle-Nose scared him off from talking to Pietro for a while. The catch is, Eagle-Nose doesn't have such good connections with Pietro. Sooner or later Salerno has got to explain that five grand to Pietro."

She was silent for a while, worried; then said, "So what do you think's gonna happen tonight?"

"Your guess is as good as mine. But I think you should just go along and sing and try to pretend there's nothing wrong."

"The five grand scares me. It's gonna make Johnny crazy."

"Please don't worry about the five grand, Angie."

"How can I not worry about it, Arnie?"

I was silent for a while, worried too. "Cause I'm gonna cover it," I finally blurted.

"You're gonna cover the five grand for me? Why should you do that for me?"

"I don't know why. Don't ask me to explain. I just want to, okay? Now stop gabbing. Save your breath for singing."

"Hey, kids, you want to deal me in on the matter?" Spieler had snapped out of it and was looking at us with a concerned expression. "I'm a few months older than either of you guys, and maybe I know a few angles you haven't thought of."

Neither Angie nor I knew what to say. I drove along awhile, looking at the people walking under the street lamps along Douglas Park. In the back, Randy kept swigging from his bottle and he got funnier and more off-color as he reminisced about his escapades with the Chicks. One when he was warming up in a bullpen, some gamblers had put bourbon in his Coca-Cola and he went in to pitch blind drunk, with bases-loaded and no outs, and got the side out. Vicki was also swilling out of Randy's bottle and getting high. Feeling neglected, she was saying to no one in particular that she was really going to learn to love baseball now that she knew Spieler.

"I think I should warn you, Mr. La Chance," I said at last, "that we've got a problem with some pretty bad guys. It's not the kind of thing you want to stick your nose into."

Spieler raised an eyebrow. He was impressed. "You sure you want to look a gift horse in the mouth? It's not every guy I offer a helping hand."

"Don't think I wouldn't like it."

"Do you agree with him, Angie?"

She nodded glumly. "We need all the help we can get, Spieler. But unfortunately, Arnie's right. You shouldn't get involved in this."

"So be it." Spieler shrugged. "Can't say I didn't try. I like your style, Arnie. Got some players I wish were as gutsy as you." Spieler lowered himself into his seat once more and stared up at the stars again, drifting back into himself.

I liked Spieler's style. He was the first person I ever knew who understood my feelings right away. It was a hell of a time for it to happen.

The Villa Georgio was about ten miles beyond the farthest southwestern city limit of Chicago, in open farm country. It had a reputation going back to Prohibition as a mob-controlled place, a favorite spot of Al Capone and other hoods. It was set back close to half a mile from the highway and completely hidden by a big dense grove of trees. A road circled through the trees, and I pulled up at a palazzo straight out of Venice, Italy.

A swarthy doorman greeted us dressed as a romantic gondolier: wide-brimmed flat-top hat, striped open shirt, sash around his waist. Some romantic gondolier! Even as he recognized Spieler and grunted, "Welcome to duh Villa Georgio, Mr. La Chance," his suspicious eyes were sizing us up through his toothy smile.

We passed through large glass doors into the glittery darkness of the place, through a lobby that led into the main dining room. The walls had murals of Venetian palazzos that made it seem like we were sailing down the Grand Canal. A cadaverous-looking maître d' greeted us He was wearing a white dinner jacket and had dyed jet-black curly hair like Tony Bennett, which only brought out his great age.

The cadaver came to life as he, too, recognized Spieler and gave him a cracked smile, and all the creases in his dried-up face got deeper.

"Yes, sir, Mr. La Chance," he said with oily courtesy, "for such an honored guest, I do believe we can find a ringside table."

Angie departed and the maître d' — his name was Dom — led us under an archway in the shape of the Rialto Bridge into a big dark main room with more columns and archways. We glided through the columns and past murals of naked women on the dim, dark walls, past tables of people within the columns, to a table near the raised area of the bandstand. On it, a lonely piano, bass fiddle, set of drums, and saxophone waited to be used. People recognized Spieler and Randy as we passed and called out greetings and nice things about the Cubs. Spieler took it all in stride. With a grin, he nodded and saluted at the voices from the darkness.

The table was big and round, and as we were seated and my eyes grew accustomed to the dark, I looked around. Angie had said it was a popular spot and she wasn't kidding — all the tables were filled. There were a lot of hard-eyed, beetle-browed guys staring us down like the doorman had. They were accompanied by a lot of bottle-blond tootsies with bare shoulders and bosom-revealing dresses. There were also a lot of hard-drinking fair-skinned handsome WASPs with their hard-drinking fair-skinned handsome wives, not to mention a good many noisy vulgar types who would've been at home trading phony stories with Eagle-Nose, but the main sense you got of the place was of a steely mob-infested crowd. The air of suspicion was as thick as pea soup. I saw Johnny Salerno staring knives at me from the bar. I wondered if Uncle Pietro was here too.

Spieler was in good form. He was displaying what Mike Ginsburg in one of his columns called his "savoir faire." He was going through an intricate discussion with Dom and the headwaiter, Dino, about the items on the menu and finally settled on Chianti classico and a variety of Italian cheeses for all of us. Some of the people from other tables had sent over complimentary drinks and Randy already had several bourbons in front of him. Other people came up and started to chat with Spieler and Randy and ask for their autographs. Jamey had this wondrous expression on his face, as though he were in a world he'd never known existed. It was almost time for Angie to come on.

Dom went up on the bandstand, took the microphone, and welcomed us all to the Villa Georgio. He proudly announced that there were some celebrities in the crowd. He introduced a couple of local television entertainers, a middleweight contender, a Hollywood character actor from Chicago, and, finally, Spieler and Randy. The crowd clapped and cheered. The Cubs were the darlings of the town. The two of them stood and waved and exchanged friendly banter with the crowd. Jamey and Vicki basked in the pleasure of being part of it. And Johnny Salerno slid into the seat next to me.

"You little turd."

"You just never know when you're not wanted, do you, Salerno? No one asked you to sit down."

"You screwed me this morning, turd."

I couldn't help grinning at him.

"You think you're smart, huh, turd? You think you can get away with screwing Johnny Salerno? I'm here to tell you that you and Eagle-Nose Pinsky and Angie Bishop and her stupid brother are all in trouble."

"You played that song this morning, Salerno. Is that all you can do, come on like a broken record?"

"You're the one that's gonna be broken up if you don't come up with ten grand by noon tomorrow."

"Ten grand? I thought five was what you borrowed."

"You heard me, turd. *Ten* to you. The extra five is vigorish for screwing me. Teach you to try to screw Johnny Salerno."

"You're out of your skull, Salerno. Just what makes you think I'm gonna give you ten grand?"

"I'll tell you what makes me think so, turd. You think I don't know that bitch tried to double-cross me by having the agent out here tonight without me knowing about it? Well, you got another think coming. Her screwing me is like her screwing Uncle Pietro. All I gotta do is tell Pietro what she tried to do and she'll never work again in this town or any town, you better believe it. You gonna come up with that ten grand, turd?"

I don't know why — Salerno sounded convincing — but I still didn't believe he had the guts to tell Pietro anything. He was still gonna look bad with Pietro any way you cut it. But he was capable of lousing up Angie's act if I gave him a good enough reason. I saw Angie near the edge of the bandstand. She was looking at Salerno and me and she was plenty scared. I had no choice but to string Salerno along.

"You'll get your ten grand, Salerno," I said, "on one condition. That you don't do a single thing to louse up Angie's show. Do that and I'll bust your ass good."

"This guy part of the problem you wouldn't tell me about?" It was Spieler talking as he slipped back into his seat. He was sizing up Salerno with an icy glare.

"Forget it, Spieler," I said. "You've got better things to do than bother with this punk. Randy doesn't need to know about him either." I glanced sharply at Randy across the table and Spieler got the message, understood right away that Salerno was involved with Angie in a way that Randy wouldn't go for, and Spieler would be in danger of having his best relief pitcher getting hurt in a brawl if Randy found out about it.

Now Jamey saw Salerno and anger flared up in his face. "Cool it, Jamey," I said across the table. "Remember the most important thing is Angie up there. Everything's under control right here."

My words made Randy look around at Salerno with a hard expression. I waved a friendly hand at Angie at the piano. Spieler pointed sharply to Randy to turn around and do the same.

"And now," Dom announced, "without further uhdo, the Villa Georgio is proud to present... *Miss*... Angie Bishop..."

A soft spotlight focused on Angie as she started to play her first number. But the tension from seeing Salerno showed in her face and her voice was strained as she tried an upbeat version of "This Can't Be Love." She wasn't much better with her second number, a slowed-down "The Very Thought of You." She had a lovely voice, strangely deep but like a bell, but none of her first five or six numbers were very well done; Angie just couldn't untrack herself, and the only reason the crowd had for paying attention to her was because she was so bad. Fortunately, the group accompanying her was great. They picked up quickly on the fact that she was out of sync and took off on long riffs to let her recover. Finally, even they couldn't keep people from talking and not paying attention to her as she sang. They scarcely clapped when her set ended.

During the break, we all put on a brave show and didn't mention Angie's bad performance. Spieler took our minds off it with a lot of funny stories. Then Dom came over and said there was a lady who wanted to join our party. As he put a chair between Spieler and me, Myrna, looking windblown, a perfect knockout as always, came up and sat down. She said enthusiastically to Spieler, "I just didn't want to miss Angie's show. I've got this certain feeling about her that she's really good. You know what I mean, Mr. La Chance?"

"Spieler, dear. I do know what you mean about her. I feel it myself." At that moment, some people interrupted him and got him in conversation about the Cubs, so Myrna turned to me and said cuttingly, "You don't mind if your mother joins you? She does deserve some fun out of life once in a while. You do remember that you invited me?"

"I remember, Myrn. Where's Eagle-Nose?"

"Oh, *him*. I *asked* him if he wanted to come. But he was sitting there in your room with this look like he'd seen a ghost and he wouldn't answer me. He can be such a bore sometimes."

"So you drove yourself?"

She pursed her lips before answering. "No, Irwin drove me," she said irritably, looking away from me and ordering a glass of red wine from the waiter. But she felt my questioning stare and looked back at me and said defensively, "Why shouldn't Irwin drive me out? After all, he'd lost all his money and his cab was parked in front and he needed a fare. Anything wrong with that?"

"Nothing that I can think of. Where's Pigeon-Face now?"

She shook her head in disgust. She was really annoyed by something. Myrna took a good gulp of wine and leaned forward and screwed up her eyes in this sincere way. "I want you to know something, Arnold," she said emphatically. "I don't particularly like Irwin. He's kind of a schmucky kid when you come right down to it, but also there's something about him that makes you feel sorry for him, you know what I mean? Like the way his father treats him. I was in the kitchen when Jules screamed at him, but some of the guys told me what happened. And believe me, you're never going to get me to apologize for the abominable behavior of Jules Pinsky. That was one of the reasons I asked Irwin to drive me, so I could tell him a few things about his situation that would help him. I wanted to tell him he shouldn't *let* his father treat him like a dog. He only invites it by his kick-me need to be insulted. He shouldn't be living at home around his father. He should move out and make his own way in life. I wanted to tell him all these things out of the goodness of my heart, but you know what the kid has the nerve to tell me?" Myrna took another good gulp of wine; she was right at the nub of her annoyance. "He says I've got enough problems with my own son without telling him how to live his life. He says he didn't want my advice, just pay him what's on the meter so he can race back across the city and get back in the game. And I was furious! Imagine getting sass from this foolish kid I was only trying to help! And I said to him, 'Irwin, I don't care anymore what you do with your life, but let me give you one last piece of advice. Whatever you do, don't get back in that game. You're a lousy poker player and you should learn to play before you get involved for such high stakes.' And you know what he says to me? Unbelievable! He says to me, 'Mind your own business, Myrna. You yourself aren't doing so well with my father that you can tell me what to do about him.' An impudent young man! Headstrong! Reminds me of someone else I know who's undergoing growing pains and doesn't want to listen to anyone. Just what in the world did you say to Jules to get him so upset?"

Another zinger! Myrn at the top of her game turning things around! Luckily, Angie was returning to the piano for her second show and Myrn saw her and stood up and called out: "Hi, honey. I made it after all. I just wanted to hear you sing. I know you're great!" Spieler, taking his cue from Myrn, bought some gardenias from a cigarette girl, tied them together into a corsage with his silk handkerchief, went up to the piano and presented them to Angie. She was deeply touched by it and smiled warmly as tears filled her eyes. And it seemed to have some effect.

Right from the start everyone in the room got the sense that this was a different singer. The words flowed straight from Angie's heart. Her expressive face, with its strong bones and all the years of hard knocks on it, and those deep-set, haunted eyes that spoke all her pain, began to shine with strong emotions. Her voice went through us like a warm stream. Angie set off waves of sorrow and joy and many strange feelings in between, and all the attentive people in the crowded room began to feel what she felt, the dark suspicion began to lighten — as though Angie's voice were the sun breaking through — and was driven away by the feelings she conveyed in her songs. For a while she made us all feel deeply about the pain of life. All the hard-eyed hoods remembered they were mothers' sons. All the bottle blonds remembered when love was pure. Angie touched our souls. There was a great loud silence when she finished and then great, spontaneous applause. Even Johnny Salerno had the look of a cast-off lover. I knew in my heart that Myrna's coming and her calling out were what inspired Angie to sing so well.

As soon as Angie finished, Spieler, in his enthusiasm, raced up to her and called for an encore. He stayed near the piano as Angie responded with a haunting version of "I Almost Got Lucky with You."

Salerno may have been briefly moved, but it only made him more determined. "About the ten grand, turd," he started in again as Angie sang, "I'll be at the Wells Street Bridge over the Chicago River at noon tomorrow. You better be —"

"Hold on, Salerno," I cut him off. I called to Randy and Jamey across the table that as soon as Angie finished, they should go right away to be with her and make sure this guy didn't get near her. I pointed my thumb at Salerno.

Randy, who was plenty bombed, stared hard at Salerno and asked who he was. "Get him out of here now," I said to Jamey, and he started tugging Randy toward the dressing room. "C'mon, Randy, c'mon," he said soothingly. "I got a feeling Angie is gonna need us. Let's go to her room."

"You think *they're* gonna stop me?" Salerno sneered. "No one's gonna stop me."

"Who *is* this creep?" Myrna asked. She'd had a second glass of wine and she wasn't such a great drinker.

"Please stay out of this, Myrn," I said.

"The turd's right, lady. Don't stick your pretty face in where you ain't invited."

"Just who do you think you're insulting, creep? You've got no right to call my son names."

"Hey, lady, you and me ain't got no quarrel. It's not my fault that your son is a turd who owes me money."

Myrna looked sharply at Salerno. She looked sharply at me. "Arnold, you do a lot of things that you shouldn't do — sometimes I think the only reason you do them is to make me think I haven't been a good mother — but I know you don't owe this creep money. Tell me you don't owe him money."

"For once you're right, Myrn. I don't owe this creep money. But that's not the point, because he thinks I do. I really appreciate your standing up for me — you'll never know how much I do — but I want you to leave us alone now. Please go get ready to leave with Spieler." He had just come back to the table.

But Myrn wasn't ready to go. Those two glasses of wine had really gone to her head. "I want you to know," she warned Salerno, squinting her eyes and shaking her finger, "that my son has some pretty good connections in this town. If he tells them he doesn't owe you money, you can be damn sure they're going to believe him rather than you."

Salerno gave her a withering look. "Oh, yeah, lady? Like who?"

"Like..." Myrna stopped to think about it, her face screwed up in thought. "Like Jules 'Eagle-Nose' Pinsky, that's who. I'm sure you've heard of him."

It deflated Salerno like a balloon. He sighed with exasperation and eyed her wearily. "Look, lady, my patience is just about shot with all of youse. The turd and I both asked ya to stay out of this. Tell her, turd, I know all about Eagle-Nose Pinsky."

"He does, Ma. Look, it's complicated. I haven't got time to explain. I'm so proud of you for sticking up for me, but I want you to go away now. Please take her away, Spieler."

He'd been standing there, a gleam in his eye, totally fascinated by the scene.

"Why does this guy think you owe him money?" he asked.

"I told you before, Spieler, I don't want you involved in this. Please take Myrna away."

Spieler nodded. But he didn't move. Instead, he said nicely but firmly to Myrna, "I want you to leave us now. Go back to Angie's dressing room. And don't worry. Arnie and I will be along soon."

It wasn't like Myrn to do exactly as she was told. Surprisingly, she drifted away without a murmur.

"Okay," Spieler said to me sternly, "being-a-hero time is over. I want to know what's going on."

I did what he wanted, just like Myrna; told him the whole story.

"I figured it was something like that," Spieler said. He glared at Salerno. "Okay, vulture," he said disgustedly, "let's see if we can't do something about you right away." He motioned to Dom, who, sensing trouble, was standing nearby.

"You got a problem, Spieler?"

Spieler whispered into Dom's ear. I heard Uncle Pietro's name mentioned and saw Dom nod and gesture behind him toward a dark section of tables. Dom went off in that direction. He came back in a few minutes and whispered again in Spieler's ear. Spieler got up and followed him into the darkness.

He returned just as Angie and Randy and Jamey and

Myrna and Vicki came back to get us. He abruptly ordered them all to wait for us at my car. He sat down and asked me, "Can you pay off that five grand tomorrow?"

"I can get it just as soon as the banks open."

"The kid says he can do it," Spieler said to Dom. The latter nodded and disappeared again.

Spieler handed me a Villa Georgio matchbook. He said there was a guy's name and an address written inside. He said to get the money to the guy by noon tomorrow. That would take care of the debt, free and clear. Now there was only one thing.

"What's that, Spieler?"

"What to do about this vulture here. I hope I didn't make a big mistake."

"What k-kind of mistake?" Salerno asked fearfully.

"I didn't tell them back there how you were trying to put the screws on. I think you know what would've happened to you if I did. I think you'd better take off, pronto, don't you, Salerno?"

Salerno stared at Spieler for just a moment. A look of relief, a look of hate, no gratitude. But he took his cue and got up and left without a word.

I didn't know what to say, just stared at Spieler in awe.

"What's the matter, kid? I got dandruff on my lapels?"

"I don't know how to thank you, Spieler."

"No thanks necessary. Let's get ready to go find an all-night spot for omelets and coffee."

"No one in my whole life ever stood up for me the way you did just now."

"I'm sorry I can't agree with you on that score. I was only taking my cue from your mother here. She was one tough chick against that bum."

"I suppose she was ... I don't know what came over her."

"Ladies are loony. Don't try too hard to figure them out.

Just give her credit for coming through when you needed her."

"People are so strange, Spieler. I'll never figure them out."

"Life is strange, kid. The older I get, the more I realize how full of surprises it is. Bet that's a surprise coming from a know-it-all like Spieler La Chance."

"Yeah . . . I guess it is."

"You don't have to look so skeptical. It's really been some night. Say, I almost forgot to tell ya, I even remembered the name of that violin piece."

"You did?"

"Sure thing. It was the Tchaikovsky Trio in A Minor. My old man was a gypsy violinist and he used to do a schmaltzy version with his buddies. Gorgeous piece. Rich as chocolate cake."

"Your father played the violin, Spieler?"

"He sure did. Worked for thirty years in Europe and the States. If I'd had his talent, I'd have done it too. I loved hearing him play the fiddle."

I was silent. Life *was* full of surprises. I hardly knew what to say about it.

Part Two

CHAPTER

6

IT WAS WONDERFUL! The town was going wild! In July
the Cubs went on a tear, won 22 and lost only 7 and took
over first place. They were 3 games up on the Dodgers going into the last weekend of the month. It wasn't easy.
Time after time they hung onto a lead or rallied miracu-
lously to win. They never lost without a struggle.

All the guys were coming through. Though still bitter
that his holdout failed, Elmo Speakes was slashing the ball
all over the lot, hitting .360, making spectacular catches
and throws and running the bases like a demon. Wally
Koslowski had 22 homers and nearly 70 runs batted in.
Joey de Angelo, the little shortstop and lead-off man, was
hitting .350, had stolen 40 bases, was making impossible
plays in the field. Royal Farrell at second, Lonnie Block at
third, Ironhead Sykes the catcher, Lance Lawrence in
right, Mark Cacoyannis in left were playing the best ball
of their careers. That pitching staff, which Jamey and others said didn't have much depth, had been a tremendous
surprise. Elijah St. John, that amazing pitching machine
from the Dominican Republic, was going the distance and
winning tough game after tough game, 8–6, 5–4, 6–5, 7–6,
always getting stronger in the late innings. The fact that

he finished almost every game he started saved a lot of wear on the bullpen. Lefty Monroe and Dale Wishnikopf, the number-2 and -3 starters, were winning consistently too. As for the bullpen situation, though right after Jimmy Weatherford was injured the Cubs had acquired veteran reliever Mickey Malone from the Cincinnati Reds and brought up their best reliever from their triple-A farm club in Los Angeles, neither of them could oust Randy Dodds from the number-one slot. For more than a month he'd been a tower of strength, saving game after game, coming to the rescue in cliff-hanging situations, firing his hard sinker on the knees and making the batters bang it into the ground. Of the 22 games the Cubs won in July, Randy won 4 and saved 12; he was right at the heart of things in 16 wins. He was pitching his best ever in his 13-year big-league career, and the person he publicly gave all the credit to was Spieler La Chance. "Without his confidence from the moment Jimmy was felled, I'd probably be back in the bushes. He's been like a father to me."

Ah, Spieler. He was really something else these days. His magic was working like something down from heaven. Every move he made seemed blessed, pinch hitters got pinch hits, hit-and-run plays kept the Cubs out of double plays, guys put in the game for defense kept coming up with great plays, Spieler's instinct was uncanny in pulling pitchers or letting them stay, someone was always delivering for him in the clutch. Reading about Spieler in the papers, seeing him on the tube, he was, as Mike Ginsburg put it in his column, "a whirling verbal dervish," cheering his gang, backing them up and jacking them up and making people finally believe that this really was the Cubs' year. The truly amazing thing about it was that though it seemed the players had to be feeling pretty good about everything to play so well, it wasn't that way at all.

I got to know Randy Dodds fairly well, and it was

Randy who clued me in that a lot of dissension was brewing among the guys. The fans pouring into Wrigley Field and the pile that Bobby Wentworth was making from it had made them madder than ever about the way Bobby had slammed the door on their salary demands. Making the most noise in the locker room was — you guessed it — old Elmo. The thing about him was that he was a foulmouthed grousing loner, which made him about as popular with his teammates as the owner. His bitching and moaning in the clubhouse every day about everything imaginable — meal money, dirty uniforms, travel arrangements — really stuck in the guys' craws, especially because he was right and they hated like hell for him to be the one to say it, and the situation was getting worse every day. It'd reached the point where resentment was running high again against Spieler for being Bobby's front man on the contracts. For a while Spieler had kept the peace by telling the guys that this was the first time Bobby Wentworth ever realized he could make money from baseball. When he knew what it was like to profit from winning the pennant and then the Series, he'd learn to be more generous with his players; but even Spieler had to grin when the guys told him it was a lot of garbage he was spewing.

Then from somewhere the rumor started that in return for helping him hold off the players' demands, Bobby Wentworth had given Spieler a big bonus. Royal Farrell approached Spieler in a bar and asked him pointblank if this was true. Spieler's eyes turned to ice as he glared at Royal, and didn't dignify the question with an answer. Instead, he sent Royal sprawling across the room with a right to the jaw and said he'd better be prepared to defend himself in an alley the next time he made a remark like that to him. It was, in Mike Ginsburg's words, "vintage Spieler," splitting opinion about him right down the middle, like the old days. Some guys appreciated Spieler's sense of honor;

others thought he was full of crap, as usual. It didn't cut a drop of ice with the latter that right after the incident with Royal, Spieler immediately demanded a session with Bobby and came out of it twenty minutes later with eyes blazing, saying to reporters only that he had no comment on the matter. But you knew they hadn't discussed the weather.

Even at this, everything might've gone along okay if Bobby Wentworth himself hadn't gotten into the act. You've got to remember that Bobby had plenty of resentments against Spieler for the large, multiyear pact he'd squeezed from him. So when reporters ran into him that same night after his session with Spieler, and asked him if he'd given Spieler a bonus for helping keep the players off his back, Bobby answered, half-crocked and bitterly: "La Chance and my wife are a lot alike. They put a high price tag on everything." In less than half an hour the remark had gotten back to the players in their different bars around the city, and so the whole thing was blazing again.

But what the players were starting to resent the most was that though they were the ones who had stormed into first place, it was Spieler who was getting most of the play from the radio and tv and newspaper guys. Though Spieler bent over backwards to put the spotlight on the players, the fact of the matter was that he was the one who made the best copy and gave the best interviews. He had a real talent for promotion. Though Bobby Wentworth didn't like it, there was nothing he was going to say or do as long as Spieler was making the turnstiles click. Though the players stewed, there was nothing they could find to do except go on winning. It was a real crazy situation.

While to the public Randy Dodds gave all the credit for his success to Spieler, to his friends he made no bones that Angie Bishop had even more to do with it. You didn't have to be together with them very long to see that he was head over heels in love with her. He worshipped the ground she walked on. Before he knew her, he was scared to death every time Spieler used him. One more bombing and he'd be on his way back to the Pacific Coast League. But knowing Angie gave him the confidence not to be afraid to go out there and do his best. She'd given him back his lease on life. He wanted to marry her as soon as the time was right.

One problem with this was that he already had a wife. And two kids to boot. Though they'd been separated for quite a while, his wife still loved him and wouldn't give him a divorce. She showed her love by putting the squeeze on him for more money for their kids. He worried about what she'd do if she ever found out about his going with Angie, if she ever knew that what made Randy prouder than his own comeback was that the agent who'd seen her at the Villa Georgio was really impressed with her. He got her a six-week booking at a top club, Nightwind, on the near north side. She opened in the middle of July. At her opening, nearly the whole Cubs ballclub and a lot of visiting Giants and Spieler and Vicki and Myrna and Eagle-Nose and Bobby Wentworth and Darlene and even Uncle Pietro and a lot of his boys and their gussied-up dolls all showed up and Angie was great and got rousing hands. Good word of mouth got around town and right away she began to draw nice crowds.

Randy admired the way Angie had struggled to survive in Chicago in the years since she'd first come north from Mississippi, a country girl who didn't know peadoodle about anything. He liked to tell the story of the way they met. They were sitting near each other at a bar and got to talking, and he got drunk and spilled out his problems. Angie drove him back to his apartment and put him to bed, and when he got up the next morning she was sleeping on the sofa next to his bed. He asked her why she'd stayed and she said she knew what it was like to be lonely and scared, with no one to tell your troubles to, and she didn't want him to wake up alone feeling as bad as he had the night before.

I could see why Randy needed Angie. She gave him all kinds of strength. Randy was honest in admitting that the thing he feared the most wasn't having to leave the majors — every ballplayer had to come to terms with that; it was having to leave Chicago and Angie that gave him sleepless nights.

I also admired Angie an awful lot. As I got to know her more, the thing that struck me most about her was that she wasn't very easy to know. She didn't let on her feelings about everything she thought. On the one hand, she could be an angel the way she was the night she met Randy. You could never for a moment doubt that she cared a lot about Randy, her feelings about him were more than just being grateful for the way he'd helped her with the Italian record deal.

But there was a part of her that was distant from him too. She could get completely involved in her music and her career and not care about anything else. And between her new engagement and rehearsing and other work her agent was getting her, and finding an apartment on the near north side, she had less time for Randy than before. He'd complained about it quite a few times at the start, to her and me and his buddies on the team, but he soon began to smile bravely to hide his pain and shrug and say this was the way things had to be for a while. Everything would be okay once Angie settled down in her new life and the danged pennant race was over. He even reluctantly agreed with Angie that they shouldn't do anything about his marriage situation until after the season was over.

Jamey had the same problem with her. You couldn't

doubt that Angie truly loved her brother. She spent a lot of time with him his first couple of weeks in town, but what with the move to the new club, she just didn't have much time for him after that. The thing that really disappointed him was that after he and I searched for an apartment for her and found one on Dearborn Parkway, not far from me, then supervised the moving of all her stuff, including her piano and her ton of music, from the southwest side, she sprung it on him that she didn't want him to live with her. The way she explained it to him was that though she hated to hurt him, she needed to be free to think about her music anytime she wanted to, night or day, and that someone else's presence in the apartment would distract her from it.

To some people it might sound selfish, and maybe it was, but all the same, you had to respect Angie for saying the way she felt and not creating complications in her life. She wasn't lying about feeling bad about having to say it, you could tell that from the pained look on her face. But she was determined to be successful and she couldn't lie about that for a minute.

So Jamey stayed with me until he got his own place and found a job, which didn't take long at all. He was a whiz at repairing cars, and he got hired at a gas station over on La Salle Street. He took a little place on West Huron Street, which was also not far from me.

Angie had said that living in Chicago might be a hard adjustment for Jamey to make, and though Jamey denied it, she was right. He really hadn't seen too much of the world and had a way of getting his nose out of joint over lots of people and things that were new to him in the city. He was suspicious of people he met, the musicians Angie knew, the sports crowd that hung around Randy and the rest of the Cubs, my friends from high school that I introduced him to. But he had enough good sense not to criticize anyone openly. We would never be the best of friends, but he was a likable guy who would do anything for me on account of the help I gave him, and whatever his strait-laced way of looking at things, he tried his best never to let it get the best of him.

He even admitted he was wrong in thinking Randy was all washed up. In fact, he had come to admire him a lot. More surprising was that he shifted his allegiance from the Cards to the Cubs. Like every other baseball fan in Chicago, he had gotten pennant fever and wanted the Cubs to win as much as I did. He was more upset than I was when Randy told us what was going on with Spieler and Bobby Wentworth and the Cubs. But he didn't say to me I told you so about Spieler in any way. If he had any feelings about Spieler's role in things, he was smart enough to keep his mouth shut. I suspected this was one of his ways of being nice to me for helping him find Angie.

As for me, I was doing pretty well . . . I guess. My problems with Myrna hadn't changed a bit. I talked to her a day or so after she showed up alone at the Villa Georgio and she acted like nothing at all had happened, would've probably denied showing up there if I'd pressed her on it. Instead, she acted like she'd never gotten disgusted with Eagle-Nose and everything was swell with them, and she was all over me for a change about going to work for him and what was I going to do with my life starting in the fall.

My grandfather Max was all over me for the same reason. Though I'd made applications to several schools, I'd done it mainly to keep Myrna and Max off my back. I frankly didn't know what I wanted to do and didn't feel any great urge to make a decision. The great summer and the Cub run for the pennant were keeping my mind off of those kinds of things. I was enjoying my apartment on North State Parkway. It was on the top floor of a grand old Chicago mansion, one huge floor-through room with part of two walls spreading out into a circular turret with big rounded windows looking out on other grand old mansions on the elegant tree-lined street. The most important thing, though, was that I'd made a new friend.

A couple of nights after the Villa Georgio I was sitting alone at Candido's, when who should come by but Kim, beautiful as ever. She nodded at me.

For her, a nod was as good as a smile, a real breakthrough. I nodded back and asked her to join me.

She surprised me by sliding into the booth, across from me. "You ever find Angie Bishop?" she asked.

"Yes, we did."

The faintest curve of satisfaction touched her lips. "That good thing you did."

"We almost got in a lot of trouble."

She looked curious, so I told her the part about Johnny Salerno at Angie's place.

She actually smiled, so I told her what happened later at the nightclub.

"Tewific ... tewific ...," she kept muttering. The story really loosened her up. She said a strange thing: "I wish I there with you."

"Why, Kim?"

All of a sudden her smile vanished and she became the beautiful grim face again.

"Well, next time something like that pops up, I'll take you with me. Would you like that?"

"We'll see," was her short answer.

I tried to think of other things to talk about, asked her if she'd like something to eat.

She shook her head.

"I hope you won't go now."

"I want ask you something."

"Sure."

"What you think about me?"

I was puzzled, didn't know what to say to such a blunt thing. "Is there something I'm supposed to think?"

She said more bluntly, "You think I hooker?"

I looked at her carefully. "What makes you think I'd think something like that?"

"Yes? No?"

"Well ... seeing the way you're putting it ... I guess I kinda got the impression ... you might be ..."

She was staring hard at me, her lips pursed.

"But what do I know, Kim? And what difference does it make what I think? Whatever you are, it's no business of mine."

"You mean you no care one way or the other?"

"Now wait a minute. I didn't say that. Do you want me to care?"

She was still staring hard at me, but her eyes were softer.

"I wish you'd tell me, Kim. I'd really like to know." I waited for her answer, looking sincere. "You're really not being very fair," I said, "seeing as how you're the one who brought up the subject."

She eyed me a few moments longer. "Hokay. No, yes. That your answer."

"No, yes?"

"No, I no hooker. Yes, you right to think I one."

"Okay ... ?"

"But it more complicated than that."

"So tell me. You seem to want to."

She eyed me some more, deciding whether to go on. "You think you trust me?" she asked.

"I guess I do. Is there some reason I shouldn't?"

She changed the subject. "You bet on baseball games?"

"Yes, I do. What of it?"

"You make money from bets?"

"I do okay. Do you need some money?"

"I need borrow money."

"How much money would you like to borrow?"

"You sure you trust me?"

"How much would you like to borrow?"

"Two thousand dollar."

I thought about it. Lately Weasel Arnie had become a banker. The five grand I'd given Pietro had reduced my savings to about thirty-five hundred. I'd loaned Angie some money too. But so what — easy come, easy go. It was only money. "Okay, you got it."

"You understand, I pay back with interest."

"It's not necessary."

"It necessary!"

"You don't have to get mad about it."

"I also pay back two-month time."

"There's no hurry, Kim."

She shook her head angrily. "No sirree. We can't be friends until I pay back. Can't be close until then. You know what I mean?"

"I understand. You'll pay me back with interest in two months' time. There's only one question I'd like to ask."

"What is it?"

"You wouldn't want to tell me why you need the money?"

She glared at me. "You schmuck. You know why I need money. To pay guy to get me out of no-yes situation. Any more stupid question?"

As a matter of fact, I did have one; got it out weakly. "How'd you know I bet on baseball games? I thought you never noticed me."

"I notice you," she said hotly. "I notice you for long time."

Why was it that Kim's anger didn't bother me? I wanted to think about it, but not right then. At that moment, something else seemed more important. I wanted Kim to go to the ballgame with me today. I asked her.

Tight-lipped, she looked at me. "You won't try get personal?"

"Personal?"

"You know I mean."

"No, I swear I won't try anything like that. I never dreamed that we —" Her hard look cut me off.

"Hokay, we go ballgame. What time start?"

It started like always at 1:30, only eleven hours from now. I picked her up at her place at 11:00; we had a fast lunch at Tony Zale's and settled into our box seats behind the Cub dugout as Elijah St. John was about to throw the first pitch.

Kim had never seen a baseball game. She didn't know a thing about how it was played. I tried to fill her in as the game went on. With those firm lips and wary eyes, she gazed around in wonder at everything going on. It wasn't so much the game itself that made her curious as it was the sight of all these people sitting in the sun in this strange-shaped place and eating hot dogs and ice cream and peanuts and drinking beer and lemonade and enjoying the things going on on the field.

It was a game I'll never forget, one of those wind-swept kind that Wrigley Field is famous for. The wind was whipping around in different directions at the same time. Balls hit high in the air were bouncing around up there like corks in the ocean. Routine flys were going into the bleachers for home runs. Balls were falling safe all over the lot as outfielders chased after them and stopped on a dime and reversed directions like Keystone Cops. Runs were being scored in bunches by both sides. Duke Snider and Gil Hodges and Roy Campanella and Carl Furillo had hit homers for the Dodgers. Wally Koslowski and Elmo Speakes had connected twice each for the Cubs. Going into the eighth the Cubs were leading 16–11. But the Dodgers rallied against Randy Dodds. It wasn't Randy's fault that guys collided and balls fell just out of reach and the Dodgers were leading 17–16 going into the bottom of the ninth. Then, with two on and two outs, Elmo Speakes did it again, slammed a line drive under the wind into the right field seats — a ball that never was more than ten or twelve feet off the ground. The Cubs won 18–17. It was the wildest wackiest game you could ever imagine. It made you think the Cubs could do anything. Even Kim trembled with excitement as the crowd roared with happiness.

Maybe no one on the team may have liked Elmo personally, but they all converged at home plate to greet him as he circled the bases. Spieler was laughing and whooping as he clapped the smiling Randy on the back. I was so happy for the team, but even happier for myself. The Cubs had won and everyone could see the beautiful girl with me. I loved her big straw pink-ribboned hat and pretty slender white linen blouse unbuttoned to show her smooth throat. What difference did it make if Elmo Speakes, after he touched home plate and was headed to the dugout, had this sullen look as he stared at Kim; if Elmo needed to be sullen to keep hitting, that was fine with me. I was shouting at Spieler as he came back to the dugout behind Elmo: *"Hey, Spieler, you have definitely got a winner this time. The Cubs are going all the way."* And Spieler heard me. He came over to the railing and smiled and waved. "I would say that you too have a winner, Arnie." Spieler doffed his cap and bowed low from the waist to Kim. "A real pearl of the Orient," he said with a grin. Even Kim had to smile.

Back at my car again, I asked Kim if she'd like to take a drive with me. To my surprise, she said she would. I started north on Sheridan Road toward Evanston. I figured we'd go through the northern suburbs and have dinner somewhere up that way.

To my surprise again, Kim asked me to tell her about myself. I told her about being kicked out of Illinois. She wanted to know why I started betting on basketball games. I said I wasn't sure I knew the reason.

"What you think reason?" she demanded.

"Well, the shrink my mother sent me to said it was on account of low self-esteem. I didn't feel good about myself and I wanted to show people how bad I felt. That's why I didn't feel so good about my grandfather's lawyer getting me off. I didn't feel like I deserved it. You understand anything I'm saying?"

"Maybe. What else your shrink say?"

"Nothing else. I stopped seeing him. The stuff he wanted to discuss with me was stuff I wanted to discuss with my mother. But if she didn't want to discuss it with me, I sure as hell wasn't going to discuss it with her paid substitute. What do you make of that?"

"You no get along with your mother?"

"I no get along with her."

"What about father?"

"You sure you want to hear this stuff? It's such a beautiful day. That sunset is really something special."

"I want to hear about whole family."

Since she wanted to know so badly, I told her. Unloaded a lot. Felt kinda ashamed because I couldn't stop talking, but also felt good because I realized it was these things I wanted to unload on Kim from the start.

My earliest strong memories of my family together started when Zach came home from the war. Aside from Myrna being beautiful and Zach having a kind of sly wit and charm, I never could imagine what my parents saw in each other in the first place, because they seemed to have absolutely nothing in common. I don't remember one single day of total harmony in the house. They couldn't agree on the smallest thing — which restaurant we should eat at, which orthodontist Dan should go to, what kind of wallpaper to put on the bathroom walls, whether I

should buy Nova or some other kind of lox at the delicatessen.

With their friends Zach was lively and funny, but it was
a mask he took off whenever he was home with us, when a
kind of great sadness came over him. It was like he was
disappointed about something very important that he
wouldn't discuss with any of us. Maybe it was because
he'd stopped playing the violin since he'd gotten out of
the service, said he no longer had the patience or the dis-
cipline for it. Though he'd gotten a job as a tile salesman
and started to do real well at it — made a lot more money
than he ever had in his best years as a musician — it
didn't seem to make him any happier at home. He started
the habit of wanting to be left alone on weekends to listen
to his favorite violin music. Myrna accused him of deliberately cutting himself off from her and Dan and me and
you didn't have to be a psychologist to know she was
right. Or that Zach had to find some way to close himself
off from her.

Because Myrna also had a kind of sadness hanging over
her, and her way of dealing with it was to be totally nuts.
She could go for days lost in a teenage world of her own,
of movie magazines and tube watching and telling Dan
and me how great someone else's kids were because they'd
said or done some stupid thing like being voted best-
dressed sophomore or giving their mother a fur coat in
August. You could only deal with her as though she were
a spoiled child, always changing her mind and driving
everyone crazy trying to cope with her. She was always
dissatisfied, with the drapes she ordered, the paper plates
for a birthday, the size of the corned-beef sandwiches a
counterman gave us, something Dan or I didn't say or do
when we'd bent over backwards to please her for some
occasion. She was always shifting her affections from one
member of the family to another, playing off one person

against another, driving us crazy with screwy demands
that tested our love and then changing her mind before
those demands could be satisfied.

What was Myrna's problem? We all wished we knew.
Part of it, I guess, was the fact she was always Max's
favorite child — he crushed her two younger brothers, setting them up in business after business and then gloating
over the fact of how they'd run them into the ground and
needed him to bail them out — and he always spoiled her
something awful. He had great plans for Myrna, wanted
her to marry into wealth and social status, and he never
really forgave her for marrying Zach in the first place.

It was Sarah, Myrna's mother, who protected Zach and
Myrna from Max and his attempts to poison the marriage
during the thirties. But when Sarah died in 1940, and Zach
went off to war, and Max got rich from his lousy firing
pins, the way was clear for him to move in on Myrna by
spoiling her some more with money to live in a style better
than Zach could ever give her. I heard some things from
relatives that all during the time Zach was away in Europe, Max tried everything he could to get her to leave
him, even introduced her to guys. Was always saying that
Zach didn't make enough money and was never going to
amount to anything in business, that he didn't treat her
the way she deserved.

Max did a pretty good job on Myrna to make her believe a lot of this stuff, which only made things harder for
her, because when you came right down to it, whatever
their problems, she really did love Zach. Myrna's problem
was that she didn't know how to show it, and, worse, she
didn't know how to feel loved. She never felt secure
enough to feel the love we all tried to give her without
making us all jump through flaming hoops to prove it.
This was what both Dan and Zach couldn't put up with
after a while, and it drove them out of the house.

Dan got deeply involved in his classes at the Art Institute, and it wasn't long before he decided to live on the south side for his courses at the University of Chicago. Not long after, Zach, though he'd worked himself up to one of the top salesmen for his tile company, changed jobs and went on the road selling home talent shows all over the Midwest. He would be away for two or three weeks at a time and would never stay home more than a few days before taking off again. Which left Myrna and me home together. I was the only one unlucky enough to have nothing to turn to. I had to take all her crap as she went totally out-of-her-head bonkers. Zach's and Dan's taking off really shook her up, and she would machine-gun away at me for hours about how they'd run out on her and not returned her love. She'd drop into her teenage world and endlessly discuss with her friends the problems of *their* kids, who Alvin was dating and what kind of cream Regina was using for her mockies and who Eliot was taking to the prom. And always, of course, there were the movie magazines and her crazy prattling about Hollywood marriages, how great it was that Fred MacMurray met June Haver, could Frank Sinatra stay together with Ava Gardner, ditto Fernando Lamas and Esther Williams, how unfaithful Ingrid Bergman was to Peter Lindstrom in leaving him for Roberto Rossellini.

It wasn't bad enough while Myrna was worrying about these perfect strangers that I knew that Dan was her favorite son; wasn't bad enough that she never realized that I might have some feelings that needed caring for; no, at the same time a weird thing was happening. It was like Myrna was making me the parent and she was becoming the kid in the house, only wanting me to understand *her* feelings, and I didn't know what to do.

I'd said everything I wanted to say to Kim for the time being. It was nearly dark and we were driving along near the Wisconsin border. I was looking for a nice restaurant and Kim was thinking with her lips pursed. I asked her what she was thinking about.

"I think maybe we should go to hotel."

"I thought you said I shouldn't think about that kind of thing."

"I changed my mind. Look for hotel."

"Don't you want to eat dinner first?"

"I want eat dinner after."

"Why, Kim? What made you decide you want to go to a hotel?"

"You keep asking questions, I change my mind again. You want me change my mind?"

"Definitely not."

"I don't either. So shut up and find hotel. Not every guy I want go to bed with." She said it angrily, as though something beyond her control was forcing her to like me. I was beginning to get the idea that being angry was her way of showing affection.

7

EVERYONE KNEW THE CUBS couldn't keep winning at their July pace. There had to be a letdown. Better for it to happen now, Mike Ginsburg said in his column, than like last year, in September.

But the Cubs continued to amaze! They went on a 2½-week road trip at the start of August and *kept* winning. They increased their lead over the Dodgers to eight full games by taking three out of four from them at Ebbets Field. They swept a four-game series from the Giants at the Polo Grounds while the Dodgers were splitting four games with the Cards. It was only after they started heading back toward Chicago that things suddenly started to go wrong. In Philadelphia, they dropped two out of three to the Phillies. In Pittsburgh, the same thing with the Pirates. Cincinnati was a total disaster as they dropped four straight to the lowly Reds.

Some losses every Cub fan had been prepared for, but *not* the way the Cubs were losing. This wasn't the same team of June and July and the first part of August. *Everything* went wrong at once! The team stopped hitting, nearly everyone stopped delivering in the clutch, the pitching stank, the defense was awful, all of Spieler's strategy was useless; overnight, it seemed, he'd reached all the way up his sleeve to the shoulder and discovered there were no more tricks to be pulled out.

What the hell was going on? There was no explaining the way the team was screwing up. In the seventh inning of a game in Philly, with two out, Lance Lawrence, a good fielder, drops a routine fly ball and three runs score to give the Phils the game. In Pittsburgh, Dale Wishnikopf, pitching a 2–0 shutout into the eighth, throws a three-run gopher ball to a weak-hitting third-string catcher who's pinch-hitting, and the Cubs lose again.

In Cincinnati, Joey de Angelo, the best in the business in hauling in flies hit over his head, loses one in the sun, and the Reds keep an inning alive and go on to score the winning run when Mickey Malone throws a wild pitch with a man on third. All of a sudden balls are going through the infield for hits that used to be swallowed up for routine outs. There's no consistency, like most pennant contenders. It's almost like the guys suddenly don't want to believe they're leading the league and've got a great shot at the pennant.

Fortunately, the Dodgers weren't able to gain as much ground as they should have, and the Cubs returned to Wrigley Field at the end of the month to meet the Braves still three games ahead. The Cubs still had some good things going for them too. Elijah St. John was throwing like the best pitcher in the majors. Elmo Speakes, still mad as a rabid dog, was stroking the ball at a .360 clip, doing everything humanly possible at the plate and on the field to single-handedly keep the Cubs in first place. Randy Dodds, though he took three heartbreaking losses on the road, was still pitching brilliantly in relief.

Then there was Spieler, the stalwart skipper, always optimistic, refusing to panic or make excuses or concede an inch that the Cubs weren't going to win the pennant. As the pressure mounted, in the interviews he gave on the road, he gave the impression that the worst would soon be over, the Cubs would soon be winning again.

I was heartened by Spieler's words. I'd made money all season long betting on the Cubs, but even when the long-awaited letdown came, I refused to stop betting on them on account of Spieler. Their losing streak cut into my winnings a lot, but I didn't care. Like Jamey said, I was betting my heart instead of my head.

On the day the Cubs were opening at Wrigley Field with the Reds, Kim and I were sitting in Candido's. It was like one or two in the morning. She was looking at a fashion magazine and I was doing the usual, studying the pitching match ups for today's games. Suddenly I felt a presence over us. I looked up and there was this black dude in a white zoot suit and a summer-weave porkpie hat with a little red feather in the band, glaring down at me, studying the things I was writing on a pad. His boozy breath hit me in the face. Suspicion was in his eyes. He was bristling with anger. It took me a moment to realize it was Elmo Speakes. "Where's La Chance?" he growled. He had something serious on his mind.

"Spieler La Chance? How would I know, Mr. Speakes? Why ask me where he is?"

"*Bull*-shit you don't know! I seen you talking to him all the time at the ballpark. In the clubhouse and on the field. One time I seen you and this fox here talking to him near the dugout. You tell me where he's at. I need to talk to him."

"Mr. Speakes, you've got the wrong idea. Just because you saw us talking doesn't mean I know what he does at night. We're not *close* friends or anything like that."

Elmo didn't believe me. My answer only made him more outraged. He was pretty drunk and he took a swig from a pint bottle in a brown bag and looked around the restau-

rant in frustration. He lived on the south side, a good ten
miles away, and the white north side was definitely not
his scene at night. He usually never went anywhere alone,
usually had beautiful women and flunkies for company, so
it was strange he was by himself. Whatever was bothering
him must've been pretty important for him to drive all
this way. One thing for sure was that if he kept drinking
he was likely to get in some kind of trouble. The Cubs
couldn't afford for him to miss today's game, or any game,
and he seemed determined to find Spieler. I got an idea.
"Look, Mr. Speakes," I said, "if you need to talk to Mr.
La Chance that badly, maybe I can help you find him."

That suspicious look again. "*You* wanna help me find
him?"

"That's what I said."

"You ain't gonna con me, man, take me where he ain't
gonna be?"

"Why should I do something like that, make you mad
at *me?*"

My answer was too simple, caught him off guard. He
blinked, didn't know what to say.

"We're wasting time," I said. "You're the one that
wants to find him. Let's go."

I looked at Kim. She was glaring as hard at Elmo as he
was glaring at us. I asked her if she wanted to come.

"You think I helpful?"

"I think you could be."

She nodded. "Hokay."

I threw some money on the table and started toward
the door, already thinking about where to find out where
Spieler might be. Elmo came after, mumbling about how
I better not be conning him. Kim pushed him along.

A huge gold El Dorado convertible was double-parked
in front of the restaurant. A line of traffic each way was
backed up on the narrow street. Guys were shouting from
their cars. A cop was about to write out a ticket and Elmo

ran up to him and started complaining, "She-it, man —" I
raced between them to explain that this was Elmo Speakes
and the car belonged to him and that we had to find
Spieler La Chance right away, it was an emergency, the
pennant race was at stake. In the confusion, I also slipped
twenty bucks into his hand. The cop, an amiable Irishman,
did his civic duty and put away his pad. "Go get 'em,
Elmo, you black bastard!" He grinned behind his back.
Fortunately, Elmo didn't hear him and I got into the driver's seat, with Elmo next to me and Kim in the rear.

I got the key from Elmo and shot east on Oak Street,
to the Outer Drive. Knowing Spieler's ways at night, he
could be anywhere in the city, but I was hoping he would
be drinking at one of the spots near the area where he
lived, around 4000 north on Sheridan Road, where a lot
of the Cub players drank at night. If he wasn't at any of
these places, maybe one of the Cubs would know where
he was.

I turned onto the Outer Drive. Lake Michigan was on
our right and the smell and the sounds of the wind and the
waves swept over us. The elegant buildings of the Gold
Coast and the near north side were on our left. The Drive
was like a long empty landing strip stretching before us
in the bright darkness of the moonlight. I floored Elmo's
caddy.

The wind had sobered him. He took a swig from his
brown bag and glared at me. "You sure you know what
you're doin', boy?"

"Maybe you'll thank me before the night is over."

"Maybe I'll kick your butt. Ever think of that?"

"Want to tell me why you want to see Spieler?"

The question started him up again. "He doin' some bad
shit on me. I told him when he came I ain't goan take no
shit off him. I said, 'Spieler man, you can con all the suck-
ers you like with your honey tongue and your fancy-ass
ways, but don't do me like you did when we was with the

Cards together.' I told him Elmo Speakes ain't never goan put up with that shit again. And he looks at me all innocent, with hurt in his eyes, like how could I accuse him of conning me, and he raises his right hand and swears on his mother's grave that he would never ever do such a thing. 'You is too big a man to con,' he says. 'You are the great Elmo Speakes, my number-one man, and I wouldn't dream of doin' you dirt in any way.' Well, you know what I got to say to that? One thing. *Bull*-shit!" Elmo took another swig and glared furiously at the road ahead.

He glared at me. "Do you know what number-one man hit last year?"

"Three twenty-five, Mr. Speakes."

"Three-two-five, that is right. And how many did he bust out of sight?"

"Thirty-one."

"You is right again. Thirty-one. And how many RBI's?

"One twenty-seven."

"You got it. One hundred twenty-seven mothers crossed the plate on account of Elmo Speakes."

"You had a truly great year, Mr. Speakes. You were probably the best ballplayer in the National League."

"No 'probably' about it, man. They screwed me out of the M.V.P. because Elmo Speakes ain't no Stepin Fetchit for the National League. Elmo Speakes speaks his mind. *No one* goan stop him!" He glared straight ahead again. Whatever he wanted to see Spieler about really pissed him off.

"Let me ask you somethin', man," he said.

"Sure thing."

"Back in the restaurant, I saw you makin' notes on the games. You make money workin' the games?"

"I do all right. I'm lucky to win more than I lose."

"Just how much bread you figure you gonna make from it?"

"Oh, I don't know. Nothing great. I'm kinda conservative. I've got a system that I try to stick to. Maybe forty, fifty grand for the season."

Elmo nodded his head quickly. My figures set something off in him. "Um-huhm, um-huhm," he said with angry satisfaction. "You is aware, of course," he said bitterly, "that Elmo Speakes was involved in a holdout with the Chicago Cubs management?"

"Every Cub fan couldn't help but be aware of it, Mr. Speakes."

"You got any idea what the best ballplayer in the league was offered for his great year?"

"You know the Cubs management doesn't tell salary figures in the newspapers."

"Damn right they don't. It would show what thieves they are. Does you know what they wanted to give Elmo Speakes for a raise? Would you like to guess?"

"I'd like to know, if you want to tell me."

"Five ... thousand ... shit-ass bucks! Ain't that a pisser? Five thousand shit-ass bucks for the year Elmo Speakes had. I would've held out all year if those foxes of mine wasn't tapping me for bread. And where, you want to know, was the chief supporter of his number-one man, old mother Spieler? Nowhere to be found, that's where. Except to show up and say when Elmo don't want to hear it that Bobby Wentworth ain't got no bread to give Elmo. Spieler-man has the nerve to tell me that Bobby has got to pay off his so-ciety wife for getting caught with another fox. Well, what does he think my problem is? I got my own foxes breathing after me for nonsupport. I need the bread just as bad as Bobby Wentworth does. But Spieler says, next year, Elmo, next year, this year we is gonna win the pennant and next year there is no way the man can refuse you anything.

" 'Next year,' he says. Ain't that a pisser! *Bull*-shit!

They conned me and I ain't goan forget it. They has conned me into holding up this mothering team. And I know what they up to!" Elmo was speechless with rage.

But he wasn't through yet. He glared at me one more time. "Listen, man," he said, "take a guess what you think Elmo makes."

"You don't have to tell me, Mr. Speakes. I understand how you feel without knowing."

"Don't jive me, man. Speak up. You think I got too much pride to talk. I ain't got too much pride to talk. The whole world should know my shit-ass deal. Elmo Speakes makes thirty-eight thousand shit-ass bucks for holding up this mothering team. What you think about that, man? *You* makes more than me. Ain't that a pisser?"

It *was* a pisser. I didn't know what to say. Kept my mouth shut.

"Kind of shocks you, don't it? Mantle is gettin' his one hundred g's, Teddy Williams is getting his, but Elmo Speakes is getting shafted by Bobby Wentworth and *his* number-one man, the one and only Seymour de Spieler La Chance. Well, I'm here to tell you, I know what's going on and I aim to tell La Chance I know. Them mothers think I'm goan carry this team for nothin'.''

I had no idea what Elmo was talking about. All I could think of was to calm him down. "Well, you've got to remember one thing, Mr. Speakes, what Mr. La Chance said. You *are* going to get a lot of money if you win the pennant and the World Series."

Elmo laughed out loud with contempt for what I said. "Hah! You is so right, man, *if* we win the pennant and the Series. That's Spieler La Chance's line for holding off Elmo Speakes. 'Cause it won't matter by that time. 'Cause there are people who don't want to see Elmo play in the Series and earn all that bread. They don't want old Elmo to get his fair share, though Elmo is carrying this mothering team on his back and putting everyone in a po-sition to cash in."

"I don't know what you're talking about, Mr. Speakes. What is it you're trying to say?"

He glared at me. "You be patient, man. You goan hear a lot of things real soon. Soons we catch up with mother Spieler."

I pulled off the Drive at Irving Park, 4000 north, and drove a few blocks to Sheridan Road. There was a bar on Irving and Sheridan called the Magic Lantern where the Cubs and visiting ballplayers hung out. Whatever Elmo was talking about, it didn't sound good. To make things worse, he'd taken another pint out of the glove compartment and started to swig it. If he went into the Magic Lantern with me and started mouthing off, it could cause all kinds of trouble. Other Cub players would get riled up. Someone might take a swing at him. Elmo could get hurt. I decided to keep him out, if I could.

Fortunately, his eyes were getting glazed again. As we waited at the stoplight at Irving and Sheridan, me looking around for a parking space, he slid down with his head back on the seat, his eyes closed, muttering, "You won't get away with this, mother Spieler . . ."

I turned onto Sheridan Road and pulled into a space down the block. "Do you mind staying with him a few minutes?" I asked Kim.

"Hokay. You hurry."

I hopped out and ran into the Magic Lantern. It was a big dark joint with a bar up front and tables and a dance floor in a room at the back. It was medium crowded and I looked around for Cub players, didn't see any, and asked a bartender if there were any around. He said that Joey de Angelo and Wall Koslowski and Royal Farrell were drinking in a booth in the back. I hurried to the back and spotted them.

"Mr. de Angelo, Mr. Koslowski, Mr. Farrell, would any of you happen to know where Mr. La Chance is?"

They were all smashed.

"Mr. La Chance?" said Royal Farrell, looking slyly at his teammates, "do you happen to mean now Mr. Seymour La Chance, frequently called Spieler by the press and other followers of our fabled national pastime, not to mention the loyal and admiring band of men he is astutely leading to fame and fortune? Would that be the Seymour La Chance you had in mind?"

"It sounds like him."

"I don't know where he is. *But* . . . I might know where an outrageous two-faced, double-dealing, lying son of a bitch named Spieler La Chance might be. Could it be him you'd be looking for, lad?"

"That could be him too."

"Aha, in that case I may be able to help. Let me see . . ." Royal looked mock-thoughtful. "Could the good Spieler be working one of many outstanding local civic organizations tonight, collecting a not-so-wee honorarium that might best be going to one of his less well paid minions? Or could he be cadging a dinner at some well-known bistro, pressing flesh and waxing eloquent for his supper? Or could he be out with some chippy, trying to con the busty maiden into bed with him with his gypsy blarney?"

"I . . . don't . . . think so," said Wally Koslowski, sounding for all the world like John Wayne. "I hear he's got . . . a new broad . . . that he's seeing. Real . . . class . . . number, I'm told." Wally had a lewd grin.

"Do you know where he is, Mr. Koslowski?"

Wally looked at Joey. "Do you know where he is, Mr. de Angelo?"

Joey looked at Royal. "Do you know where he is, Mr. Farrell?"

Royal stood up and called out to the room. "Does anyone in the joint know where our illustrious leader, Seymour the Spieler La Chance, happens to be passing this most ordinary night in this most infamous year in the history of baseball?"

"Shut up ... Royal," Wally said. "You know ... we agreed ... not to talk about that."

A voice spoke up from down the bar. It was Mike Ginsburg himself. "You might try the Polynesian Room of the Edgewater Beach Hotel."

I went up to bespectacled Mike. "Are you sure about that? I need to find him fast."

"No one can be sure where Spieler La Chance is going to turn up of an evening, son, least of all Spieler himself. But I did talk to him today and he told me he had a special date tonight, and he thought he would take her dancing at the Polynesian Room."

"What if he's not there, Mr. Ginsburg?"

"If he's not there, try the Aragon Ballroom. If he isn't there either, try his apartment at the Sunnyside Arms on Sheridan and Grace. Give the doorman a tip to call him. *Don't* interrupt him yourself. Might lead to premature ejaculatum." There was a chorus of laughs from Mike and the group around him.

I left the Magic Lantern on the run. Back at the car, Elmo was blithering drunkenly to Kim about how little money Bobby Wentworth was paying him. She was listening with a bored expression. We were lucky he hadn't gone in with me.

Sheridan Road was deserted in the glare of street lights as I drove fifteen blocks north. Then there was life again as I pulled into the curving driveway of the grand old Edgewater Beach Hotel. In the daytime, with its flags flying from the roof of its tall sand-colored walls, it always had a gay and luxurious air. Under its portico, I gave the car to an attendant and we hurried through the glass

doors into the gaudy lobby. The breeze had revived Elmo.
He was his usual surly self. Though people recognized and
called to him, he ignored them and kept repeating, "You
better not be conning me, man. Elmo Speakes ain't in no
mood for conning."

A big sign in the lobby said that Desi Arnaz and his
Cuban band were performing in the Polynesian Room.
From far down the lobby we could hear the music with a
wild Latin beat. We could see through the entrance that
the place was packed. I asked the host if he'd seen Spieler
La Chance come in. He said that Spieler *was* in the room,
at a table near the dance floor.

The room was sweaty and noisy. I led Elmo and Kim on
a snakelike path through the milling people in the dining
area. It was set in a jungle decor with life-size coconut and
palm trees and plaster lions and tigers and bamboo chairs
and tables.

We reached the foot of the dance floor and found every
inch filled with dancers. That Latin beat was vibrating. On
the bandstand, Desi himself, in a white shirt with sleeves
ruffled from wrist to shoulder and green pants tied with a
sash, was pounding a long cone-shaped conga drum and
wailing:

*"La cumba-cumba-cumba-charro! La cumba-cumba-
cumba-charro!"*

I looked through and around the dancers, looked at all
the tables and couldn't see Spieler anywhere.

*"La cumba-cumba-cumba-charro! La cumba-cumba-
cumba-charro!"*

Then I saw him. He was dancing with his date. They
were a few feet apart, not touching but moving together
like each other's shadow to the pounding rhythm. I saw
both his expression and her behind at the same time. His
arms swinging, his fingers snapping, his body shaking as
though he had no joints, Spieler was hypnotized by his
partner's face.

I was hypnotized by her behind. It was the greatest behind of all time. She had a great pile of silver hair and the
most exciting hourglass figure inside a skintight silver-
sequined dress, with great gams showing under her short
hem.

"LA CUMBA-CUMBA-CUMBA-CHARRO! LA
CUMBA-CUMBA-CUMBA-CHARRO!"

Desi had stepped up the beat. He was singing faster,
the band was playing louder, the room was throbbing with
sound.

Something else was happening. Other dancers were no-
ticing Spieler and his partner. They stopped dancing to
watch them. Soon Spieler and his date were the only dancers on the floor. The sexual connection between them was
as strong as the heat. Everyone watching them could feel
it. It was like the heavy air before a thunderstorm. Every
eye was fixed on them.

Desi began to control the movement of the dancers. He
sang slowly and softly, "La cumba-cumba-cumba-charro,"
leaning forward as though he were whispering delicious
sexy things, stirring them up. As he danced, Spieler
worked his white dinner jacket off and flung it away. That
head of silver hair was rotating sensually, that great figure
was shaking this way and that.

Desi sang loudly, *"La cumba-cumba-cumba-charro,"*
whipping the dancers into a frenzy as though he'd turned
on a switch.

Spieler and his date were like one! Every swing of the
hips, every finger snap and wiggle. And Desi drove them
into one incredible exciting frenzy — "LA CUMBA-
CUMBA-CUMBA-CHARRO!!! LA CUMBA-CUMBA-
CUMBA-CHARRO!!! LA CUMBA-CUMBA-CUMBA-
CHARRO!!! — *CHARRO!!! CHARRO!!! CHARRO!!!*
— he paused and then one more electric time —
"CHARRO!!!" — and the dance was over and the crowd
roared its approval.

The only person who didn't care for it was Elmo. As the applause died while the two dancers stood there frozen, eyeing each other with smiles, he called out, "You mother, Spieler. I want to talk to you." He raced out onto the floor.

Kim and I followed him. But Spieler was cool as he snapped out of it and saw Elmo coming. He looked amused as Elmo laid into him: "You think you can con me, huh? No one goan con Elmo Speakes anymore."

"What are you talking about, Elmo? I wouldn't dream of conning you. Would I con my number-one man?"

"You would con your mother if you could."

Spieler grinned at Elmo's comeback. He didn't say anything one way or the other. Finally, though: "Well, if conning is what you want to talk about, don't you think it's better that we do it in private, at the table?" He smoothly guided Elmo by his elbow back to the table.

Kim went with them. I was about to go, too, when I got a good look at Spieler's date. I was struck dumb, because I hadn't recognized Myrna in her silver wig.

She came up to me, patting her brow with a handkerchief.

"Arnold, what are you doing here?"

"I guess I could ask you the same thing, Myrn."

"I think you can see it with your own eyes. Mr. Seymour La Chance and I are having a night on the town."

"I guess he's going to give you his Cub jacket soon."

"He's already given me a lovely emerald ring."

"I gotta hand it to you, Myrn. You're nothing if not expensive."

"It was an expression of deep affection. You shouldn't badmouth it."

"What about Eagle-Nose? Does he know you're seeing Spieler?"

"I don't care what Mr. Eagle-Nose Pinsky knows. He and I are on the outs."

"Sounds serious. I guess you've given him back his Siding King jacket."

"You know something, Arnold? You and Jules are a lot alike. Very childish."

"You're only saying that, Myrn, because I don't treat you like the child *you* want to be."

Myrna rolled her eyes upward. "Why, God, have you given me such a smart-ass son?"

"I bet Spieler treats you like the child you want to be."

"You almost don't deserve to know that Seymour La Chance is one of the finest gentlemen I've ever met."

"Can I quote you on that for Kup's Column?"

"You can tell the world I've finally met a man who fully appreciates me."

As usual, Myrna and I were off to a great start. There was nothing to be gained by asking her anything more, at this point. Besides, I wanted to get back to Elmo and Spieler. They were seated and Elmo was leaning across the table and pointing a finger at Spieler: "You con me and I promise I'm gonna tell the whole world what's going on. You ain't goan cut me out of what I deserve."

Spieler heard him clearly. His mouth curved thoughtfully and he nodded his head several times. Then his look got tolerant and he talked to Elmo like he was talking to a child. "Elmo, Elmo," he said soothingly, "you are one of the greatest players in the history of the game and one of the dumbest. *No one* is cutting you out of anything. How could anyone? Aren't you the key to winning the pennant?"

"Don't hand me that shtick, man. You may be able to sugar it over on a lot of folks, but you ain't sugaring it over on Elmo Speakes. You ain't taking away the best chance I'll ever get to make some bread in a pennant year. I waited too many years to get into this league for you to con me out of pennant dough."

Spieler shook his head and sighed. "Elmo," he said sincerely, "I promise you you haven't been cut out of anything. I swear it to you. I think that you and I should go have a cup of coffee somewhere and get down to some straight talk. Okay? Fair enough?"

"Okay. But you better not be conning me, man. I'm warning you." Suddenly Elmo looked around and spotted me. "I want this kid along too. I promised him he was gonna find out a lot tonight. I want a witness to see if you're conning me or not."

I could see Spieler didn't like the idea of me being with them. "He's just a kid, Elmo. He doesn't need to know what you know."

"I want him, Spieler. I want him to know what we know."

Spieler was still cool. He threw his hands up. "Okay by me," he said amiably. "Okay by you, Arnie?"

"I guess so." I tried to be nonchalant about it.

"Myrna-sweets," Spieler said. She'd come back to the table and was preparing to go off and fix her face. "I gotta do something that's gonna disappoint you. I've gotta send you home right now in a cab because I've gotta have a cup of coffee with this gentleman here, who assures me it is quite important. Uh, I don't believe you've ever met Mr. Elmo Speakes, the center-fielder of the Chicago Cubs and my number-one man. Elmo, this is a person I also think is number one, Mrs. Myrna Barzov." As Myrna and Elmo shook hands, I saw Spieler looking thoughtfully at Elmo, trying to figure out how to handle him.

"Pleased to meet you, Mr. Speakes," Myrna said, withdrawing her hand quickly and looking at Spieler with a pout. "Can't you even wait until Desi sings 'Besame Mucho'? I've been looking forward to it all evening. It would be quite rude to Desi to go now. You know how you made a special request of him to sing it."

"I know I did, honey, and I'm real sorry about it. I don't

like to hurt Desi's feelings and we'll come back real soon and apologize to him and we can hear him sing everything we want him to. Okay, hon?"

Myrna still looked miffed. "Okay," she said at last. "I guess you have to do what you have to do. But there is one thing I wish you'd take a minute to tell this young man here. That he shouldn't forget that in September his mother is expecting him to go to his cousin Selma's son Alvin's bar mitzvah, and that if he doesn't go, it will be a much bigger disappointment to her than having to miss Desi Arnaz singing 'Besame Mucho,' which is a big disappointment too."

"I will, Myrna."

"You should also tell him that it's about time he made up his mind about what he's going to do with his life. If he doesn't go back to school the army is going to get him. You should tell him to ask his cousin Tillie's son Hiram how much he liked spending two years in the army, catching pneumonia from marching in the rain."

"I will, Myrna. I promise you."

"You should also remind him that he should call his grandfather and thank him for getting him out of all that trouble he got into recently. It's an ungrateful boy who won't even take a minute to thank his grandfather for keeping him out of jail."

"I will, Myrna, I will. Relax. You can count on it."

"It also might not be a bad idea if he gave his mother a call once in a while. You'd think she'd done something so terribly wrong, the way he treats her. He makes it seem like she doesn't care about him."

"Hey, sweets. I'll take care of all those things."

The funny thing was that Myrna's craziness didn't ruffle Spieler. He was as cool with her as he was with Elmo.

"Honey pie, sweets, you just put your mind at rest now

and trust old Spieler to make things right. Okay, now?"
He smiled warmly at her.

Like a coaxed child, Myrna smiled back. "Okay, Seymour."

As we left the Polynesian Room, that Latin beat was
throbbing again as Desi wailed "Babalu."

Spieler, Elmo, Kim and I put Myrna into a cab at the entrance to the hotel. Kim was plenty pissed when Spieler
motioned to me to put her in one too. She said she wanted
to come along with the three of us, but Spieler nixed the
idea with strong shakes of his head. He said he figured
what Elmo had to say to him, not to mention what he had
to say to Elmo, should be heard by as few ears as possible.
"Right, Elmo?"

"Wrong, Mr. Seymour the Spieler. I don't care who
knows it if the deal don't include Elmo Speakes."

Spieler nodded. He got the message. He motioned again
for me to put Kim in a cab. She got in, glaring at us, and
the cab pulled away.

Spieler was back in his white tux jacket. He dug his
hands into his pants pockets, leaned back on his heels,
raised his head, and sucked in the nippy breeze. His eyes
studied the starry night. "Suppose the three of us take a
walk down to the beach," he said amiably. "The only company we'll have will be the wind, the sand, the stars, and
the water."

"Cut the crap, Spieler. I mean it. You ain't goan sugar-
coat me ever again. Let's get going." Elmo took a swig
from his pint and started walking north on Sheridan Road.

Spieler and I started after and caught up with him. We
walked until the first intersection, which was where Bryn
Mawr Avenue crossed Sheridan and became the Outer
Drive, circling out behind the hotel. We started up the
Drive and crossed it and walked on a grassy area until we

came to the beach. We walked across the sand to the edge of the water. It was dark and rumbling. The silver-tipped waves rolled in and died as foam within a few feet of us.

We'd walked in silence. Now Spieler spoke: "Jeez, my feet." He removed his white jacket, folded it shoulder to shoulder, and carefully laid it on the sand. He sat down and took his shoes off, then unfastened his garters and removed his socks and put them in his shoes. He stood up and carefully rolled up each leg of his pants three times until they were at his knees, then he marched into the lake. Ten yards out he turned and faced us. He dug his hands into his pockets again, rolled back on his heels, and examined the stars again as he took a deep, exhilarating breath. "Ah, the water's great," he said. "You sure you guys don't want to join me?"

"No thanks, Spieler."

"Cut the crap, man. You ain't throwing cold water on what I got to say. I done come to tell you something."

Spieler chuckled and eyed Elmo in a friendly challenging way. He smiled and raised an eyebrow. "I'm listening, Elmo."

"Do you recall what you told me when you personally came as a messenger from you know who and assed me not to hold out for the season?"

"I do, Elmo. I most certainly do."

"Would you repeat it for the benefit of the wind and the sand and the stars and all the fishes in the lake and, mos' specially, for this young man here?"

"You sure you want to make the boy a witness to all this? Like you said, he's a young man and might not understand."

"Was you sure you wanted to screw me?"

"Okay, Elmo, I understand how you feel. What I told you was that if you accepted a certain raise at that point,

124

later, if the Cubs won the pennant, you'd get everything you asked for. If the Cubs won the Series, you'd get another bonus as well as the Series money. The deal still stands. Nothing's changed. The Cubs win the pennant and take the Series, you're going to pick up a very heavy piece of change."

Elmo was shaking his head as he listened. "Man," he said, "people has always told me you were a real con man and now I finally believe it. Let me ask you something else, mother. Is I or is I not having the kind of season that's goan get the Chicago Cubs into the World Series?"

"You are indeed having a great season."

"And if the Cubs does win the pennant, who would be the person that most made it happen?"

"Only you, babes. No one else remotely close. You are indisputably my number-one man."

"You wouldn't be pulling my dong, would you, Spieler?"

"Pulling your dong, Elmo? Why would I do something like that to my number-one man? Remember, Elmo, I've never won a Series. You know what winning a Series means to me."

"Yeah, I know what winning a Series means to you. Makes you look mighty big, like a real live miracle-working saint. New long-term contract, lots of bread, more steppin' out in high so-ciety with expensive foxes, like tonight. That's what it means to you, Spieler man."

Spieler grinned. "I hope so for my sake. But, Elmo, you aren't saying what's on your mind. Speak up, man. Come to the point."

"I's at the point. I done heard somethin' that makes me think there is somethin' more important than winning the Series for you. I done drove a lot of miles to find out the truth."

Spieler raised an eyebrow again. "Go on, Elmo."

"I done heard some bad shit. It got to do with things

goin' on with the Chicago Cubs. You know what I'm talkin' about, Spieler man?"

Spieler looked fondly at Elmo. He still had his hands dug in his pockets so that his suspenders were taut off his chest. He slowly shook his head. "I haven't the foggiest, Elmo. You'll have to tell me."

Elmo looked very dubiously at Spieler. He stared hard at him and shook his head in disgust. "What would you say, Spieler man, if I was to say maybe things ain't so kosher with this pennant race?"

"I'd say what makes you think so? Who's been bending your ear?"

"You mean you really don't know nothin' about it?"

"I swear this is the first I've heard of it."

"And you don't think nothin' funny has been goin' on, on the field? All them miscues and bad pitches and guys messing up and not coming through like they was, and this losing streak we're on, you don't think there's nothin' funny about it?"

Now Spieler was looking hard at Elmo. He didn't answer his question. "I think maybe you better tell me who you've been talking to."

"Don't matter who I been talkin' to. Just a guy on the team."

"But this is serious stuff, Elmo. Did you find me tonight *not* to tell me what's going on? Stuff like this getting around could ruin the morale of the ballclub."

"Screw the morale of the ballclub! A thing like this could do Elmo Speakes out of what he deserves for having his greatest year. Elmo didn't break into the majors early like a white jiver. Elmo Speakes had to pay his dues for lots of years on black-ass teams. He ain't got no one-hundred-thousand-smacker deal like DiMag or Teddy Williams or Mantle. Elmo Speakes is a nigger workin' for nigger wages and he can't even hold out for what he's worth 'cause he don't have enough bread not to play for nigger wages.

"This is the year Elmo Speakes is supposed to lead the Chicago Cubs to the pennant and the World Series and pick up all the extra chips that Spieler man, fronting for Bobby Wentworth, promised him. And all of a sudden Elmo Speakes get the impression that it ain't gonna happen that way at all. You hear me, mother Spieler? Elmo get the idea that Seymour de Spieler La Chance has got a plenty-good reason for not giving a shit about the pennant and the Series."

Spieler had a kindly expression. He smiled and shook his head. "You're wrong, Elmo," he said soothingly, "you're dead wrong about what's going on. The Cubs are going to win the pennant, and you're going to the World Series, and you and me are gonna have the pleasure of winning the whole blessed thing."

Elmo was startled. His mouth dropped open. His look got fearful and his eyes bugged out. "Hey, Spieler," he said urgently, shaking his head, "you got it all wrong. I think maybe we is pulling each other's dongs. I don't give a rat's ass about no pennant or no Series. What riles me is that it's *my base hits* that's settin' things up for the Cubs to take a dive. The rest of you mothers ain't goan make your bundles on the sweat of my labors and cut me out of it. Screw that noise! I want in on the fix!"

Unflappable, Spieler grinned. Then laughed loudly. "That's wonderful, Elmo," he chuckled, "one of the best baseball yarns I've ever heard. When they do my biography, that one has gotta be in it. It's so rich I hate to spoil it with what I've got to tell ya. Elmo, if there's a fix on, I swear I don't know it. I also promise ya that I'll look into it, 'cause that's the last thing I want connected to any club managed by Spieler La Chance. I don't know who you were talking to, but *he's* the one who's pulling your dong.

Completely, categorically full of shit. Just someone trying to get your goat. *You* may not give a damn about the Series, but I do, and don't let me hear you say it again. I'll fine your butt for it."

Elmo glared at Spieler. That very dubious look. "I don't trust you, man. I know all about what happened on the Cards in '48 when your guys blew the last six games of the season."

"That was something completely different, Elmo. That was for laughs and pocket money. It didn't matter in the standings. It wasn't worth a piss in the water I'm standing in."

Elmo still wasn't satisfied. "You better not be conning me, man."

"What can I say?" Spieler shrugged. "Except maybe that we're all niggers together in this game. I know exactly how you feel about everything and I sympathize, but you gotta remember I played in the majors on white-assed teams and I didn't get paid too well either. No one except the greats did, and they had to spit blood nearly every time to get it. The owners were the masters and the players were the niggers. If I'm making fair bucks these days, don't hold it against me. I've paid my dues too. Now let's go back to my place. You can sleep overnight. White nigger and black nigger, we'll sleep in the same bed together." Spieler came out of the water and put on his white jacket and picked up his socks and shoes. With his other hand, he took Elmo's arm and led him along.

"I don't trust you, man," Elmo said stubbornly, as we walked.

In Elmo's car, I drove the three of us to Spieler's apartment. He lived on Sheridan Road at a point where it ran right across from the Outer Drive, and his place looked out over Lake Michigan. As he and Elmo had a last drink in their underwear and Spieler kept reassuring him that he wasn't conning him and was going to get to the bottom of things, I sat in a window seat and stared out at the first white signs of dawn rising over Lake Michigan and Belmont Harbor. Finally Elmo keeled over on the sofa. Spieler raised his legs onto the sofa and put a pillow under his head and a blanket over him. "Gotta take care of my number-one man," he muttered, as he went about caring for Elmo like his mother.

He came over with a cold can of beer for me and one for himself, and together we sat in armchairs looking at the dawn rise. He asked me how I ran into Elmo.

I told him the whole story, from Candido's to the Magic Lantern to the Edgewater Beach Hotel. Spieler shook his head in wonder and said, "Hell of a night for you, Arnie. Thanks for looking after Elmo."

I shrugged. "Glad to do it, Spieler. Anything to aid the Cub cause. Do you think there's anything to what Elmo said?"

But Spieler had that faraway glint in his eye as he watched the dawn come up. I knew that Elmo wasn't what he was thinking about. "Your ma's a terrific kid," he said at last, "I have great times with her. It's been a long time since I felt so comfortable with a woman."

I didn't say anything. Spieler smiled at me like he expected me to. "I guess it surprises you to hear me say something like that," he said.

"I only know Myrna as my mother. I guess I don't see the side of her that you do."

Spieler laughed. "You think I don't see that she's as screwball as they come. Sure I see it. But for some strange reason I can't put my finger on, I like the way she is. The chemistry's just right between us. She's for Spieler La Chance and I'm for Myrna Barzov. How do you like them apples?"

All I could do was shake my head. I was really confused. I didn't know if I liked the idea of Spieler and Myrna going with each other. Somehow I resented it.

"Myrna Barzov is also for Arnie Barzov. She worries a lot about you, kid. She told me a lot about you and I want to talk to you about it sometime soon. I hope you won't think I'm intruding."

"I don't know if I'll agree with you, Spieler — as a matter of fact, I don't know if I like you going with Myrna — but I'll listen to whatever you have to say."

"Good boy, Arnie. Your mother's gone through a lot and she doesn't know how to handle everything. But underneath it all, she's a real gem."

Even if Spieler was right, I didn't like hearing it. I'd make my own decisions about Myrna. "How about Elmo, Spieler?" I asked, changing the subject. "What are you gonna do about him?"

Spieler's face twisted with thought. He didn't like dealing with Elmo but knew he had to. "Yeah, old Elmo," he sighed, "the guy makes a real case for himself. One of the greatest players the game will ever see and he's been screwed right and left in his career. Broke into the majors after he was thirty. Was never paid a decent salary by the owners. Never will get the recognition he deserves because he's such a hard-nosed, loudmouth son of a bitch. No one will lift a hand to help him when his playing days are over and he doesn't have a dime. It's a cruel shame, but that's the way life is ..." Spieler looked at me philosophically.

"And now he's got this crazy notion that some guys on the Cubs are deliberately going to blow the pennant? How can you straighten him out, Spieler?"

Spieler didn't answer me. He took a sip of beer and looked thoughtfully out the window. It was almost morning now.

"He's going to start shooting his mouth off to the whole world if you don't show him that he's wrong, Spieler."

"I'm not worried about Elmo, Arnie. I'll take care of him. I'm just sorry that you had to get involved in this."

"You don't have to worry about me, Spieler. I'm not going to say anything to anyone. I promise."

Spieler turned and looked at me. He had an affectionate look in his eyes. "That's just the problem, Arnie. I didn't figure you'd say anything to anyone. But that can get you in trouble if the thing ever blows up."

"I don't follow you, Spieler. What are you trying to say?"

"I'm saying that Elmo isn't wrong, Arnie. Never trust a ballplayer to keep his mouth shut. Some schmuck leaked the thing to Elmo. I told the guys it would never work." He shook his head sadly and finished his beer as he looked at the bright white morning.

"Are you saying what I think you're saying, Spieler?"

"You're hearing me right, Arnie. I'm saying the fix is on. I'm sorry you gotta know about it."

Part Three

8

SPIELER ADMITTED THE FIX WAS ON, but he wouldn't say who or why or how. The only thing he added was that the guys who were in on it didn't want Elmo in on it because he was an ornery troublemaker who couldn't be trusted to keep his mouth shut. Spieler agreed they had a point. But it was a risk they were going to have to take from this time on, because whether they liked it or not, they couldn't afford to keep him out. Spieler would see that Elmo was cut in on the deal.

I didn't say anything when Spieler finished. My feelings were on my face.

"I'm sorry to disappoint you," he said sincerely. "Like I said, I wish you didn't have to know about it."

"I guess I am disappointed. I don't know why I should be. I'm really not surprised. I myself was only recently telling someone that money and gambling are part of sports, and that leads to things like fixes. I guess Myrna didn't tell you about my being kicked out of downstate for gambling."

"As a matter of fact, she did. I got the impression you didn't do it for the money."

134

"How'd you know that, Spieler?"

He shrugged. "You learn something about human nature when you've been managing as long as I have."

"Are you in on this for the money?"

Spieler's face twisted up. My words pained him. He didn't answer, looked at me thoughtfully. He looked at his watch. "Good God, do you know what time it is? After six. I gotta get some rest for the game today. You're welcome to sleep over."

I was plenty tired too and it was a tempting offer to stay at Spieler's. But I wanted to be alone with my thoughts as soon as I got up. I told Spieler I'd better go. He saw me to the door.

"Thanks a lot, kid. I won't forget all you did tonight."

"Forget it, Spieler. You were a big help to me a little while back and I'm glad to repay the favor. And don't worry about me. I may be disappointed but I'll get over it. It would've been nice to see the Cubs win the flag. But if you can take it, I guess I can too. I guess you've got good reasons for being in on it.

He still wouldn't comment, still looked thoughtfully at me. "Sit tight. I'll be in touch. We'll talk."

I took a cab back to my place but was too tired to sleep at once. When I finally did fall asleep, someone leaning on my buzzer woke me up. It wasn't even nine o'clock. I staggered up and opened the door.

It was Jamey Jackson. He'd just got off work and was wearing his greasy attendant's uniform. He started pacing back and forth with a worried look.

I could barely keep my eyes open. The room kept fading out and I sank into a rocking chair. "Jamey, I've been out all night. Can't it wait until I've had some sleep?"

"I'm sorry, Arnie, for busting in, but it can't wait. It's awful important and I thought you'd want to know."

I sighed and told him to make some coffee. I staggered up, put a robe on, washed my face with cold water. I sat absolutely straight in my rocker, trying to make my mind work as the coffee perked.

I drank a cup and asked what was so wrong that it couldn't wait.

"You think there's anything funny about the way the Cubs are playing lately?"

It was about the only question that could make me more alert. I said casually, "What makes you say something like that?"

"I got my reasons. I'll tell you soon enough. But you tell me now if you think there's something funny about the way the Cubs are playing."

"Funny? You call their losing funny? To me it's more like sad. They're going to blow the pennant for sure if they keep it up."

"That's not really what I mean. What I mean is, does it really seem possible to you that the Cubs could play so terrible after playing so good for so long? I mean don't all these errors and other freaky things seem strange to you?"

As he talked, I made up my mind I wasn't going to let on a thing until he told me what he knew — and maybe not even then. "No, I can't say there's anything funny going on. Just a team going through a real bad screw-up time. What makes you think there's something funny going on?"

He began to pace back and forth again. Suddenly he wheeled around, a look of distress on his face. "You won't tell anyone what I'm going to tell ya?"

"You know me fairly well, Jamey. Don't tell me if you don't think you can trust me."

His face tightened as he spoke. He hated what he had to say. He said he was at Angie's last night when Randy came over unexpectedly. He said he needed to talk to

Angie about something personal and asked Jamey if he would leave for a while. Jamey said he would take a walk. Only he didn't do it. Instead, he only pretended to leave and slammed the door to make it seem like he had. Then he ducked into a little room off the hallway and put his ear to the wall and listened to their conversation in the living room. He said he figured Randy was going to tell Angie something new about his situation with his wife, and he, Jamey, couldn't help wanting to know about it too.

But that wasn't what Randy started in about. He came right out and said that the reason the Cubs had played so bad on the road trip was that certain players were losing the games on purpose. There was a deal worked out with big-time gamblers for the Cubs to win or lose each game for the rest of the season by a certain number of runs — whatever score would beat the spread worked out in Las Vegas — with the end result being that the Cubs would blow the pennant in the final series of the season against the St. Louis Cardinals.

Randy said that ever since the Cubs had moved into first place in July, big-time gamblers had been making tantalizing offers to key Cub players to throw the pennant. They kept reminding the guys how Bobby Wentworth had slammed the door in their faces on their raises in the spring, and now Cub attendance was soaring and Bobby was making money on their labors but didn't appreciate his team any more for its success. Bobby's contempt for his players was well known, and the gamblers didn't let the guys forget it. It rankled the players an awful lot, and the ones approached had gone back and forth for nearly a month on whether to do it but somehow managed to resist the urge.

They didn't finally take the plunge until the team left New York after the winning series against the Giants and the Dodgers. That's why things suddenly started going wrong in Philly and Pittsburgh and Cincinnati. What broke the straw was an incident in New York, on Sunday night after the Cubs swept the Giants. Randy didn't want to get into it too much. He said it had something to do with Bobby Wentworth.

He also didn't want to name the players involved, said only that there were seven of them and that though they'd made the commitment to the fix, their feelings about what they'd done changed from day to day. Sometimes some of them were pro and some of them were con and some of them didn't know what they thought, even during the course of a game.

That was one reason why the team was winning and losing such weird ballgames. Another reason was that though the guys directly in on the fix had made deals with the other, less important players on the team to take a percentage of their cut, there were certain key players who either didn't want any part of the fix or weren't included in it and who played only to win.

Angie asked Randy where he stood on the matter. He said that in the beginning, when he first heard about it, he was dead set against it. He'd pitched all these years in the majors and kept his nose clean and he didn't feel right about doing something wrong. However, certain things got him thinking. Important as his role was, he began to see that he couldn't stop the guys from going through with it, or keep them from throwing games. And if he continued to stay out of it, then he was going to miss out on the best dough he would probably ever be able to lay his hands on in a lifetime. He was tempted, but in his heart the fix disgusted him, he would feel guilty about taking part in it. So he stayed on the fence, unsure about what to do, as he pitched three magnificent outings in relief and lost them all as his teammates gave the games away. It was only after he got back to Chicago that something happened to make him see things in a different light.

There was a letter from his wife waiting. She was saying one more time that she would never give him a divorce. She would never let him marry someone else. She wanted him to come back to California after the season and help her open a restaurant. She had already made arrangements for nearly half the financing. Opening a restaurant with him was Barbara's dream, the thing she hoped would bring him back and hold them together.

Randy went out and sat in a bar. He had several bourbons and thought about the letter for a long while. Finally he decided to go see Angie. After telling her about the Cubs and the leter, he said he had something to ask her. He said he wanted to know what she thought about his joining the guys who were in on the fix. There were a couple of reasons why he'd considered doing it. One was that he could go to his wife and tell her he had no intention of ever returning to her, and in return for her giving him a divorce, he would give her the rest of the financing for her restaurant. He said that if he played his cards this way with Barbara, he thought he had a pretty good chance of succeeding.

The second reason was that his divorce would leave him free to marry Angie. Were these good enough reasons, he asked Angie, for him to throw the pennant? This was the real reason he'd come over tonight. Jamey paused and looked at me.

"And what did Angie say?" I asked him.

His face screwed up again. He apparently wasn't all too happy with her answer. He was also puzzled by it. "My sister is the strangest girl. She never lets on too much about what she thinks. All she told Randy was that she was behind him whatever he wanted to do. She said it probably would be best for him to go along with the other guys now that things had gone so far. I don't know that she should've said that."

"What should she've said?"

"I think Randy shouldn't get involved. Sounds to me like the whole thing could blow up anytime and good players could go to jail for something they didn't really mean to do. I don't think the guys have had the chance to think it over and see what they're doing is not only illegal, it's immoral. Baseball is a beautiful game and they shouldn't give it a bad name. What do you think we ought to do, Arnie? I can't say anything to Angie because she'd be furious with me if she knew I listened in on the conversation. I think someone ought to talk to Randy and show him he's making a mistake."

Silence.

"And you think that someone ought to be me?"

"You're probably the only one who can make him see what a devil that Spieler La Chance is. He's the evil influ—"

"I told you before to cut it out about Spieler. You don't know one single thing to tie him to this. Until you do, I don't want you to say another bad word about him. If you're so concerned about Randy's moral welfare, why not talk to him yourself?"

Jamey didn't answer. The question caught him off guard. He had this uncomfortable look. " 'Cause I can't do that, Arnie. I just can't. Angie wouldn't want me to do that. It wouldn't be right for me to do it."

Jamey could be as strange as his sister. I didn't know why he didn't want to tell Angie he knew about the fix, or why he didn't want to tell Randy to get out of it, but I did know he wasn't being completely honest. "And what did Angie say about marrying Randy?"

"What's she's been saying all along. That they should talk about it when the season's over."

I was too tired to think about it then, too tired to think about anything. "Jamey, I just gotta get some sleep. I can't function another minute. Call me tonight and we'll talk some more."

The next thing I knew the phone was ringing. I'd forgotten to set the alarm and it was nearly two o'clock. Shit, I'd missed the start of the game. I picked up the phone and said hello.

"Hello! This is Myrna Barzov. Remember me? I'm your mother."

"As though you could ever let me forget, Myrn. To what do I owe this unexpected pleasure?"

"You mean it's almost too much to expect you to be glad to hear from your mother?"

"I'm glad, Myrn. I'm glad. What's on your mind?"

"You know what I was doing at the Edgewater Beach last night. Now I want to know what you were doing there."

"Fair enough, Myrn. That ballplayer you met last night, Elmo Speakes, he asked me to help him find Spieler."

"Why should he ask you, of all people? What are you, a private detective for schvartzas?"

"He'd seen me talking to Spieler at the ballpark. He saw me in a restaurant last night and said he was looking for him. I volunteered to help him find him. We found out he was at the Edgewater Beach by going to a place where ballplayers hang out."

"Do you know what they talked about?"

"You mean Spieler and Elmo?"

"No, I mean Seymour and Sid Caesar. Of course I mean Seymour and that schvartza player."

"Yeah, they let me listen in."

"Arnold, one thing about your mother, she doesn't ask you for many favors. She doesn't pry into your life a lot. But I would like you to tell me now if there is anything wrong with Seymour and the players on the Cubs."

"What makes you think there's something wrong, Myrn?"

"It's a certain feeling I get about Seymour. He's been very upset about something since the team got back to Chicago, but when I ask him what's wrong, he won't tell me. I thought maybe that Elmo player had something to do with it."

"No, Ma, it wasn't important at all. Just a minor matter they had to straighten out. If there's anything wrong, I don't know about it."

"It's a terrible thing for a mother to call her son a liar, but I don't think you're telling the truth, Arnold."

"Do you think they would've let me listen if it was anything important?"

Myrn was silent; she wasn't satisfied with my answer.

"What makes you think I have any reason to lie, Ma?"

"This reason, smartie. I just got a call from Seymour. Do you think he would take the time after a game had started to go back to his office and give me a message for you? He said he'd given some thought to what happened last night and he wanted to talk to you about it. He wants you to meet him at Stryker's Lounge on Broadway and Irving one hour after the game. You know where Stryker's Lounge is?"

"I'll find it."

"It's terrible you should start lying to me this way. I don't deserve it. I hope you aren't starting another nasty habit."

For once I had to agree with her. For good reasons or bad, telling lies was a bad thing to do. I'd already told Jamey one about Spieler and I didn't like it. I was afraid I was getting sucked into something I wouldn't like.

I called Kim but she wasn't in. Then I hurried off to the game. As I drove, I listened to it on the radio. It was another zany one. The Cubs were playing the Cincinnati Reds and losing 5–0 in the third inning. Bert Wilson was going over some of the strange things that happened. Dale Wishnikopf, an outstanding control pitcher, had already walked four batters, two with the bases loaded, and committed a balk to bring in another run. Lance Lawrence, normally a fine fielder, dropped a fly ball that let in two more runs. In the fourth inning, though, as so often happened at Wrigley Field, the wind picked up and shifted and started blowing straight out to left field. Two routine fly balls, by Ironhead Sykes and Benny Bartram, had each drifted into the left-field bleachers for homers with a man on base, and the Cubs were only down 5–4 when I got there and found my seat. Then Dale Wishnikopf had another wild streak. He walked three straight men and Mickey Malone was brought on in relief. But the Cubs failed to turn two double plays and two runs scored, and then a wild pitch brought in a third one and the Reds led 8–4. The wind continued to work in the Cubs' favor, though, and two fly balls veered crazily between the outfielders and the Cubs got three runs back. The score was 8–7 in the seventh. It seemed the Cubs couldn't give the game away faster than the Reds could legitimately give it back.

Once you knew the fix was on, it wasn't hard to see who was in on it and who wasn't. Ironhead Sykes made a perfect throw to second base to nail a runner trying to steal. But Joey de Angelo dropped it and the runner slid in safely. Benny Bartram at third made dazzling stops of hard smashes to his right and left to throw out batters. Wally Koslowski, however, waved at a couple of grounders going into the outfield that he ordinarily would've gobbled up. Royal Farrell didn't pivot as smoothly as usual at second and messed up the two double plays that allowed a couple of runs to score. Mark Cacoyannis and Lance

Lawrence, both clutch hitters, each flied out feebly when
they might've driven in a run. About Dale Wishnikopf I
couldn't have any doubts. None of these would've been
noticeable, so skillfully were they done, if I hadn't known
what was going on. The only person whose performance
was glaring was old Elmo's. He had struck out less than
thirty times during the entire season and today he had
already struck out twice with men on base. He was dead
serious about his new deal.

In the ninth inning, with Randy Dodds pitching, Gus
Bell and Ted Klusewski hit home runs to give the Reds a
two-run lead. I honestly couldn't tell if Randy had taken
anything off his pitches or if this was one of his bad days.

The first two Cub batters in the bottom of the ninth
were easy outs. Elmo Speakes was the last hope and he
grounded weakly to the second baseman, who booted it.
Elmo was disgusted as he stood fuming on first, staring
daggers at the second baseman. Then Mark Cacoyannis
walked on four pitches he couldn't have reached with an
oar. This brought up big Ironhead Sykes. With the runners going on a 3–2 count, Ironhead lashed the ball between the left- and center-fielders. The left-fielder made a
headlong dive to cut it off. He missed, and his flying body
made the center-fielder behind him lose sight of it too. The
ball bounced right past him to the ivy-covered outfield
wall. What's more, he tripped and fell as he tried to turn.
Both outfielders were on the ground as Ironhead, one of
the slowest runners in the game, chugged around first, and
the shortstop and the right-fielder chased the ball from
far away. Two runs had scored and the score was tied as
Ironhead, rounding second, was already running out of
gas. The two outfielders were up now and the four Reds
converged on the ball, but they couldn't find it — it was
lost somewhere in the thick ivy — and the third-base
coach was frantically waving Ironhead home. He stag-

gered and nearly stumbled as he rounded third as the Reds were desperately looking for the ball.

Finally it popped out of the ivy. The throw was headed to the infield. Ironhead was about halfway home, but his legs were melting under him. Benny Bartram was frantically waving him in and signaling him to slide. Elmo Speakes was frantically shouting for him to fall down. That was exactly what Ironhead did as the second baseman got the ball on the outfield grass and whirled to fire home. He collapsed on his knees and started to crawl. The throw was headed home. Ironhead went down on his face as the ball sailed over the catcher's head into the box seats. Ironhead was awarded home on the overthrow. He crawled to the plate and collapsed on it. The Reds manager stormed out of the dugout to argue, but stopped short, with his mouth open. There was nothing he could say. The Cubs won 11–10. The crowd roared. Wrigley Field seemed to shake.

After the game I drove to Stryker's. It was an ordinary neighborhood joint, and I sat at the bar and ordered a beer. I figured it would take Spieler longer than he figured on account of the reporters would be wanting him to talk a long time about the crazy win today. It was all right with me. I wanted to sit and think. It was the first time since the season started that I'd missed placing bets on the afternoon games. I still had time to get my bets in for the games tonight, but strangely I didn't care. I was so concerned about the things going on I forgot to call Kim.

Spieler, however, showed up right on time. He came quickly through the door and looked relieved when he saw me. "Good to see you, Arnie. What say we blow this joint. Let's take a walk to the supermarket and get some grub for tonight. I figured you and me might have some dinner at my place. Talk about things without the outside world looking over our shoulders, you know what I mean? A couple of big sirloin steaks and baked potatoes and lots of salad and ice cream sound okay with you?"

"Sounds fine, Spieler. I hope you'll let me supply the booze and beer."

He nodded approvingly. "Spoken like a true sport," he said. "I like your style, kid."

We got the food and drove to Spieler's place, just a few blocks away. As Spieler showered and shaved, I put the food away. I tried to call Kim again but she still wasn't in. I opened a bottle of beer and sat in one of the window seats with the view overlooking Belmont Harbor.

For the first time I looked around Spieler's place. It was a one-bedroom furnished apartment with a large, airy living room and a sense of being unused except for the immediate area near the three tall windows with window seats and two large armchairs placed side by side to take in the view of the harbor and the Drive and Lake Michigan. Except for his clothes, all the things that had any use to Spieler — books and newspapers and magazines and mail and a portable radio and his checkbook and bank statement — were carelessly piled in one of the end window seats. In the bedroom, shirts and ties and socks and underwear were similarly draped on his dresser and a chair. A television set on a portable stand and a record player on the floor and bottles of liquor on a dolly stood not far away from the twin chairs. There was something strangely familiar about these chairs, as though I'd seen them someplace else.

I was curious about the things Spieler liked to read. Magazines like *Life* and *Time* and, of course, the *Sporting News*. There were different racing forms. There were mysteries by Raymond Chandler and Eric Ambler. There was the big new novel that everyone was talking about, *From Here to Eternity*, by James Jones. Thank goodness he didn't have anything by my brother. I'd never read Dan's novels, but people told me they were pretty good.

Spieler came from the kitchen with a cold beer for me and a bucket of ice. He made himself a Scotch and water and sat down in one of the armchairs. He was wearing self-belting beige slacks with a sharp crease, a black-on-black silk sports shirt, and tan alligator shoes. There was a large square-cut diamond ring on his pinkie. I could smell his sweet barbershop hair oil from where I sat. He looked ruddy and refreshed and as perky as ever.

"I'm awful glad you could make it, Arnie. You asked me a good question this morning about whether I got involved in it for the money. It struck something deep in me and I couldn't concentrate on the game today until I called Myrna and asked her to arrange this meeting. I figure I owe you an answer.

"I want to tell you how things like fixes get started. You gotta understand that a guy pays a price for being a major-league ballplayer. The longer he sticks around, the more it costs him. A guy who's gone ten, fifteen years in the bigs — a good player who's still not a star — that's the guy with the hardest problem. Some day soon he's got to accept the fact that his playing days are gonna stop. The little boys' game is over and he's got to cut it in the real world overnight.

"Now the problem wouldn't be half so bad if it weren't complicated by the fact that every guy who stays in the game for a lot of years knows in his heart he's getting screwed. Getting screwed by the club owners who want to pay him zilch for his labors. For every DiMag or Musial or Williams or Mantle that takes big bucks from the owners, the owners turn around and make it up by turning the screws on the other players.

"Why don't the good players that last do better, you ask? Good question. The answer is, the way baseball is set up, the players have no choice in the matter. Do you know what the reserve clause is?"

"I think it gives the owner the right to renew a player's contract when it's up."

"That's right. But not only that, the owner can renew the player's contract at any salary he wants to give him. The player doesn't have any say in the matter. The only thing he can do is hold out like Elmo tried to, but they all have to give in after a while because what they're doing is holding out on their own wage-earning time. The owner's got money to pay his rent and the landlord's knocking on the player's door. You follow me?"

I followed.

Spieler went on: "In most cases the nonstars learn to live with it. They come to accept the fact that they're never gonna get paid like DiMag. They make do with whatever they can squeeze out of the bastards for the privilege of playing this game year after year. Once in a while, like I say, a genuine star like Elmo makes a stink, but not often. Most players aren't cut out for giving owners trouble and holding grudges — all they really know how to do is play baseball — except when sometimes something can happen that can get them all aroused. It usually happens when an owner is so dumb as to constantly remind the guys that they're only peons and he doesn't give a shit about them. That's what happened in New York with Bobby Wentworth."

Spieler explained that on the Sunday night the Cubs took a double-header from the Giants, making it a four-game sweep, a bunch of the players went out to a famous nightclub, the Copacabana. Even New Yorkers were coming over and congratulating them on how well they'd played. All of a sudden one of them spots Bobby Wentworth in the place. He's with his Chez Paree Adorable and having crêpe suzettes and magnums of champagne. A couple of the guys go over to say hello.

Bobby is soused and he looks at them with this bewildered expression and asks them what the hell they're doing in New York. Royal Farrell explains to him that they've just taken seven of eight games from the Dodgers and the Giants and they've moved eight games up in first place, but Bobby continues to blink and gets this furious look to the roots of his white-maned hair. It's bad enough that it's obvious to the guys that Bobby had no idea what had happened, let alone where the guys were playing, but Bobby has to make things worse by growling that the guys better understand that he wasn't paying for them at the Copa.

That did it! From that moment the die was cast. There was no turning back after Bobby, with one dumb stroke, stripped the guys of their sense of pride and made them feel like absolute dirt. The guys got smashed and called up the fixers when they got back to their hotel, and once the fixers moved in to set up the deal, though the guys might've had second thoughts, there was no getting off the hook — the fixers wouldn't let them.

Spieler took a gulp of Scotch and looked out the window. He spoke quietly: "You ever heard of the Chicago Black Sox scandal of 1919? That White Sox team was one of the greatest ever. My God, Shoeless Joe Jackson in left and Happy Felsch in center and Buck Weaver at third and Swede Risberg at short and Eddie Collins at second and Ray Schalk catching and Cicotte and Lefty Williams and Dickie Kerr pitching, with the exception of Elmo and Elijah they make all my guys look like minor leaguers. Well, eight of the guys got it into their heads that they were going to throw the 1919 series with the Cincinnati Reds. Why did they want to do it? You guessed it. Same shit as now. Cheap grubbing owner who kept reminding them that he owned them. They hated old Comiskey so much it made them bold enough to dump the Series.

"And you know what happened? Right again. They got found out. You want to know why they got found out? 'Cause ballplayers just don't know how to keep their mouths shut. Some dumb reserve infielder was overheard shooting his mouth off in 1919. Some dumb reserve infielder shot his mouth off to Elmo in 1955. Same shit. What was it the French guy said, the more time goes by, the more nothing ever changes. And one thing now you can count on more than anything else, the harder my guys try to blow it, the more they're going to screw up.

"Look at the game today. The Cubs handed the Reds eight runs in the first three innings. You'd think that would be more than enough to do it, that they should've saved some of those runs to blow another ballgame. But what happens? The Reds start to give it right back to them. The guys win in spite of everything. Old Ironhead takes five minutes to round the bases and nearly dies of a heart attack before he collapses on the bases and *still* he scores. My guys can no more blow this game than they can tell the wind to blow the other way. They can no more control this fix right down to the end than they can get messages from God. Only one thing's for sure. If the deal blows up and they're exposed, they're the only ones that are going to suffer for it."

Spieler turned and nodded knowingly at me. "When the Black Sox thing blew up in 1919, there were more different kinds of guys involved than Carter's got liver pills. There were big-time gamblers all over the country who were in on it. Comiskey himself knew about it. The presidents of both leagues knew what was going on. The politicians and the cops and a lot of lawyers in Chicago knew the score and I don't have to tell you what they did about it. They all played the string out to the end, lining their pockets on the way.

"Yet when the thing blew up and the story made headlines, who were the only ones in the public spotlight? You got it: the players, of course! They were the ones that went to trial and got kicked out of baseball as the owners and the cops and the pols and the lawyers and the newspapers made a lot of noise about how swell it was that their hallowed game had been saved from shame and the wicked players had got their just deserts. These were the same miserable hypocrites that made ten times more than the players while the fix was on. Want another beer?" Spieler asked.

I shook my head. He got up and freshened his Scotch and water. He sat down again. "So why am I bending your ear like this, you want to know? Who gives a shit what happened in 1919? What's your part in it, Spieler, you want to know? Okay, you got it.

"It wasn't my idea to begin with. The guys only came to me because they knew they could never get away with it without me knowing about it. So they decided to approach me right after they realized they were committed themselves and it wasn't going to be so easy to get out of it. They didn't want to take a chance on *my* sticking it to them good after I found out what was going on.

"Well, I thought about it and I decided I wasn't going to be either for them or against them. I came to that conclusion because I couldn't think of anything better to do. The circumstances didn't give me room for anything else. The average fan doesn't know how sensitive the guys've been all season long on account of the contract problem in the spring. Half a dozen times they were ready for a fix. That incident with Wentworth at the Copa broke the camel's back.

"My own position with them has been kinda tricky too. A lot of them want to believe that Wentworth paid me off to front for him on the contract talks. Ballplayers aren't the brightest guys and they'll never realize what I told them was for their own good. I realized in spring training we had a genuine shot at the pennant, and if the team got off to a decent start they might begin to believe it too, and that would become more important than their raises. My figuring was that if they wanted to be in a winning situation, what you might call a negotiable position with the gamblers, let them get off to a winning start and they would have the option of playing for keeps or cutting a deal.

"If I'd told the guys to go screw themselves when they came to me with the deal, that's exactly what they would've done, in my opinion. They would've choked up and started losing without trying and taken themselves out of their negotiable position, if that's what they wanted. No, if there was going to be any reason for calling off the fix, it seemed to me it had to be a good and convincing one, and I figured I would be better able to convince the guys if I was neutral, rather than for them or against them. A lot of the guys may not love me. A lot of them may not trust or believe me on a lot of things. But one thing they can all mortgage their souls on is that I'll never blow the whistle on them. You sure you don't want another beer?"

I shook my head.

Spieler was looking at me intently, as though he was trying to gauge what I was going to think about the next thing he was going to say. He had kind of a guilty grin.

"To tell you the truth, what I've just said isn't exactly the truth. I also wanted time to think about the kind of bread involved in the deal. There were nice numbers for everyone involved, including yours truly. Look around you, Arnie. What you see is what I am. A baseball vagabond who's spent most of the last thirty-five years of his life living out of a suitcase in apartments with only bare essentials for furniture. I still say I got news for Elmo

Speakes: you don't have to be black to get screwed in baseball. You know what bubkas are? That's what I've worked for most of my career, and I've been around a lot longer than Elmo.

"Everyone's jealous cause of the three-year contract I got out of Wentworth, but no one wants to hear that it's my ex-wives who get the lion's share. It's been a lifetime of easy come, easy go, and now I'm fifty-two years old, and like every other schmuck in baseball, only as good as my next paycheck. But suddenly the pot of gold is there for the taking. To be absolutely candid about it, Spieler La Chance needed time to think about it.

"He needed time because of something special that happened to him. I'm sure you know what it is. Look around you again, kid. See anything familiar?"

I looked around. Nothing caught my eye. I started to shake my head —

"What about the armchairs we're sitting in? Don't you recognize them?"

Aha, I did! I *had* seen them before, I'd sat in them maybe a couple of thousand times. They were the big square deep armchairs that used to be in Myrna's bedroom. She'd recovered them in new ivory-colored material, which was why I didn't recognize them at first.

Spieler saw the recognition on my face. "The first time your mother was up here," he explained, "she saw what an awful mess it was. She knew that I liked to look out at the lake at night, and she remembered how much I said I liked the armchairs when I was over at your place one time, so the next day she had the two chairs brought over for us to sit in. Had an upholsterer come up and redo them. Now she's made it a real pleasure for us to be up here. Our favorite thing is to sit here late at night and look at the water and watch the cars like shooting stars speed up and down the Outer Drive.

"But the chairs are only a small sign of how your mother's changed my life. I don't know why I'm so nuts about that wacko dame. The other night we were sitting here with the lights out and looking out the windows, and I was trying to think about the guys while her mouth was going ninety about the most trivial stuff, like did I know that Ricardo Montalban was married to Loretta Young's sister, or could I name all the husbands of Sylvia Sydney, or who were all the actresses who wanted to be Scarlett O'Hara, and I say to myself what is it I'm letting myself in for with this half-woman half-child and why do I want it?

"I don't know the answer. It's something more than liking to be with her. It's something more than her liking to be with me. Last night when her mouth was going nonstop about a dozen things at once, and I'm not listening, suddenly I realize there's only silence, and we sit there for a bit and she still doesn't say anything and I ask her if everything is okay. And she says, 'Seymour, do you think I talk too much?' and she's silent again. And I think about it for a while and say finally, 'No, Myrna, you don't talk too much. Never ask me if you talk too much. I'll tell you when you're talking too much.' And she says, 'Thank you, Seymour,' and I can tell she's close to tears but she goes back to doing seventy about George Sanders being Tom Conway's brother and they both played the Saint and who were all the lady costars of all the guys who've ever played Dr. Jekyll and Mr. Hyde and it dawns on me that your old man leaving her busted her up pretty good and it's not easy for her to show she cares, but I'm glad that she can care for me because we're not the likeliest twosome you're ever gonna meet. I feel real good that I've got someone like her that needs me and I can take care of. It's like something I've been looking for without ever knowing it.

"So when this fix business came up, I got to thinking about it in terms of Myrna. If the bucks ain't coming in for me, she's not exactly the type who's gonna go out and get a waitress job and say we can live the simple life, on love and peanut butter sandwiches. She's become accustomed to a certain better style of living and I'm certainly not going to be the one to change her ways. After all, they're my ways too and a leopard doesn't change his spots. And taking care of Myrna is one of the reasons I've been hedging on which way to go.

"The way I see it is that I've got a little time. Not much, but enough to help me decide. Including today, there's eleven games left in the season, two with the Reds today and tomorrow and three with the Braves over the weekend to close it out at Wrigley Field. Then next week three with the Pirates and three with the Reds on the road and that's goodbye. If I want in, I don't have to bet on every game up to the end, I can wait till the final series with the Reds and ante up real big. I think you understand what I'm saying, Arnie. You ran your operation at Illinois."

I understood very well what Spieler was talking about. What I didn't understand was how he could get out of the situation clean if he wanted to, since the gamblers weren't about to let the other guys out of the deal. I asked him.

He smiled shrewdly at me, appreciated the question. "That's another one of the problems. I've given it some thought. For me to get out of it, it requires a stylish act, something that everyone will sit up and take notice of and know what I'm up to, without my saying a word. You got any ideas?"

I shook my head. "And what about the guys?"

Spieler smiled shrewdly again. "That's another kind of problem. For the guys to get out of it, assuming that they *can* get out of it, they've got to do it all together. It's not a halfway thing. It would be too hot a potato for anyone to dare point a finger at them if they all washed their hands together. The fix would just wash away in the tide. But if each guy decides to act for himself...well, that would be a disaster. And who can guarantee that so many guys will ever think the same thoughts at the same time when there's so much money and hatred of Wentworth involved? So that's why I'm riding the fence as long as I can. To see what, if anything, *I* can do about it. To see if I have any choice in the matter."

I didn't say anything. Was thinking about what he said. "I guess I know what you mean, Spieler, about that each-guy-for-himself thing. You'd have a lot of trouble getting Randy Dodds to pull out now."

"You already know he's part of it?"

"Angie Bishop's brother, Jamey, overheard them talking about it last night. Randy wants the money so he can stay in Chicago with Angie."

"Oh, yeah! You see how many people know about it already. No sirree, no way of keeping it in, the stink is coming up from the sewer."

"Do you know who the high rollers are?"

Spieler stopped talking. He looked keenly at me. "Yeah, I do. But it's for me to know and for you to never find out. You don't wanna know, Arnie, believe me. Even the guys don't know. *I* know because I'm Spieler La Chance and I've spent a lifetime being in the know about these kinds of things. Be glad you don't know, and stay cool and go out and make love to that lovely Oriental chick I've seen you with. She's quite a looker, that one. Is there anything going between you?"

"Yeah, I go for her. I'm not so sure how much she goes for me."

"Why don't you ask her?"

"She's not the kind to tell."

"You'll know anyway. Don't leave yourself in the dark about such an important thing. Hell, I'm fifty-two years old. You're nineteen. If I'm still trying to find out where I stand in life, maybe it's time you started too. Eh, what?"

"Maybe you're right, Spieler."

"Okay, then. Let's eat now and talk about other things and get to know each other. I want you to tell me more about yourself and what's been happening since Zach took off. Sorry to bend your ear like this, but, like I said, I figured there were some things you'd want to know. If we're gonna be friends, sometimes you gotta listen to Spieler's spiel."

9

WHEN SPIELER MENTIONED KIM, I remembered that I still hadn't talked to her today. It was after eight o'clock, and while he went into the kitchen to broil the steaks, I tried to call her again, at the restaurant where she worked as a cocktail waitress. The manager said she hadn't shown up or called in. It was the first time she'd ever done either. I called her at home and there was still no answer. For the first time I got worried.

Spieler saw that I was worried. He asked me what was bothering me. I told him. "I've got a funny feeling about it," I said.

"What could be wrong?" he asked.

"I don't know exactly. It's not like Kim not to get in touch. She's secretive about certain things, goes off on her own some days, but she always lets me know when she's going to be away and when I'll hear from her again. She's real dependable that way. It's just not like her not to let the restaurant know she wasn't coming in."

"What do you mean 'secretive'?"

"I mean there are people she sees and things she does when she's alone that I don't know about. It bothers me that she won't tell me, but she absolutely refuses. It's been

like that since I met her, and she says I've got to accept it
or not see her." That was all I wanted to tell Spieler. I
didn't want to get into the money I'd lent her or the reasons she might've had for needing it. Not yet, anyway.
"Maybe I'd better go home. Maybe Kim's been trying to
call me."

"Yeah, maybe you'd better. But take twenty minutes
and eat some dinner. I'm kinda washed out from last night,
so I'll be home all night. I think Myrna's going to come
over later. Write down my phone number. Give me a ring
if you need anything."

I left Spieler's around eight-thirty and drove to my
place. I double-parked the car outside my apartment and
sat there thinking. Should I go up to my place and wait for
her call, or should I go on to her place first? I thought
about Kim.

It was weird how little I knew about her. She told me
her entire family had been killed in China when the Com-
munists took over, and she had escaped with relatives to
the United States in 1950. The relatives had settled in San
Francisco, and she had come to Chicago to look for her
mother's sister, but the sister wasn't here, and ever since,
Kim had been getting by on her own. It seemed she'd done
some things I didn't like to think about, but I was sure in
my heart she wasn't doing any of those things anymore.
The reason I was sure was that Kim took pains to make
me think so. It was the one thing she felt really passionate
about.

"It spoil things for us if I hook around," she said one
time, after we'd been going together a few weeks. And I
believed her. Lots of times I got the feeling that Kim didn't
want to talk about herself because she thought she was
protecting me from finding out something bad about her.
Sometimes it made me laugh that she treated me like some
innocent child who wouldn't be able to take the truth

about a lot of things. I tried to tell her that I was just as aware of life as she was, but she wasn't having any. "It spoil things for you, me if you know too much," she insisted, on the verge of getting mad. "You just got to take my word for it, hokay?" It was okay with me. I didn't want to lose her for any reason.

I started the car and drove up North State Parkway, through the great crowd and the glitter and traffic in the Rush Street area on this warm September night, foolishly hoping to spot her walking along these familiar streets. I turned west on Chicago and drove three blocks to La Salle, turned south on La Salle for one block, and turned east on Superior, Kim's street. I parked on her block between La Salle and Clark.

I pressed her buzzer and there was no answer. I stood across the street and stared up at her dark apartment on the fourth floor. I stood there for half an hour, waiting for her to show up. She didn't. I took out my notebook and wrote a message for her to call me and stuck the page halfway in the side of her mailbox. I drove back to my place and parked and started up my stairs. Halfway up, the phone started ringing. I rushed in and grabbed the receiver. It was Spieler calling to find out if I'd heard from her. I told him no. In the background I could hear Myrna telling him to remind me that she expected me to be at that bar mitzvah in Lake Geneva on Saturday. Spieler paid no attention as he told me again to call if I needed him.

It was after midnight when I sat down in the dark in my big leather armchair, the phone next to me, and waited for it to ring ... The next thing I knew, the light streaming through the bay windows waked me. It took me a few moments to realize I'd slept until morning in the chair. It was after eight o'clock. I stared at the silent phone.

I called Kim. Let it ring ten times but there was still no answer. Helpless, I stood there with the receiver in my hand, not knowing what to do next, when my buzzer sounded. I heard heavy footsteps coming up the metal steps. I knew it was Jamey again.

Like yesterday, he was in his grimy mechanic's suit, just as riled up. As I made coffee, he paced back and forth across the room. I asked him what was up. He whirled and stared grimly at me; asked me if I'd thought about what he'd told me yesterday.

"Yeah. Some. I've got a lot of things on my mind."

"So many, I guess, you don't have time to think about the Cubs throwing the pennant. You don't care a bit."

"I care, Jamey. You know I care."

"If they keep on playing the way they played yesterday, people are gonna figure out soon what's going on."

"The Cubs *won* yesterday, Jamey."

"It wadn't their fault they won. They tried their best to give it away. I went to the game. I was watching."

"All right, Jamey. I'm not saying they're not doing it. But today is no different than yesterday. There's still nothing *we* can do about it."

"Sounds as though you don't *want* to do anything about it."

"What are you trying to say?"

His face reddened. He muttered something.

"Are you trying to say that I'm in on it?"

He shook his head briskly, waved his hands to deny it. "I'm sorry I said that, Arnie. It's just that I don't know what to think. This whole thing has been getting to me. It's not right the Cubs throwing the pennant. There oughta be somethin' we can do about it."

"Like what?"

"I don't know. But I've got the feeling that if we told someone important that's involved in it that we know what's going on, then we could get that someone to get the guys to call it off."

"You gotta remember something, Jamey. The guys that got involved in this did it on their own. Nobody broke their arms. You may not like what's going on, but it's not your problem. It's really none of your business. You can't play God."

"I'm not so sure nobody twisted their arms. I'll bet you anything Spieler La Chance had plenty to do with it. Remember when I warned you that things like this could happen to teams he's connected with. He's the devil in all this. Can't you see, Arnie, Spieler La Chance is no damn good for base —"

"I don't think you know what you're talking about, Jamey. You're shooting off your mouth without knowing the facts."

"What makes you so sure I don't? Look at his record. Look at the kind of guy he is. Who else on the team would be more likely to sell out baseball?"

"Things don't happen the way you think, Jamey. Don't say things you don't know anything about."

"You're sure a funny guy, Arnie. Spieler La Chance is destroying the most beautiful game in the world and you want to let him do it. You've waited all your life for the Cubs to win the pennant — it's as important to you as anything else you can name — and now you're not willing to let it happen. I ask you, Arnie, do you want the Cubs to throw the pennant? Say that you do and I promise I'll never say another word about it."

"No, I don't want the Cubs to throw the pennant. It's the last thing I want to happen."

"So, all right. So we gotta find someone who can get to Spieler and get him to call the whole thing off."

I was silent; couldn't keep saying that Spieler wasn't part of it or Jamey was sure to ask me how come I knew so much. And I couldn't let Jamey blow the whistle and get everyone in a jam. I didn't want to play God either, didn't want to be put in the position of protecting the fix, but I knew that Jamey's way wasn't the right one. His heart seemed like it was in the right place, and maybe it was, but like before, there was something he wasn't saying that bothered me. I still couldn't put my finger on it. I asked him if Angie had found out anything more from Randy.

The question made him uneasy. "You know I can't ask her about it. She'd know I overheard something."

"I want to tell you something," I said. "You don't have to answer me now. You don't have to answer me ever if you don't want to. I don't believe you're telling me your real reason for not wanting the Cubs to throw the pennant. It's something else and you know it."

Jamey fidgeted and looked embarrassed. "You just come right out with it if you think it's something else."

"I told you we don't have to discuss it now. I don't have the time right now. I've got a problem I can use your help on. I haven't been able to get in touch with Kim for over a day. She may be in some kind of trouble."

Jamey was glad to get away from the thing we were talking about. He also was grateful for the help Kim had given him and was instantly concerned about her. We decided that he should stay at my place in case she called and I should go to her apartment and see what I could find out from her janitor and people in the neighborhood.

I drove to Kim's, parked, raced up her steps. My message was still there. I pressed her buzzer, still no answer. I ran to the phone booth in the drugstore on Clark Street and called her. Still no answer. I went back to her building and pressed the janitor's buzzer. He said what he'd told me the last time I'd bothered him, that he hadn't seen her for a while, but it wasn't unusual because of the hours she kept. Kim didn't have any friends that I knew of. She was friendly with a few store owners on Clark — the druggist, the grocer, a waitress at a luncheonette — and I went back and asked them if anyone had seen her recently. No one had. I called Jamey and asked if he'd heard from her. He hadn't. It was around eleven A.M. I didn't know what to do.

I walked back to her building and got a sort of idea. I removed my message from its crack and pressed someone's buzzer so I could get into the building. I went upstairs to her floor. There were two apartments in front and two in the rear. I sat down against the door of a rear apartment, ready to wait as long as I had to, right here.

Hours passed. I'd gone out only once, for a take-out sandwich and to call Jamey. It was after four o'clock when I finally heard the click of high heels coming up the stairs. They weren't Kim's usual clip-clip-clip — more slow and tired. I stood up and waited, hidden from her.

She already had the key in the door when I spoke: "Kim. Where the hell have you been?"

She was startled, looked at me, looked away, raising her hand to cover her face. I went up to her. "Please tell me where you've been. I didn't know what to think."

"I 'preciate, Arnie, I 'preciate," she said quickly, "but I no talk now. Don't bother me. Go away."

Her usually perfectly groomed hair was messy. Also, she kept her hand over her face and turned away from me as though she were hiding something.

"What's wrong, Kim? What's the matter?"

"You go away now, Arnie. You stay away until I call you. No time for you now." She started to open her door.

I was confused; reached out to touch her arm. "*Get lost!*" she screamed. "I no want to see you now!" She started to push me away and I saw the other side of her face.

There was a terrible bruise around her eye. Big and blue and ugly. "Kim, what happened to you? I'm not going anywhere until you tell me." I pushed past her and went into the apartment.

She was still trying to push me away in the middle of

her little one-room place but suddenly she was dizzy and staggered over to the bed and fell on it. She glared fearfully at me, too exhausted to speak.

I went to the bathroom and ran cold water over a towel, then went back to Kim and washed the blood and dirt off her face. She didn't try to stop me, but cried once as I touched her bruise. I asked her how she got it.

She didn't want to tell me; eyed me as she thought about what to say. "I tell if you tell something first."

"What is it?"

"Is Cub team losing games on purpose?"

Holy Christ! Jamey, Myrna, Kim — who else was going to know? Were Elvis Presley and Ed Sullivan going to call and ask the same question? "Maybe I'll tell you," I said sarcastically, "if you tell me why *you* want to know. Fair enough?"

It wasn't, as far as she was concerned. She dug her teeth into her lower lip and thought hard, her eyes unblinking. "Hokay, hokay, I tell you. Certain things you ought to know."

"That's damn decent of you Kim. I've only been looking for you for over a day. Take off your clothes and lie down and tell me certain things I ought to know."

She did. She took off her raincoat and dress and shoes and lay down with her head raised against the headboard. She said she'd had a business appointment yesterday afternoon. While she was meeting with this guy after they got done talking about what the meeting was about, he asked her out of the blue if she knew what Elmo Speakes wanted to talk to Spieler La Chance about the night before. She asked him why he wanted to know. He said he was asking for a friend who'd gotten the word about Elmo looking for Spieler and finding him at the Edgewater Beach.

Kim said she wasn't there when they talked, so she didn't know what they talked about. Even if she did, she wasn't going to tell some guy she didn't know. Why did his friend want to know?

The guy told her that his friend told him the Cubs were fixing to throw the pennant and what Elmo and Spieler said to each other might have something to do with it.

Even if Cubs throw pennant, Kim said, why should she care? She didn't give a damn what they did.

Her friend told her that she *should* care. His friend had told him that if word got out about the Cubs, it especially wasn't going to be good for a couple of pals of the guy she went with, Arnie Barzov. He was referring to Spieler La Chance and Randy Dodds who were going to be in plenty of trouble with the cops. Maybe I would be in it too. The guy's friend said that he wanted her to find out from me all the details about how the Cubs were going to throw the pennant and get the information back to him by six o'clock tonight. If she didn't, the newspapers would have the whole story for their morning editions. I and my buddies would be up shit's creek without a paddle.

Kim said she didn't know what to do. She came back to her apartment and thought about it.

"Why didn't you try to call me?"

"I did. Lot of times. You no home."

This was true. I was at Wrigley Field and then I went to Spieler's. "You still could've waited for me to come home."

"By that time, I knew what I want to do."

"You didn't figure you could use all the help you could get?"

"I knew what I want to do! I called my guy and told him I couldn't get in touch with you. I needed more time. One more day. I tell my guy I want to see his friend as soon as possible."

"And did you?"

"Yeah, I see him."

"Who is he? What's his name?"

"No give name. Just a guy. Dime-dozen in this town."

"What's he look like?"

"Nothing special. Usual hustler. He said you no know him."

"What did you talk to him about?"

"I tell him I no know much about baseball. No know how to ask or how to explain what he want to know. That's why I need more time. He told me questions to ask you. You tell me now. Are Cubs going to throw pennant?"

"Kim, you know better than that. Even if I knew, I wouldn't tell you. Not so you could pass it on to some guy I don't know from Adam."

"Then you know what going to happen. He spill beans to papers."

"What if I want to tell him myself?"

"That impossible. I no let you do it. You tell me what to tell him. I take care of him myself."

She wasn't leaving me much choice. I thought about it. "Kim, I get the idea there's something you're not telling me. Something important. How'd you get that bruise? What happened? Did *he* give it to you?"

"Bruise have nothing to do with him. Something else," she said impatiently. "You want me to take care of this thing or no? You want all your friends to get in trouble? You better tell me how to save your ass."

She sat against the headboard, breathing hard, too tired to talk for a while. Then she started up again: "You no want do it my way, you get out of here. We no more see each other. You get out of my life right now. Get hell out of here!" This exhausted her altogether. She slipped down on the bed and rolled on her side and stared at the wall.

She'd made up her mind not to tell me any more. I didn't know what to do. I grabbed at her raincoat on the bed to hang it on a standing rack in the corner. But as I moved toward it, a closed switchblade knife fell out of her pocket. I picked it up and stared at its intricately enameled crescent-shaped Oriental handle. I opened it and stared at its long moon-shaped blade. I stared at Kim, still staring at the wall. I closed the blade and put it in my pocket.

It was after five. Kim had fallen into a kind of troubled sleep. I thought about calling Jamey. Better not. In his state of mind, he'd only complicate things. There was no one to turn to. Nothing now but to wait.

Six o'clock, the time she should've been at her meeting, Kim was still asleep. The phone rang. She bolted up, alert. It rang two or three more times. She glared at me with her hand poised over the receiver. "I go see him. You no go with me."

I shook my head. "Tell him to come up here and talk to me. He won't spill anything because he wants to get in on the fix. Tell him he has to talk to me for information. I won't leave you alone."

She saw I wasn't kidding. "Hokay, hokay, you some stubborn fool. I would take care for you. You should trust me." She answered the phone and made arrangements for the guy to come up. She told me he was just down the block, would be up in ten minutes. Kim looked around for her raincoat, spotted it on the rack, got up and felt inside her coat pocket and withdrew her hand. She didn't let on for a moment that what she was looking for wasn't there. She put on her dress and shoes and sat on the bed and waited.

The buzzer was pressed right on time.

"What kind of a guy is he?" I asked Kim.

She looked hard at me. "You be careful. Something real crazy about him."

A knock at the door. Kim opened it. Somehow I knew who it was going to be, and I was right. There was Johnny Salerno, with a loony look. "Surprise, punk," I said.

He had this evil leer. "Well, look who's here. Glad to see you, turd. Might as well get what I need from the horse's mouth." He swaggered into the room.

"Is this the friend of the guy you went to see?" I asked Kim.

She nodded grimly. Her hatred for Salerno was all over her face. He'd done something real bad to her. It was more than the bruise on her face.

"You got the info I need?" he asked, grinning.

"Why don't you ask me, punk? I'm the one that's supposed to know."

He looked sharply at me and broke into that cruel grin. "Okay, turd, I'll do that little thing. I'm asking. For your sake, I hope you know the answers." He was all swelled up with himself. There *was* something crazy about him.

"What makes you think I know?"

"You know, turd."

"Even if I do, what makes you think I want to tell you?"

"Lots of things." He smirked. "We'll start with your buddies La Chance and Dodds. They'll be wearing prison stripes for a long time if it gets out."

"That wouldn't do you much good, Salerno, if being in on the fix is what you want."

"That's right. It ain't my intention to blow the whistle on them if I don't have to."

"You realize you're trying to horn in on big action. The heavy rollers have already got this thing set up."

"I don't want no part of their deal. I only want a small deal of my own. It won't have nothing to do with the big action."

"What if I call your bluff, punk? What if I tell you to go ahead and blow the whistle? You think the big action won't find out that you did it?"

Salerno was shaking his head confidently. "I don't think so, turd. You ain't bluffing me this time. I see our Chink friend here hasn't filled you in on everything." He grinned spitefully. "Have you, Chink?"

"What's he talking about, Kim?"

She glared murderously at Salerno. "You bastard."

"You tell him or I will. Makes no difference to me, Chink."

"I'll tell him. I'll get you, too, for making me. Get out of here now, Salerno. Come back in half hour. I want to talk to Arnie alone."

"You wouldn't be thinking of screwing me, would you, Chink?"

"You holding all cards, Salerno, so how I screw you?"

"I'm glad you know it. I'll be back in thirty minutes. You know what I need to know, turd. Don't you forget it, either." He left the apartment with that smirk.

Kim looked at me. "It not too late for you to get out of this. You let me handle him."

"We're in this together. That's the way it is. What's going on, Kim? No holding back anymore."

She *still* didn't want to tell me, was still thinking about how to get out of it. But finally she realized she had no choice, took a deep breath and started in. She said that the guy she owed money and went to see each week wasn't at their meeting place this time. Instead, Salerno was waiting for her in the booth in the back of the restaurant in Chinatown. She asked him where her guy was. He told her to sit down. She asked him who he was. He said he'd bought out her contract from her guy and she'd be making her payments to him from now on and she'd better sit down because he had something important he wanted her to do.

Kim sized him up. She saw right away there was something dangerous about him. Without a murmur, she sat down across from him.

Again she asked him who he was. He said his name

didn't matter. He told her he knew about the fix and what he wanted her to do. Though he tried to be cool, Kim felt an anger in him he couldn't control. As he talked, his eyes widened and his words spewed out with hate. She tried to find out more about it.

It didn't take long. His second Scotch and Salerno spilled out the story of how Angie had run out on his record deal and how much he hated me and Jamey and Randy and Spieler for helping her. He'd been humiliated in the eyes of Uncle Pietro Celli. Uncle Pietro had called him in and raged at him for an hour. He thought it was his last day on earth. But because he was the son of a friend that Pietro owed a favor, Pietro spared him. He told him to get out of town and never show his face again in Chicago. Told him he'd better never catch him in businesses he had no business being in, like the record business or any other racket. Screwing up and being banished wrenched like a knife in Johnny's heart. But it didn't hurt half so much, Kim realized, as losing Angie.

I'd mentioned Salerno's name to Kim in connection with Angie, and she realized who he was as he talked. She also realized something else about him. He was an incredible fool. Only a fool would talk so easily. Only a fool would come back to Chicago after being warned to stay away by Uncle Pietro.

He'd gone to Las Vegas and worked as a 21 dealer, but returned less than a month later. He couldn't help himself. He wanted to get back at all the people he thought had done him in.

He laid low; didn't get in touch with any of his old contacts. Stayed in a crummy hotel near Hooker and Wilson, in the tough, seedy area near the Lawrence Avenue El station. He knew from the newspapers that Angie was playing Nightwind, but he fought off the urge to go and see her. He had this burning idea that he wouldn't go see her until he had a reason so strong she wouldn't have any choice but to go back with him. Maybe he would have a lot of money. Maybe it would be something else. His dream only made him crazier as he checked up on me.

Salerno found out that Kim and I were going together. He followed her as she left her apartment one morning and took a streetcar on Clark Street going south. He got off when she did, at the corner of Clark and Cermak, 2200 South, in the heart of Chinatown. He followed her into a Chinese restaurant and saw her sit down in a booth in the rear with a Chinese guy. He took a booth on the other side of the room and watched their conversation. He could tell from the anger in Kim's face that the Chinese guy had some hold over her that she couldn't get out of. He decided to find out more about it.

When Kim left, Salerno stayed and followed the guy out. He followed him to a travel bureau in Chinatown a block away. He peered in and saw the guy working as an agent at a desk. He got in touch with a guy who could check out the Chinese guy. The guy found out the agency was a front for something else. Salerno raised some money and made a deal with the Chinese guy to buy out Kim's debt from him. He decided to wait for the right time to let Kim know he owned her.

It wasn't much later that he bumped into a guy who told him an amazing thing. The guy was dating a stew who roomed with a cocktail waitress who'd just broken up with Mark Cacoyannis because she discovered Cacoyannis was sleeping with her sister on the sly, and the cocktail waitress was spreading the story that the Cubs were going to throw the pennant, which was what Mark had told her. Now maybe Salerno was onto something. It made him itchy. It made him bolder. He needed a way to get in on it. Risking the chance that he might be seen by Pietro's crowd, he began to follow Kim and me around.

One time, around two A.M., he was across the street when he saw us go into Candido's. He stood there on the sidewalk, wondering what, if anything, he should do about it, when a big amber-colored convertible pulled up, and who should get out but a drunk and angry Elmo Speakes. From the way Elmo left his Caddy double-parked and went into Candido's in a hurry, Salerno had a hunch it had something to do with the Cubs and the fix.

He kept standing there, wondering if he should risk going into Candido's to see if he could find out more, when he was saved the trouble, because, at that moment, the three of us — Elmo, Kim, and I — came out of the restaurant. He saw me talk a cop out of giving Elmo a ticket and then the three of us drive off in Elmo's Caddy. He jumped in a cab and followed us to the Magic Lantern. When he saw me go in alone, he figured I'd probably soon be out, and sure enough, when I reappeared, he followed us on to the Edgewater Beach.

Salerno decided to follow us into the Polynesian Room. In the crowd, it was easy for him to get close and hear Elmo call out to Spieler on the dance floor. He followed our whole party out and saw Myrna and Kim take off in separate cabs and Spieler and Elmo and me go off together.

He couldn't follow us anymore, but he didn't need to now. Now he knew exactly what he wanted to do. He called the Chinese guy that he'd made the deal for Kim with and told him he'd be taking over and dealing with Kim directly. Then he waited half an hour for Kim to get home. He called and introduced himself and told her he wanted to see her in the morning.

It was on the sidewalk after that first meeting that Salerno hit Kim. Drove his fist into her face and said that was what she could expect if she tried to screw him. I was waiting for her when she got back to her apartment. "That story," Kim said. "You know everything now."

"Not everything," I answered. "You're not telling me the whole story. What kind of debt did Salerno buy from your guy? What's it all about?"

She was firm-lipped, not about to tell. "I tell you much as I tell you. You no need to know rest."

"You mean I don't need to know why you were carrying this knife with you?" I showed it to her. "Why you would've killed Salerno if you had the chance? It's not fair for you to hold out on me."

"Life not fair, Arnie. You much better off not knowing. I do you favor not telling. Hokay?" She pressed her lips together and looked away.

What could I say? She was determined not to tell me any more. And Salerno would be back soon.

We waited, Kim sitting still on the edge of the bed, me standing still near her. The buzzer sounded. I pressed Kim's buzzer, opened the door and stood in the hall listening to the footsteps coming up the stairs.

It was Jamey. I'd forgotten I'd asked him to come over. He came in with an anxious look, wanted to know what'd happened since he'd seen me. I saw by Kim's expression that she realized the last thing we needed was for Jamey to meet up with Salerno here. No telling what *he'd* do to him. "I'll fill you in later," I said. "Right now Kim's got someone coming over she doesn't want to see. I wish you'd take her back to my place. Don't you think that's a good idea, Kim?"

She frowned at me. But she couldn't disagree. "Hokay, hokay, I see what you mean. Jamey, I 'preciate if you take me to Arnie's place." She looked angrily at me. "You be sure call me when you get done." She put on her raincoat and gave me her apartment keys. I gave her my apartment key and Jamey my car keys. "Go quick," I said. Kim nodded and she and Jamey left.

I prayed that Salerno and Jamey wouldn't see each

other on the street, hoped that Kim had enough sense to hustle him along. I waited for Salerno to return.

He came back ten minutes later and looked around the room for Kim. "Where is she?" he asked suspiciously, his eyes getting that wild gleam.

"We didn't have any agreement that she had to be here. This business is strictly between us, Salerno. You want me to find out what the situation is with the fix? I'm telling you I don't know right now. I'll have to find out. I'll need some time, at least a day, maybe longer. Only one thing you'd better know. You harm anyone I know and I'll get you, Salerno. You can count on it, I promise."

Salerno sneered. "Big talk for a little turd. I don't need to lay a finger on anyone anymore. What I got on the Chink it pays me to keep her healthy. Healthy and on the hook. She tell you what I've got on her?"

"I don't need to know what you've got on her. When Kim's ready to tell me, she'll do it. If she doesn't want to, that's all right too."

"Noble turd, ain't you." Salerno laughed at me. "You really think the Chink is worth it?" He laughed again. "No broad is worth it," he sneered.

I stared at him. Maybe he had a point. I didn't want to discuss it. "Let's get out of here now," I said.

"You've got till one o'clock tomorrow afternoon," he warned me. "Keep me waiting a second and you're out of business, you hear me, turd?"

I kept staring at him. The guy was such a putz. He was plain pathetic. He was off his rocker all because Angie had given him the shaft. And you just knew he was bound to screw things up somehow.

He left. I locked Kim's door and went down the stairs too.

10

I WASN'T SURE what to do next. I walked a couple of blocks north on Clark until I came to Bughouse Square. The park was quiet and nearly deserted at this hour, and I sat down on a bench in the shadows, scared but glad to be alone for a while.

About a week before, I had waked up in the middle of the night with Kim beside me and waked her.

"What matter?" she asked drowsily.

"If you ever decide to leave me, you will tell me about it first, won't you, Kim?"

She was wide awake now, on her elbow, looking at me hard. "That what you want to know?"

"That's what I want to know."

"Sure, I tell you about it first, damn fool."

"You wouldn't just run out like other people?"

"Go sleep, Arnie. Don't think 'bout it. I no run out like other people."

I walked to Nightwind. It was on a dark lonely street on West Ohio, across from a block-long brick factory wall. The white letters of its frost-colored neon sign flickered like a match in the distance.

It was after two and Angie was playing her last set. A pretty good crowd in a mellow mood was settled in. I found a spot at the bar and ordered a beer and listened too.

Since she'd opened here I'd heard Angie a few times. This intimate room was perfect for her. The blue spot on her created a warm tone. The deep feeling of her voice, her phrasing of the material, her subtle playing, the pain and strength of her expressive face, filled the crowd with happy-sad feelings. Angie moved through a string of lovely ballads — "These Foolish Things," "Looking at You," and my very favorite, "I Almost Got Lucky with You" — and moved us all. If anything, she'd gotten better. Angie was a great performer, sure to get famous in my book.

She'd seen me from the piano and waved. Afterward, I felt important when she came straight through the crowd to say hello. "What brings you here, Arnie?"

"A couple of things I'd like to talk to you about."

"About Jamey?"

"Yes. And something else, too. Have you got time for a bite with me?"

"Sure thing." She sensed the importance of the things on my mind and seemed to have something important on her mind, too.

We took a cab to Charmets on Chicago and Michigan. There weren't many people in the big, bright place and we sat in a round leather booth.

"You sure were great tonight," I said.

"Thank you, sir. We work hard to please. And you're still one of the people I have most to thank for it."

We were silent for a bit. Angie lowered her eyes and smiled tightly, with a look of regret.

"Why should you be unhappy about being successful?" I asked. "Is something the matter, Angie?"

She looked up and pleasantly chided me. "Whoa," she said. "One problem at a time, young man. You were the one who said you wanted to see me about something. About Jamey, you said."

"Yeah, I do. I've got something I need to find out. Back when you were in Mississippi, was it hard for you to leave him?"

Angie was struck by my question. She realized how important her answer was to me. She nodded slowly. "It wasn't easy, I'll tell you that. There I was, getting along close to thirty, with a burning ambition to be a singer but stuck in the smallest of small towns with a younger brother whose father had run away and mother had passed away and needed more than the usual amount of love and attention on account of it and depended on me to give it to him and what was I gonna do? Can you imagine what it is to have the kind of burning I had inside of me? Sometimes it was so strong I thought I couldn't bear it a day longer. I loved Jamey, I knew how much I meant to him, but I also knew I couldn't become a drunk and bitter woman like our mother, pining away her life with alcohol until it drove her to her grave. *I couldn't* let that happen to me. I *had* to run away. But how could I explain it to Jamey? Make him believe that he was better off with his grandparents down in Alcoma? That bringing him up to the city would've been trading off my life for his, with neither of us getting anything in the bargain? It wasn't worth my coming here if I was going to do that! Yes, it was a very hard decision, it's not good having to hurt someone the way I hurt Jamey, but I did it because I had to." Though Angie's eyes were pained, her mouth was firm. "Am I telling you what you want to know?"

"Yeah, I guess . . ."

"You look like you've got something hard to do right now."

"You're right. I've got a couple of very hard things to say. I know you know what's going on with the Cubs. I know you know that Randy is one of the guys in on the fix. It's a dangerous situation because all kinds of people know about it already, like your old friend Johnny Salerno. He's back in town and making trouble."

Angie's eyes widened. "What kind of trouble?"

I told her.

She shook her head in disgust. "What are you going to do?"

"I don't know yet. I'll think of something."

"Have you talked to Spieler?"

"He's the person I was thinking I'd have to see."

"Randy says he hasn't committed himself one way or the other."

"So far as I know."

"He handled Salerno once. Maybe he can handle him again."

"If only it were just a matter of that."

"There's something else?"

"Unfortunately it's more complicated. Jamey and Randy are part of the problem too."

"What do you mean?"

"This is the other thing I got to say. Jamey also found out about the Cubs and what's going on. He overheard you and Randy talking about it. He said he wants to expose the whole thing to the newspapers because he doesn't believe the game of baseball ought to be corrupted this way."

Angie was shaking her head. She didn't believe that was Jamey's reason. "It must be something else," she said.

"I think so too. I think the corruption thing is part of his thinking but not the main thing. His real reason is that he's afraid Randy's going to make enough money from being in on the fix so he can give some to his wife and get her to agree to a divorce so he can marry you."

Angie's look got real disturbed. Her eyes glowed with regret again. For a moment there was panic but she pulled herself together and tightened her mouth and nodded. "You're perfectly right about Jamey's reason. But he shouldn't have worried. I'm not going to marry Randy."

"Does Randy know that?"

She shook her head. "Not yet," she said sadly. She was thoughtful for a bit. "You know, when I made that decision to leave Jamey behind in Mississippi, I used to think that was the hardest decision I was ever going to have to make. I was so wrong. The hard decisions never stop, all through life. Arnie, I can't marry Randy and I can't stay with Jamey. I'm afraid I'm going to have to disappoint them both. I got an offer last week to work a club in New York. I'm supposed to start as soon as my gig's up here at the end of the month. The people that hired me said they were real impressed. They say they can get me bookings all over the country. They say I can count on making New York my home base. I don't like the idea of running out on them, but what else can I do? It's *my* life in the balance."

I didn't answer.

"Arnie, I'm asking you, am I right or wrong?" For a moment she had some doubt.

I nodded in agreement. Angie wasn't wrong. I understood her point of view. Even more, I understood the way Jamey and Randy were going to feel. Even, strangely, the way Salerno felt right now. We were all out at home.

I tried to get Angie to stay overnight with me or Myrna or in a hotel. Anywhere but her place was okay until I figured a way to deal with Salerno. But she insisted that she had things to do at her place in the morning to get ready for New York. She promised she'd be careful, wouldn't take any chances, would be alert at all times. I couldn't talk her out of it, so I went with her in a cab to her place on Dearborn Parkway and saw her into her apartment. Then I went downstairs and told the desk clerk and the doorman to watch for characters asking about her and to pass the word to their replacements. One thing Angie did agree with me on was that she ought to tell Jamey and Randy about her new situation as soon as possible.

I called Spieler. He wasn't home. How could I reach him? It was too late to start looking all over the north side. Maybe Myrna knew where he was. I called her. There was no answer. She was probably out with Spieler. I didn't know what to do. Kim had the keys to my apartment. Jamey had my car. I dialed my number and there was no answer there. Damn Kim! God only knew where she was!

I called Jamey at his gas station, but the other attendant told me he'd taken the tow truck out on a call and didn't know when he'd be back. I left a message for him to leave my car near my apartment as soon as he got off work; also that I'd call him in the morning. It was just as well not to see him now. All the same, as I walked ten blocks north on Clark Street to Myrna's place, I felt so depressed having to deal with everything alone.

I let myself into Myrna's. It was after four but she wasn't home yet. Maybe she was staying with Spieler. I dialed his number but there was no answer. I dialed Kim again; same thing. I had no choice but to wait.

In my room, I put Tchaikovsky's Trio in A softly on my record player, took off my clothes, and lay down in my underwear. I set the alarm on my bedside clock for one hour from now. I put my head on the pillow and waited.

I remembered another night when I lay here and waited for Zach to get home. This time he was driving from somewhere in Indiana. He usually arrived between ten and midnight and usually called if he was going to be delayed. It was ten-thirty and he hadn't called, so I knew he wouldn't be long. I was extra anxious for him to arrive. Something special had happened to me that week.

After a while I started to pace back and forth in the short hall space between his den and my room, going nervously in and out of each room. I'd opened his violin case and would return each time to stare at the shining brown wood in its plum-colored satin setting. I was thinking about something he'd said when we were on the road together: "Sometimes I think the only two things I have to cherish in the world are my violin and you." Somehow I was never jealous that he'd said that. I cherished all the pleasure he'd given me, playing his violin.

I remember I was in his den when I heard the front door open. I closed his violin case and went down the hall to greet him. I saw him coming toward me, smiling, the billiard-ball dimples pooched out on his sweet, squirrelly face. "Hi, dad," I called out.

I kissed him. We embraced. I could smell the familiar dried-sweat smell about him from the long ride. "How was the trip?" I asked. He nodded and continued smiling with his mouth closed, like he was thinking about something unpleasant. I wondered why he didn't say anything.

He took off his suit jacket and laid it on the bed. Loosened his tie and rolled up his sleeves and went into the bathroom to wash his face and hands as he usually did when he returned from a trip. He usually left his suitcases in the foyer until after he'd washed, and I went to get them for him. They weren't there. I was puzzled and returned to the bedroom.

He was drying his face and hands.

"Was it a good trip?" I asked again. His not saying anything was making me nervous.

As he buttoned his shirt collar and cuffs, raised the knot in his tie and straightened it, he continued to smile at me in this pained way. But then he came forward and took

me in his arms and kissed me on the forehead, held me at
arm's length and looked at me with his warm, sweet smile.
"It was a trip," he said curiously, "I won't forget. Where's
your mother?"

"She's playing mahjong at Pearl Schwartz's."

He got that special pained look whenever Myrna frus-
trated or disappointed him. He shook his head a couple
of times and went to his closet and took down a couple of
suitcases.

"Is something wrong, Zach? Is Myrna supposed to be
here?"

"Not really," he said quietly, not quite able to hide his
anger. "Your mother is supposed to be anywhere she
wants to be. I called her this afternoon and asked her to
be here tonight."

"She never mentioned it to me. But she was in one of
her crazy moods when I got home from school. She left
after dinner like she didn't want to be here tonight."

"No, I guess she wouldn't. Maybe it's best this way."

"What's wrong, Dad? You just got home. Why are you
opening those suitcases? Where are the ones you took
with you?"

Zach didn't answer. He put the shirts he'd taken from a
dresser drawer into a suitcase and turned and faced me.
He had that painful look again. "Arnie, I've got something
to tell you. It's something very important. It's the hardest thing I've ever had to do, but I have no choice any —"

"I did it, Dad."

"— more. I've got to do it."

"I made the junior basketball team. Got my uniform
today."

"I'm going away, Arnie. I've made up my mind that I
can't live with your mother any —"

"Coach is counting on me to be one of his most dependable reserves."

"It's not good for any of us, you included. There's no way to make things better ..."

Zach couldn't look at me any longer. He walked out of the bedroom and down the hall into his study.

I followed after him. "All right, I can understand what you're doing. I pretty much agree with you that it can't get any better between you and Myrna. I don't blame you for doing it. I want to go with you, Zach."

He picked up his violin case and held it pressed to his chest with both arms as he turned to face me, with a sad look. Trembling, he slowly shook his head. "No, Arnie," he said, "I thought about that. I thought very hard about it, but I can't do it. It's not possible. You see, I'm going away with someone. A woman I know. It just wouldn't be fair to anyone involved for the three of us to go off together. Maybe there'll come a time when we can all be together, but not now. Now I've got to take care of first things first. I've got to straighten out my own life before I can help you with yours. I don't expect you to understand that now, but maybe someday you will. I want you to understand that I don't love you any less because I'm leaving. I'm asking you to take care of Myrna for me."

"But what about me, Zach? What about me? What am I supposed to do without you? You've got your friend to love. Who am I supposed to turn to? It's not fair. I made the team for you."

Zach stared sorrowfully at me. The pain showed in every corner of his face. He slowly shook his head. "I'm sorry, Arnie. I'm so sorry. I don't know what to tell you. I don't have any answers. You'll have to carry on the best you can. That's all any of us can do. Carry on the best we can." He walked back to his room with his violin.

As he finished packing, Zach explained that his bags were still in his car. His friend was waiting for him and that was why he was in a hurry, they were starting off for the West Coast tonight. He said he had asked Myrna to be here tonight so he could tell her too. But she must've sensed what was on his mind and didn't have the courage to face him. He said he had already made arrangements with his attorneys to take care of things. He finished packing and put on his suit jacket and combed his hair. He looked at me sadly. "Maybe someday you'll be able to forgive me. I don't know. Anyhow, goodbye, son. I love you. I know you made the team for me. I'm very proud of you."

He asked if I would like to go down to the car with him. He wanted me to meet his friend. He wanted her to meet me. But I refused. It was bad enough that it was his violin, not me, that he'd come home for. I didn't need to look into the face of the thing I'd been dreading for the longest time.

I heard the front door open and voices in the foyer. Funny, I was prepared for Spieler to come home with Myrna, but now that he was here I didn't like it. I turned off the radio and the alarm. I waited on my bed, putting off going into the living room and seeing them together. But I needed to tell Spieler about Salerno. I couldn't wait any longer.

I put on my pants and shirt and tiptoed down the hallway in my stocking feet. I stood in the darkness of the foyer, looking into the darkness of the living room. Myrna had turned on a couple of dim-lit lamps at different ends of the big space. She and Spieler were covered in shadows in the middle.

They were making out on one of the sofas. Myrna was stretched on top of Spieler. Her legs were doubled under her, and her skirt had risen to show her calves and thighs. Spieler's head was raised on a high armrest. Myrna was stroking his face as his hand stroked her thigh. They were too involved to notice me.

"Oh, you are so good to me, Seymour. So thoughtful and kind. No one has ever treated me the way you have."

"You've been pretty good to me, kid."

"You make me feel so alive."

"You make me tingle, too."

"I've never met anyone like you."

There was the sound of kisses and Myrna moaned as Spieler put his hand inside her blouse.

I coughed.

They looked up.

"Spieler," I said sharply, "I need to talk to you."

"Arnold, what are you doing here?" Myrna shrieked, springing up and straightening her skirt and tucking her breast back into her blouse in the same motion.

"I'm sorry to break in on you, Myrna. But it couldn't wait. It's important."

" 'Sorry to break in'!" she repeated, her face reddening with embarrassment. "You've got some nerve, sneaking up and spying on me. Aren't you asham —"

"Hold it, Myrn," Spieler said. He said it calmly but firmly. "Arnie doesn't mean no harm. Why don't you bring us some Cokes or something." He sort of waved her out of the room.

Glaring at me all the way, Myrna backed obediently out.

"What's up, Arnie? Come on in and sit down." Spieler pointed toward a chair near him.

I sat down. But all of a sudden something was wrong with me. All of a sudden I didn't want to tell Spieler about Johnny Salerno. "I guess I just wanted to find out what's happening with you and the guys."

Spieler nodded. He appreciated my concern. "Then I'm glad you came, Arnie. I do have a little something to tell you about that." He leaned forward with his hands on his knees and his elbows out, looking in the direction of the kitchen, trying to hear if Myrna was coming. He was still leaning forward as he spoke softly to me. "She still doesn't know what's going on. I tried to get in touch with you a couple of times today, but you never seem to be at home, fella. I wanted you to know what I'm gonna do before it makes the news tonight." He looked in her direction again, didn't hear anything, leaned closer to me, and whispered: "I'm leaving the team today."

"You are?"

"I am indeed. I've made up my mind about which way to go. I don't want any part of the fix, and that's the message I'm going to give the guys. It's beginning to stink real bad, and a lot of people are getting a whiff of what's going on. I think there's a better than even chance it's going to blow up in their faces. I hope the guys get smart for once in their lives. But whatever they do, my not being at the game is a message to whoever cares that Spieler La Chance has got clean hands. The reason I gave your mother is that I had an argument with Wentworth about running the team. It should hold her for a while. We're taking off for Lake Geneva right after I say my piece. Myrna's been all over me to remind you that she expects you to be there too, but I'm not going to pester you about it, 'cause I sense you got other, more important things on your mind. Sure you don't want to tell me about it?"

I didn't, and I still wasn't sure why. "What if the guys change their minds and decide not to go through with it? Will you come back to them?"

"I'll come back if they want me back. They'll know where to find me. Arnie, it's not smart not to tell me what's on your mind. Let me help you if I can."

"I don't need any help, Spieler. It's nothing I can't handle by myself."

Spieler shrugged. "Well, then," he grinned sheepishly, "at least say you're sorry to your mother when she comes

back in. You kind of broke in on us at an intimate moment. Embarrassed the hell out of her."

"Embarrassed is not the word for it," Myrna said, bristling in with sandwiches and bottles of soda on a tray. She
was livid with anger. "Just what do you mean lurking
around in my apartment? Don't you think your mother
has a right to her private life?"

"You have every right to your private life, Myrn, and
I'm sorry it seemed like I was spying. It's hard to explain
but I wanted to see both of you and I didn't know where
you were. I was waiting to tell you something."

Myrna eyed me warily. "So tell."

"If you don't mind, I'd also like to join you at that bar
mitzvah. I'll drive up tomorrow after I take care of some
business. Tell Cousin Selma she can count on me being
there."

Myrna was still dubious. She kept eyeing me as she held
the tray out for Spieler to take a sandwich and a soda.
"Don't do me any favors, young man. You only come if
you want to come. If it's too hard to enjoy yourself, stay
away." She extended the tray toward me but I waved my
hand.

"I'm not trying to do you a favor, Ma. I really want to
go."

But Myrn wasn't buying it. Her eyes narrowed as she
tried to think of my ulterior motive. "Why should you
want to go all of a sudden? Why, suddenly, are you so hot
and bothered?"

"I'm not hot and bothered, Myrn. I thought you'd be
glad that I'm coming."

"Leave the boy alone, Myrna. He's only trying to please
you."

"Trying to please me, is that what he's trying to do?
Well, maybe it's just a little bit too late for that. I'm not
so sure that's his reason. Listen, young man, don't do me

any favors. If you want to come, it should only be because you truly want to come. Is it fair to Selma to wear a long face and make everyone around you miserable?"

"Myrn, honey, give the boy a chance. He means well."

"I'd even like to bring some friends," I said.

She just didn't want to believe I had good intentions. "Oh? Just who are these friends, if I may ask? Don't tell me you want to bring that schvartza Elmo?"

"No, Ma, I wouldn't dream of doing that. I know the only schvartzas there will be the entertainers, and Elmo doesn't sing or dance. No, one of the persons I want to bring is Chinese. I don't know what her religion is. She doesn't either. The other person is a Baptist."

"That Chinese girl you brought to the Edgewater Beach? You want to bring *her* —"

"Cut it, Myrn," Spieler interrupted. "You promised me you wouldn't start that stuff about Arnie's friend."

She whirled on Spieler, shaking her finger. "Now just a minute, Mr. Buttinski, don't be so quick to defend. It was a girl like that that took away my other son. It was a woman like that that took away my husband. It's not fair for him to invite people like that to Selma's bar mitzvah. I think he's doing it to spite me."

"That's not his reason, Myrn. You've got the wrong slant on things. Arnie's not trying to spite you in any way. He likes the girl and it'd be nice if you'd like her too. Come off it now." His look was firm and kind.

Myrna stared back at him. She knew he was right but wouldn't admit it, set the tray down and gestured with her hand. "Likes, smikes. It's a bar mitzvah. At least let her be Jewish."

"Spieler isn't Jewish."

She whirled on me. "Spieler is Jewish enough. Spieler is my friend."

"Kim and Jamey are my friends."

"Hey Myrn," Spieler cut in again, "you don't have to be Jewish to enjoy a bar mitzvah. What's the big deal about it? The boy wants to go. What else matters?"

Finally Myrna gave in. She stood there in the middle of the living room nodding at both of us. All of a sudden her face crumbled and her look got distraught. The tears rolled down her cheeks. She was worried about something, dropped wearily into a big overstuffed armchair and leaned forward, looking down with her elbows on her thighs and her fist pressed against her chin. "To tell the truth, Seymour," she said haltingly, "maybe we shouldn't go to the bar mitzvah after all. There's going to be a lot of people, and they're going to bother you with a lot of questions and you don't need that kind of bother with everything you're going through and I thought maybe it would be better if you and I went someplace quiet, a resort like Starved Rock or Elkhart Lake, where no one would bother you, you know what I mean? Don't think you'd be doing any favors by taking me to this affair. What do I need another bar mitzvah for, anyway? You'd think I hadn't been to enough of them to last a lifetime. I think you're absolutely right, it's not such a big deal."

Spieler stared at Myrna with this admiring look in his eyes. "You know something, Myrna-sweets, you are really some kind of broad. The very best thing in my life that could've ever happened to me. That is the most considerate thing you could've ever thought of. And don't think I don't appreciate it. But I wanna tell you something. I really don't mind going to the bar mitzvah. Not a bit. Really look forward to it, if you want the truth, now that you've told me Tony Martin's going to be there. I know Tony. Know his wife, Cyd Charisse. Dated her a few times in the old days. It'll be nice to see them again. People will be no problem for me. The more the better. Take my mind off of things. Sincerely."

Myrna took this in slowly. She thought about it for a while. She looked up. "You know Cyd? You never told me you knew Cyd Charisse."

"Lots of things I haven't told you, kid. Haven't had the time to tell you. Tell you one thing, though, I've been wanting to say. If it weren't for you, love, I'd be undecided about a lot of things. Knowing you has conquered that. Lots of things I don't need anymore."

But one thing you do need is the patience of a saint, I thought. Anyone who can put up with Myrna the way you can, deal firmly with her, make her listen to reason, deserves all the consideration in the world. I suddenly realized why I didn't want to tell him about Salerno. He'd already made up his mind not to take part in the fix. I wasn't the one that had talked him out of it. He'd made the decision on his own. A large part of his thinking was on account of Myrna. It wouldn't be fair to drag him back into it. It wouldn't be fair to Myrna.

All the same, here I was being run out on by the two of them. Myrna was taking away from me the only person I'd ever come to admire or respect. It was the same old shit, Dan and Zach and now Myrna and Spieler. What about me? I thought. Don't I count? Why does everyone assume I can go on being alone, without some understanding? I *didn't want* Spieler and Myrna to be together. If I told them about Salerno, I could screw things up for them real good.

Myrna finally accepted that Spieler wanted to go. She turned and faced me with a troubled look. I'd never seen her eyes quite so moist and keen at the same time, her look so pained and peculiar, and I braced myself for more nonsense. "Arnold dear, I want you to know I've been thinking a lot about you too. I want you to know that Seymour and I have talked about going away to Florida for the winter. We're thinking about leaving in mid-

October, even sooner if the Cubs don't get to the World Series.

"What I want to say is that I hope you won't mind our going. I want you to know that I don't feel right about leaving you. Maybe I haven't been so good as I like to think — nevertheless, I don't exactly think it's been all my fault — you haven't exactly been the easiest boy to handle or understand. But I'm very sorry that we haven't been closer as mother and son. You say one word — just one word is all you have to say — and I promise you I won't go. Don't be ashamed to say that you don't want me to. Seymour and I, we've talked it over and the last thing we want you to think is that we're deserting you. You certainly don't think that, do you?"

I didn't know what to think. My head was really spinning. One thing about my mother, she could pick the most surprising times to show her love, and be as batty as ever when she did it. What could I say? In spite of myself, my resentment melted. "No, Ma, I don't think you're deserting me."

"And I do have your permission to go to Florida?"

"You have my blessings."

"I must say, Arnold, you are getting more mature. More able to be responsible for someone besides yourself. I knew you wouldn't let me down when you understood that I'd finally found a man like Seymour. You see I'm going away with someone who cares for you."

"I care for Spieler too."

"You will come visit us at Christmas? We'll all go to Havana together. Desi Arnaz has told Spieler he wants us to use his house. Won't that be a terrific thing to do?"

"I'll think about it, Ma." What I wondered was could they make it together until Christmas. Would Myrna prove too much for him? Would his patience last? What would Myrna do if he left her? I wished her luck. I wished him well. God bless them both. Spieler could deal with Myrna and I'd deal with Salerno. I wouldn't have it any other way. "Spieler, I would like to ask a favor of you."

"That's more like it, kid."

"I'd like to be at that meeting today when you make your announcement to the guys. Would that be possible? It's not often you get to see a manager leave a team to take his lady to a bar mitzvah in Lake Geneva."

Spieler grinned. At the same time, he eyed me keenly, wondering what I was up to. "Why not?" he said agreeably. "You found me for Elmo. You're concerned about the guys and me. You deserve to be there. We'll go to the ballpark together."

"I appreciate it, Spieler." Now all I had to do was think of a way to handle Salerno.

CHAPTER

11

WE STAYED OVERNIGHT at Myrna's. Spieler slept in Dan's room, I slept in mine. Spieler wanted to get to the ballpark early, so we got up at nine and Myrna served us a quick breakfast. I only had a minute to call Kim before Spieler and I took off, but at least she was there this time. She surprised me because she wasn't difficult at all. She assured me she was all right, said calmly that when I got there, she would explain where she'd been last night, all she'd really done was go out for a walk. She added that I shouldn't worry, she wasn't going out again. I told her I'd be there as soon as I could.

We got to the ballpark around ten, before any of the players arrived. The locker room was empty. It was a long, rectangular room with lockers on each wall and benches and chairs in front of them, the permanent smell of sweat in the air.

Spieler's locker was in his little office, at one end of the clubhouse. There were two entrances to it. One faced out on the locker room, the other on a corridor that led into the locker room. As he took things from his locker and packed them in a duffel bag I sat in the big worn leather armchair behind his desk and saw the players, singly and in two's and three's, file past in the corridor. All but one of the main guys involved in the fix — Cacoyannis, Lawrence, de Angelo, Wishnikopf, Farrell — went by with frowns and didn't bother to look in.

The exception was Wally Koslowski who when he saw me, ducked his head in and grinned. "Hey, kid?... You ever find Seymour the Spieler... that night?" I nodded and for some mysterious reason his grin grew broader. Spieler told him to get his Polish ass over to his locker.

Elijah St. John also ducked his head in and asked in his merry singsong, "Hey, mon, you the new boss mon?" Spieler told him to get his Dominican Republican ass over to his locker. He laughed like a child and floated away.

Elmo Speakes was cheerful as all get-out as he passed, but when he saw me, did a double take and his eyes bugged out. He came into the office with a suspicious look and said, "Why you here, man? What kind of shit you trying to pull?" Spieler told him to get his black ass over to his locker. Elmo stood there glaring at us, his eyes moving from me to Spieler and back, then slowly he backed out with that suspicious look.

When Bobby Wentworth burst in a few minutes later — it was the first time he'd ever visited the clubhouse — he was only there because Spieler had called him last night and said he'd have something to say that Bobby would want to hear — he paid no attention to me and said angrily, "What the hell's this meeting you're calling, La Chance?" His selfish playboy's face was flaming.

"You'll find out soon enough, Wentworth. I'm making a little announcement to the boys in a few minutes. I appreciate it's probably the first time in years you've been up before noon. I promise I won't keep you long."

"Well, it better be important. I can't imagine what you couldn't have told me over the phone. There's nothing you can tell these jerks that's going to make them play any better."

Spieler stared coolly at Wentworth. "I'll be out in a few minutes," he said quietly. "Go out and meet the guys that are filling your pockets. I want to talk to the kid."

Wentworth disappeared and Spieler closed both doors. He looked sharply at me. "I know something is bothering you. You sure you don't want to tell me about it?"

More than ever, I didn't. I shook my head.

"It's dumb to be too proud when you're in over your head. I'm glad to help you any way I can. I wanna tell you something I'm never gonna tell Myrna. You don't know how close I was to deciding to go with the fix. Woulda totaled up some great big numbers in a Bahamas bank account. One of the things that stopped me was meeting you and her. It was her story about what happened to you in school — getting caught on the bucketball games, I mean — that really helped me change my mind. Myrna would've really gone to pieces if the two guys she cares the most for both were nailed for the same thing. I didn't want to risk that happening. It put a certain shade on everything else I had to consider. And that's why I'm glad to be of service. You and Myrna have been a great help to me. Spieler La Chance is a guy who shows his gratitude. What about it?"

"Thanks but no thanks, Spieler. I'll take care of it myself."

Spieler looked sharply at me again. He nodded quickly. "Okay, I said my piece. I understand it's a weekend-long bash in Geneva and I guess Myrna and I will see you there. Excuse me now. I gotta say my piece to the guys." He went into the locker room.

I went to the door to watch. No one noticed Spieler at one end of the room with one foot on a bench, stroking his chin and grinning at the guys in this thoughtful way. They were going to know something was up when they saw him out of uniform, in his expensive pin-stripe custom-made suit. His grin got bigger as he anticipated their surprise. He adjusted the knot of his solid-colored silk tie and shot the cuffs of his white-on-white shirt to expose large gold cuff links that caught the light, then went to the middle of the room and made signs to guys that he wanted to say something. The room got quiet real quick. The silence was deafening. I looked down the rows of guys and saw the tension in their faces.

He said in the most friendly way, "Gentlemen, I've come to a decision. As of this moment, I'm resigning. You all know the reason I'm doing it. I'm not saying it's right, I'm not saying it's wrong, I'm telling you I don't want any part of it. I'm not trying to tell you guys what to do, but I've got a bad feeling in my gut about it. It's a great big open secret already and I don't think the secret is gonna keep. But even if it does, it's not the kind of thing you want to live with. At least I don't. Not for any amount of money. You know I've never lied to ya, so that's it guys. I've said my piece."

Spieler looked around the room. You could hear the guys holding their breath. A lot of them looked stunned. A lot of them looked shaken. Some looked at Spieler like he was a traitor. Quite a few faces got stiff with resistance. I was mistaken thinking Spieler was going to sway them completely.

As he was talking, Elmo Speakes had stood up and glared at him. Now he said angrily, "Man, you is so full of shit. Where does you come off with this man-of-honor bit? Next thing we know you'll be trying to tell us you ain't full of shit. I know you is up to somethin'." He shook his head in disgust, was so put out he couldn't speak.

Spieler chuckled. "I wish you thought better of me, Elmo," he said. "You really are my number-one man." He turned and handed Bobby Wentworth a slip of paper.

"Just what the hell do you think you're doing, La Chance? You've got a contract to fulfill. I'll have your ass in court."

"No, you won't, Wentworth. Not with what I know about what's going on. Ask some of the guys to fill you in. The last thing you need is another scandal."

Now Wentworth was fuming just like Elmo. The two of them were glaring at Spieler, speechless. Spieler raised his hand to silence a stirring among the players.

"I'm leaving my number with Wentworth here. Seeing as how he feels about me, it doesn't seem likely to happen, but if you need me for anything, I'll be at a bar mitzvah in Wisconsin. Good luck, guys. Despite my differences with some of you, I appreciate how great you've all played for me. With me or without me, I'd love to see ya in the Series. I'm rooting for you all the way. Cheers. It's been a season I'll remember the rest of my days." He winked and did a little dance step and walked jauntily out of the locker room.

He was headed back to his place where Myrna was waiting for him. True to his word, he'd pulled out in style, given notice to anyone concerned just what he thought about the fix, without mentioning the fix at all. He'd made it sweet and short and clean. The only problem was he hadn't helped me any with Salerno.

A great commotion started among the guys. There were heated conversations and worried looks and set jaws and heads firmly shaking. Bobby Wentworth was screaming at General Manager Murray Grimes that he'd better do something quick — anything! — he passed the slip of paper to him like it was poisoned and stormed out of the clubhouse saying he couldn't stand another minute of this crap and he'd be in Grimes' office. I walked into the spot where Spieler had stood and looked around as all hell broke loose, guys screaming and pleading and swearing at one another, guys ready to take a punch at one another, guys banging lockers and talking to themselves, and saw that opinion was just about divided down the middle. I figured I'd better act fast.

"*Gentlemen!*" I shouted above the noise. Everyone froze and looked at me as though they couldn't believe it was a runty kid who was butting in.

"You guys know what I've got to say is pretty important. Otherwise you wouldn't all be sitting there looking at me like maybe I know something you don't about settling this thing one way or the other."

No one moved an inch. They were waiting for me to go on. I had the strangest sense they wanted me to get them out of it. I also sensed they didn't have an iota of faith that I could do it. Elmo stirred angrily in his seat. He was glaring at me with murder in his eyes.

"The truth of the matter is that I don't really have an answer. I can only tell you the way I feel about things like reserve clauses and owners who don't pay you what you deserve."

Elmo shot up. "Just what is it you talking about, man? Sure we gets paid what we deserve. Get your butt out of here. We got a game to play."

"Let him finish, mon," Elijah St. John said, dragging Elmo back into his seat. Maybe there was a chance yet.

"Now, I'm not saying you haven't got every right to get mad when an owner doesn't respect what you're doing for him. It's not that you shouldn't think of ways to get even. But it's not as simple as all —"

"It sure ain't," Elmo said, shooting up again. "Are we gonna sit here and listen to this little sucker con us out of what we got coming? Get out of here, runt. Go back to that con man, Spieler, who put you up to this."

"For once, Speakes is right," Royal Farrell stood up and shouted. "We can't let this kid trick us into doing what Spieler and Wentworth want."

"Spieler didn't put me up to anything —" I started to say. But it was too late. Guys were standing up and agreeing with Elmo and Royal and making those guys back down who might've changed their minds. I'd failed.

I went over to Randy. I'd noticed him while I was talking and he was sad and distracted, like he was thinking about something else as I talked.

"Randy, I've got to tell you something important."

"No, you don't. I know already. Angie called me last night and had me come over. Sure was a kick in the ass. I almost got lucky, but it didn't happen."

Elmo came up in his underwear, with a bewildered expression. "She-it, man, what was you trying to do to me? Ain't you got any consideration for me at all? You was putting turds in my pot of gold at the end of the rainbow. What has I ever done to you to deserve it?"

"Come off it, Elmo," Randy said. "The kid was only trying to keep rummies like us out of jail. You should thank him for wanting you to be an honest man."

"I should thank him, huh?" Elmo looked bitterly at me. "What do you know about it, kid? You make more than me just phoning your bookie from bed each day. Don't make no difference if fix on or off, we is all meat for the slaughter. The grave and getting screwed is all we can count on. Honest man, my ass!"

Elmo really moved me. There was no arguing with him. He was right. He was one of the greatest players ever and he deserved better. All the guys did. And I just knew in my heart they were going to get caught.

"Mr. Speakes, I want you to come with me."

Elmo's look was wary. Before he could say a word, I said, "Remember when you wanted me there to see if Spieler was conning you?"

He nodded, but still looked suspicious.

"Well, I want you along to make sure someone isn't conning me."

He squinted grimly at me. "Who you talking about, man?"

"I'll tell you as soon as you put your pants on and we're on our way."

"Bobby Wentworth, man? The big mother himself? Is that who you taking me to see?" We were moving fast down the corridor toward Murray Grimes' office. "Man, I been all through this gig with Grimes. What is there left to say to Wentworth that ain't been said to Grimes?"

"What nobody thought to say to him, including Spieler. I only hope he's still here."

"Is Mr. Wentworth still here?" I said to the secretary in Grimes' outer office.

"Yes, he is, but I don't think he wants to see any —"

I opened Grimes' door and barged in, Elmo after me. Murray Grimes was seated behind his desk, on the telephone. Bobby was slouched deep in a leather wingchair, with a drink in his hand. We'd snapped him from a brooding funk.

"Mr. Wentworth, we need to see you."

"What about, kid?"

"About the Chicago Cubs baseball team and its chances for winning the pennant this year."

"I've had it up to here with the Chicago Cubs baseball team and the goddamned pennant. Take it up with Grimes here when I'm not around."

"You're the only one that can handle this." I motioned to Elmo to come forward.

"You mean I have to talk to this spade too?"

"This spade is the star of your team, Mr. Elmo Speakes. Maybe it's time you met one another."

Neither Elmo nor Bobby could find it in themselves to shake hands. They sort of wiggled their hands and nodded grimly at each other.

"Well, make it quick, kid," Bobby snapped. "I'm scheduled to sail my yacht to Michigan in an hour."

"Mr. Wentworth, I'm going to propose an idea to you that can save you a lot of embarrassment and trouble."

"You don't say. And just how much is it going to cost me?"

"Not so much that it won't be worth it."

"Maybe you ought to be telling it to my lawyers."

"I don't think so, Mr. Wentworth. From what I hear, you've already got enough trouble with lawyers. Why don't you listen, please."

Bobby looked away irritably: "I'm listening."

"I don't know if you know it, Mr. Wentworth, but certain players on the Cubs are on the verge of throwing the pennant."

His face got red. "Now just one goddamn minute, kid. If you think I'm going to fall for that bullcrap that La Chance was trying to pull just now —"

"Maybe you ought to hear the kid out, Bobby," Murray Grimes said.

"Maybe you ought to remember whose side you're on, Grimes."

"But I think maybe you can get them to call it off," I went on.

Bobby squirmed in his seat uncomfortably. He looked furiously at Grimes, who was standing stone-faced with his arms folded. Seeing no help there, Bobby reached over to Grimes' desk and poured himself another Scotch from a bottle. He glared at me. "I don't know what La Chance's game is and I don't care," he insisted. "You're nuts if you think you can get me involved in it."

"You are involved in it, Mr. Wentworth."

"That sounds like a threat, kid."

"I'm only giving you information to use the best way you can. Spieler tried to leave it up to the guys to make up their own minds. I'm not leaving it up to them. They're not smart enough to know what's right. I'm leaving it up to you."

"Like I said before, just how much is it going to cost me?"

I paused. Here went nothing. "Give the guys the raises they asked for in the spring. If you do that, I think they'll call off the fix."

Bobby looked at me in shock. Looked like he might have a heart attack. "D-did I hear you right? Did you really say I should give handouts to a bunch of jerks who think I owe them something? You must be off your rocker, kid."

"You're easily making enough in attendance to give it to them. You're going to make a lot more when they take the pennant and the Series."

Bobby shook his head stubbornly. "The Chicago Cubs baseball team is not a charitable institution. Jeezuz Christ, you must think I'm Santa Claus."

"I'm sorry you feel that way. You could really save the day otherwise. Now it looks like everyone is going to be implicated in the fix... even you, Mr. Wentworth."

Bobby glared hard at me. "Just what the hell are you trying to say?"

"I'm trying to say you can't deny you know what's going on, because you're finding out in front of people who know you know. I guess Mr. Grimes wouldn't want to spill any of it to the press, but Mr. Speakes here may feel entirely different about it. Wouldn't you, Mr. Speakes?"

I don't know why I was counting on Elmo to back me up. He'd been glowering suspiciously at Bobby, the anger simmering up, but just like Bobby, he wasn't sure what I was up to. He glared at me with this confused look. "Feel different about what, man?"

"What I'm saying," I explained, "is that I'm sure you wouldn't mind telling the press that Mr. Wentworth here knows all about the fix and hasn't done anything to stop it for whatever reason of his own — if it were necessary for you to say something to the press, of course."

Elmo got the point. His eyes brightened. "Naw, I wouldn't mind at all saying that you is one crooked mother, Wentworth."

"What good would that do you, Speakes?" Bobby said. "You'd be implicating yourself as well."

"The papers don't know who's in on it, Elmo," I came back. "If you tell the papers it was Wentworth here who tried to put you and the guys up to the fix, it'd be your word against his, and you know damn well that every last one of the guys is going to back you up on it. Think about it. You know I'm right."

Elmo was totally confused now. His eyes kept moving from Bobby to me and back to Bobby, trying to figure who was trying to con him.

Bobby wasn't confused, though. He saw the trap he'd fallen into. "Now look here, Speakes. You can't do something like that to me. We've had our differences in the past, but there's no reason we can't let bygones be bygones. What you and I need to do is sit down and have some lunch together. Get to know each other. You know I never knew much about baseball until this year. I'm just beginning to appreciate the great contribution you've made to the team. I see where I may have been somewhat unfair about your demands —"

Elmo's mouth fell open. He couldn't believe what he was hearing.

"Look, Speakes," Bobby went on, "I think maybe we better talk alone. Leave us alone for a while, Grimes. You better leave too, kid. Mr. Speakes and I have some personal things to discuss."

"The kid stays," Elmo said firmly, not so much because he trusted me, I'm sure, but because he didn't trust himself alone with Bobby. Murray Grimes got out of the room fast.

"Have a drink," Bobby said, pointing to the bottle of Scotch.

"Never drinks before a game."

Bobby nodded. He poured himself another and sat down in the leather chair behind Grimes' desk.

"Look, Speakes," he continued, "maybe you and I and the kid here can make a deal. You're the outstanding player involved. The others don't deserve what you deserve —"

"*That's* the truth," Elmo said proudly.

"So suppose we make this arrangement. You get ten thousand dollars more for this season. A sweet ten g's. Grimes will get you the money right away. Fair enough, Speakes? Shows you Bobby Wentworth can be a real sport, eh?"

Elmo stared long and hard at Bobby. He didn't believe him. He was mighty suspicious. "And what does I have to do for the ten?"

"First, you don't tell anyone else about our deal. Give the kid what he wants so he'll keep his mouth shut. As far as the fix is concerned, I'll make you a proposition."

"I's lis'enin'."

"You keep me informed what the jerks are gonna do, I'll take care of you with another ten grand."

"You mean you want in on the action too?"

"I guess that's as good a way of putting it as any. Well, this seems to be a lucky day for all of us. Let's drink to it, I say. Elmo, old man, you've just made yourself twenty grand. Not to mention" — he winked — "whatever you get from the other end."

Elmo didn't say anything. He was still eyeing Bobby suspiciously. "Hey, kid, you think he's pulling my dong?"

"No, I don't think he's pulling your dong, Mr. Speakes."

"Why don't you think so?"

"There's every reason for him not to."

"You think I can trust him?"

"I guess so."

"You think I should do it?"

"It's up to you, Mr. Speakes. It all depends on how you feel."

"How much *you* want for keeping quiet?"

"You don't have to give me anything, Mr. Speakes. I'll keep my mouth shut, but I don't want any part of it."

"Why not?"

"I guess I just wouldn't feel right about it. I don't want to take something the rest of the guys aren't in on."

"I don't owe the other guys nothin'. The other guys never done me any favors. They wanted to cut me out of the fix."

"True enough. You don't owe the other guys a thing. No quarrel from me on that score."

Elmo eyed us both carefully. He was real perplexed about it all.

"Hey, Speakes," Bobby said, "what's the matter with you? Isn't it the kind of deal you've been looking for? The chance to make big dough with two scores? This is no time to back down. Look at what I've set up for you."

Elmo continued to stare hard. You could see he wanted the deal bad, but something held him back.

"This is what I want," he said finally.

"Now you're talking," Bobby said.

"I want the ten grand for this season."

"You've got it. No problem."

"And I want another ten grand for next season. I mean ten grand more than the amount for this season, including the ten grand you just gave me. And I want it now."

"Are you mad, man? I can't give you that kind of money now. Why I've got expenses you've never heard of."

"You mean like your yacht and your ponies and your Chez Paree Adorable?"

"Well, yes, that's exactly what I mean."

"Ten grand more for next season is exactly what I mean too."

"You sure are taking advantage of my generosity. You better remember to keep your mouth shut about the fix."

"I ain't promising you nothing about no fix. You is paying me strictly not to tell the press that you know about the fix. You got that, Wentworth?"

"This is blackmail, Speakes. You've got another think coming if you think you can get away with blackmailing Bobby Wentworth. You can't prove a thing. It's your word against mine."

"And the kid's. Right, man?"

Old Elmo had thrown the ball to me. I was on the spot. "Right, Mr. Speakes."

Bobby's face flushed with anger. He stuttered, couldn't speak.

"And one more thing, Wentworth," Elmo said.

"Yeah?"

"I want raises for all the guys on the team that asked for them this year. I want them to have them raises before the game starts today."

Bobby was flabbergasted. I was stunned. "Now, why the hell would you care about guys that don't give a damn about you?" He was burning to know the reason. So was I.

"I don't know," Elmo said gruffly. He turned away. "I don't want to say no more about it either. You just do it, Wentworth. Raises for everyone that held out before the season."

Bobby nodded weakly. He looked at Elmo as though he were about to cry.

Elmo scowled at Bobby, glared at him with fierce eyes, then said the strangest thing. "We all got our heartaches, Wentworth. Welcome to the team."

We left Wentworth's office and started back down the corridor toward the locker room. Wentworth had said that Murray Grimes would make the announcement there in a few minutes about the raises. I could only hope it would stop the fix.

I had no time to stay, had to meet Salerno at one. I said to Elmo at the locker room entrance, "Why'd you do it? Why in the world did you do that for the guys?"

He was still gruff. Didn't want to say. Finally said in spite of himself, "You was right. Whatever they done to me, I couldn't screw them that way. Like Spieler said that night, we is white niggers and black niggers in the same boat together. I couldn't feel good about what I got if they couldn't get somethin' too. I know I is one dumb nigger. I know I'll regret it. Now shut your butt. Leave me be."

CHAPTER

12

Now for Salerno. With the fix off, he was in big trouble. The thing was to make him realize it and save his ass by blowing town, but who knew what Salerno would do? He was still crazy enough to spill it to the papers for spite. I worried about it as I rode a streetcar to my place.

It was five after twelve when I got there. Jamey had returned my car and I spotted it down the block.

Kim was waiting like she said. I'd never seen her so withdrawn, her mind somewhere else, but also calm and not her usual difficult self. She just nodded when I told her what happened at the ballpark, as though that was all the concern she could show about it. And she didn't squawk one bit when I said I wanted to be alone with Salerno at her place and she should wait in the car. She just nodded when I added that I wanted her and Jamey to go to Lake Geneva with me for the weekend so we could all be far away from Salerno and whatever trouble he was going to cause. She was staring blankly at the wall as I called Jamey and he refused to go with us. Her expression didn't change as I told her that Jamey said he wanted to spend time with Angie on the weekend. Angie had told him about her going to New York City, and he had enlisted in the marines and was leaving for basic training next week.

"I hope Salerno doesn't show up," I said after hanging up.

"Jamey be hokay," she murmured. "Angie tell Randy about Salerno. They watch out for Jamey." There were lots of holes in what she said, but she didn't invite any questions.

We were walking down the block to the car when I finally burst out, "What makes you so sure Angie and Randy can watch over Jamey? Jamey can go as crazy as Salerno."

She didn't answer, acted as though I hadn't said it, got in my car and looked straight ahead. It was impossible to tell what she was thinking.

I started off. "You want to tell me where you were last night?"

She nodded. Kim said she'd had a headache and I didn't have any aspirins and she went to an all-night drugstore. Then she walked to the North Avenue beach and thought about things. That was all. She was perfectly safe.

Five minutes later, I found a space near her apartment. We hurried up and she put some things in a suitcase. As she was about to go back to the car, I put my hand on her arm and stopped her. "What's wrong, Kim? I wish you'd tell me what's bothering you."

She looked hard at me, didn't want to show any feeling. "Just thinking that Salerno really screw up things." She shook her head in disgust. "I be hokay."

Through the window, I watched her go down the block with the suitcase, turn the corner and disappear. I'd deliberately parked where Salerno wouldn't be likely to see her. He really was a destructive prick. I gripped Kim's knife in my pocket.

It was five to one. Salerno should show up any minute. It was a smart idea for him to pick this time for the meeting, only a half hour before the start of the game. He wanted

210

to place his bet as close to game time as possible. If you could bet against the established odds one minute before the game started, you could make a bundle because you wouldn't upset those established odds — it would be too late for the bookies to change them.

I thought about the Cubs situation. As of today's game, they were 2½ games ahead of the Dodgers in second place. Including today's game with the Braves, there were nine games left in the Cubs' season. They would have had a good margin and plenty of opportunity to throw games in the remaining week, if that was what the guys had finally decided. It was a tempting proposition. I hoped the guys had resisted the temptation.

One o'clock came and Salerno didn't show. One-fifteen and still no sign of him. I turned on the radio and got the Cubs' pregame show. Bert Wilson made the sensational announcement that Spieler La Chance had resigned this morning and third-base coach Sid Carson had replaced him. Bert interviewed General Manager Murry Grimes, who couldn't give any reason as to why Spieler had done it. One-thirty, the game started, and still no Salerno.

Something was wrong! What could've happened to him? Could he've found out what happened at the ballpark? Should I stay or go? It didn't seem like he was still going to show. I locked Kim's door and hurried downstairs and raced down the block and across the street to my car. I saw Kim in front with her eyes lowered, her thoughts still somewhere else. She looked up startled when I slipped into the driver's seat.

I told her that Salerno hadn't shown. I told her that word was out about Spieler. She didn't speak, was strangely calm, looked grimly out the window.

I started the car and drove off. I wasn't sure where I was going. Why the hell was I so worried about Salerno? Let him get out of his own mess.

After a block, she broke the silence. "What it mean," she said, looking worried, "if Salerno was supposed to make bet but didn't do it?"

"It means the guys who put up the money are going to ask him why he didn't do it."

She chewed on my answer for a while. "What if they can't find him?"

I chewed on her question for a while. "That's a good question." I chewed some more. "I've got the funniest feeling you know where he is."

Her brains were churning as she stared out the window. "I want you do me big favor," she said.

"Sure."

"I want you take me Midway Airport. I need take plane right away."

"Where're you going?"

"Anywhere. Got to get out of Chicago."

"That *is* a big favor. Are you going to tell me why you want to do it?"

"You start car toward airport. I tell you about Salerno."

I picked up Division Street going west. "Okay. We're going to Midway."

"I hope he still in room on Diversey Avenue."

"Why the hell didn't you say so soon —"

"Salerno dead."

Silence. "What hap —"

"Shut up, Arnie. Just drive. I tell you what happen."

She told me the real story of last night. Said she was furious thinking about Salerno as Jamey drove her to my apartment. She decided she wasn't going to let him get away with it. She had his number and when Jamey went off to his job she called and said she wanted to see him right away. She said she wasn't trying to get him to back off on the fix. She said she had a good idea about how both of them could hook up and make more money from it. He took the bait and told her she should meet him at a bar on Clark Street near his rooming house.

Half an hour later, when she showed up at Buck's Iron Bucket, he was already sloshed. She flattered him. She got sexy. She stroked his balls under the table as she told him about other money she could bring into the fix along with the money he'd already lined up. They smiled real sly at each other and Salerno laughed like he was real smart and Kim said they should go on up to his place and close the deal in bed.

Salerno bought a bottle from the bartender. They stopped at a Chinese take-out place and ordered stuff to be sent up to his room. They went up and while Salerno lay on the bed, Kim undressed in the john, steeling herself to brain him with a paperweight she'd brought in her handbag.

The doorbell rang. Kim supposed it was the delivery boy from the Chinese restaurant. She never heard what happened next. When she went into the room, Salerno was still on the bed, but his throat was cut from ear to ear. The blood was gushing from him. Someone had saved her the trouble and gone.

"Who do you think did it?" I asked.

"Look, you want to know about Salerno. I tell you as much I can. I don't know who killed him."

"I don't believe you."

She glared at me. "Damn fool."

"What'd you do after you saw the body?"

"What the hell you think I do? I get ass out of there. People in bar saw me with Salerno. That why I gotta get out of town."

She had a point. I thought about it. "You said this happened in a rooming house on Diversey?"

"Yes."

"Where, exactly?"

"Couple blocks west where Clark, Broadway come together. Crummy place."

I thought some more. We were at a red light. When it changed, I turned north on Halstead.

"Hey, you not going Midway."

"Did you lock the door after you left Salerno?"

"Why the hell you want to know?"

"Because I want to."

"I even take his key. So what? Other people got keys."

"But he still might be there. It's a crummy rooming house. Who the hell knows when they change the sheets? Maybe no one's discovered him yet."

She stared wide-eyed at me. There was a light in her eyes. She saw my point but wouldn't admit it. "You crazy, Arnie. What good it do to go there?"

"Don't you see, Kim? If Salerno's still there, if no one knows about him yet, maybe we can get him out of there. We'll get rid of him somewhere. Without a body, there's no evidence against you, even if you were seen with him last night." I drove a block and let her chew on it. "No one will know he's even gone. Not even the guy who killed him." I looked at her.

That light was brighter. She saw there was a chance. Her brains were churning again. She was torn by the idea, wanted to do it, wanted to talk me out of it. She heard herself saying, like her conscience got the best of her, "No, Arnie, you no do it. I no let you."

"Why not?"

She was silent. We were getting close to Diversey. The rooming house wasn't far from where we'd turn. At last she said bluntly, "Because it no take me off hook. I no tell you all truth. I know who killers are. Killers know me. Only thing to do is take me Midway. I get out of Chicago."

"And you still don't want to tell me who the killers are?"

"Don't be schmuck. You no want to know."

I pressed my lips together and drove faster.

"You nothing but big dummy. Please stay out of it. Why you such a dummy?"

"I don't know, Kim. I really don't. Maybe I'm tired of the way my life is going, everyone pulling on me. Maybe I don't care anymore what I do." I sailed through a traffic light after it turned red.

"Don't be dumb, Arnie. Take me airport. You no know what it's all about."

"Then tell me what it's all about."

We were coming to the Diversey traffic light.

"You stupid runt! Crazy dummy! Chinese guys that Salerno got my contract from — *they* kill him. He try to cheat organization out of money he agree to pay for me. He try to bluff them and say his contacts would get them if they lay hand on him. They call his bluff."

"You saw them do it? Why didn't they do anything to you?"

"They no need to. They take picture of me with body and say I back on contract with them. They say I now start to do other things for them. If I try to leave town, or they can't find me, they send picture to police. So it do no good to see if body's still there. Do no good to get rid of it. They know I the one that get rid of it and come after me. My only chance get out of Chicago. Be somewhere else when they show my picture to police."

I drove past the rooming house, a big four-story, boatlike house on a block of boatlike houses and low-story apartment buildings, went around the block, found a space on a side street. I sat back and looked at Kim, dazed by it all. I saw Kim's urgent look, heard her saying, "Don't you see? No other way. Take me airport. Hurry. Cops may be all over place."

But I wasn't in a hurry. I sat there in that daze, looking at her.

"Real dangerous thing you up to, Arnie. I tell you something now you don't know. You know who stake Salerno to fix money? Uncle Pietro, that who. Salerno damn fool for getting killed, but you just as dumb for going up there. You no want to get involved with Uncle Pietro again. Take me airport now!"

I heard these things and I didn't hear them. My head was filled with something else. "You never told me what the Chinese guys have on you, Kim. What did Salerno know that I don't?"

She glared furiously at me, her lips pressed together. She wouldn't talk, shook her head.

I opened the door and put one foot out, looked back at her.

"You no have to do this," she said.

I didn't answer.

"I want you to do three things," I said.

"What you want?" she sighed.

"Give me the keys."

She drew them out of her pocket and handed them over. "What else?"

"Listen to the game while I'm gone. Tell me the score when I get back."

"You should know score already. What else?"

"Wait for me. I won't be long." I got out of the car.

It was about three o'clock. That late-afternoon dreaminess was in the air. The trees and people drooped. I turned the corner and walked several houses down to Salerno's rooming house. There was no one on the big porch, no one going in or out the front entrance, the place was quiet.

I went up the steps and looked into the big lobby. On one side, the clerk behind the desk was idly reading a newspaper. There was an elevator at the rear, beyond him. A woman got out of it and started talking to the clerk. They didn't notice me go past them.

The elevator had a musty smell. It jumped when I hit the fifth-floor button.

I got out and looked both ways down the dark hall. A shaft of light from an open door in the direction of Salerno's room was the only thing that broke the shadows. I looked in and saw it was a supply room, sheets and towels on shelves, a laundry cart.

I stood before Salerno's door and listened. There was no sound. For the first time I got queasy. Couldn't turn back now.

I put the key in the lock and opened the door. Salerno was still there. I slipped inside and closed the door. I felt weak as the smell of death hit me.

I steadied myself and looked around the miserable bare room. Salerno on the bloody sheets was staring up at the ceiling with his mouth open. The jerk! The dumb son of a bitch, winding up like this for no good reason but that he couldn't stay away from Angie! It seemed like he almost *wanted* to wind up this way!

A knock at the door. I froze.

"Arnie, are you there? It me, Kim."

I opened the door. "What's wrong? Why'd you come?"

She slipped in and closed the door, then leaned against it nervously, eyeing me. "I figure you found Salerno. I figure you need help."

I nodded.

"I gotta tell you something. Forget Salerno. Leave him here. Won't help me."

"Why not?"

Kim sighed. She saw she had no choice anymore. She said straight out, "No way you can save me. Anywhere I go, still in danger. Make no difference what Chicago police know about Salerno. Chinese organization will send information to FBI. Illegal alien. That what I am, Arnie. I go back to China if FBI find me. Take me to airport quick."

Illegal alien! What a bag of shit life was! And I was holding the bag all alone.

"C'mon, Arnie, let's go. You some guy. You try hard for
me. You no want to wind up like Salerno because of
me."

Kim was right. All the same, I didn't want to leave the
room. I stared angrily at Salerno. Why was he such a jerk?
I wanted to shake him and wake him up and tell him what
a jerk he was for winding up like this. I wanted to laugh in
his weak punk's face. I wanted to kick the shit out of him.
I wanted to see his expression when I told him I was just
as dumb as he was. "What about me, you jerk?" I said.

"Arnie, we gotta get out of here."

Looking at his body made me think of something else.

"What about Salerno's money?"

Kim shrugged. "I guess killers take it."

"Was it a lot?"

She shrugged again. "I guess so."

"How much do you think?"

"I don't know. Pretty good roll of bills, I guess . . ."

"How good?"

"Maybe five thousand."

"Maybe more than that?"

"Maybe more. What you thinking, Arnie?"

I didn't know what I was thinking. I thought some more.
"You're sure Salerno wasn't bullshitting you when he said
Pietro staked him?"

"You know Salerno. He couldn't stop telling me Pietro
staked him."

I nodded. I got an idea. "Stay here, Kim. I'll be right
back."

I opened the door and looked out. The hall was empty
in both directions. I went to the laundry room, looking for
the laundry cart I'd seen earlier. It was still there, a can-
vas bag on wheels, maybe three feet deep, maybe four feet

long. I piled sheets and towels into it and wheeled it back to Salerno's room.

Kim's eyes were bright. "You some crazy guy," she said. "Real dangerous thing." But she didn't try to stop me.

I asked her to help me. We put the sheets and towels on the bed. We lifted Salerno into the laundry cart. We put the sheets and towels on top of him. We rolled him down the hall into the elevator. "You've gotta distract the desk clerk as soon as we get out. Make up a name and ask him if the person lives here. Make him check it out. But don't take long. Get back to the car as soon as you can."

Kim nodded.

We hit the lobby. Kim went to the desk and I wheeled past as she got the clerk's attention. I bounced down the porch steps and headed to the sidewalk.

An old drunk with a weathered face turned up the rooming-house walk.

"Say, how mush you charge for shirts, fella?"

I shook my head as I went past him, but he came after me. "If you don't charge for shirts, fella, how do you make a living? Do you do them free?"

He followed me as I turned the corner and got to the car. "Come on now, how mush you charge for shirts? Damn Chinks I go to charge too mush."

"Look, mister, I'm not a laundry man. Please go away. Don't bother me."

"Don't tell me what to do, fella. I ashed you how mush you charge for shirts. What's the matter? You too good to do my shirts? I'm gonna tell the world you think you're too damn good to do my shirts. I'm gonna tell everyone I see. Yessir." He looked around for people. They were coming in both directions. Kim was also coming around the corner.

"Hey, miss, this guy won't tell me how mush he charges for doing shirts."

She glared at him.

"Do you think that's fair? I'm a hard-working citizen and he won't do my shirts. You'll do my shirts, though, won't you? You're a Chink. You do shirts."

There were some high school kids coming one way. There were a couple of mothers with strollers coming the other. There was also a cop car coming down the street.

"Hey, mister," I said. "It's all right. I'll do your shirts."

"You will?"

"Sure thing."

"You don't overcharge?"

"Not me."

"Easy on the starch?"

"You bet. Now you go on to your room and get your shirts. I'll wait here for you."

"Well, how 'bout that?" The old drunk was tickled pink. "Not often you find real Americans to do your shirts. I'll be right back." He hurried off.

I gave Kim the car keys, told her to get in and start the motor. The cop car turned the corner. The high school kids went by. So did the mothers with their strollers. But suddenly cars were going in both directions. And the drunk might be back at any second. Though it was perfect daylight under that broad blue Chicago sky, and people could be looking at me from anywhere, a window, a doorway, a passing car, I grabbed Salerno up in my arms with sheets and towels. He weighed a ton and stunk awful and his hands and feet were sticking out. It seemed like forever as I stood there frozen, but somehow I managed to dump him into the trunk. I slammed the lid and staggered to the driver's seat.

I drove awhile and parked near a deserted school yard. Kim hadn't said a word all the while. We sat quietly, breathing hard, trying to get calm. I turned on the radio and got the Cubs' postgame show.

The Cubs had won 3–2 in extra innings. Elmo Speakes
had singled in the winning run. Earlier, he and Wally Koslowski had hit back-to-back doubles to produce the tying
run. Randy Dodds had relieved Elijah St. John and was
the winning pitcher. The biggest news of all was that
Spieler La Chance was returning to the team. He'd be
back in charge tomorrow. No question, the Cubs had
played to win. Spieler and the guys were off the hook.

We needed gas and I drove to a gas station. I told the
guy to fill us up and told Kim I had to make a call. She
had been silent and thoughtful all the way from the school
yard, with that hard-to-know expression. She looked at me
and nodded, as though she knew what was on my mind
without my saying it.

From the gas station office, I called Spieler in Lake Geneva and waited for him to come on the line.

"Arnold, dear, are you all right?" It was Myrna, that
near-panic in her voice.

"I'm all right, Myrn. I need to talk to Spieler."

"He's right here, dear. You're not going to tell us you
can't make it? You don't know how much that would disappoint me."

"No, I'm not going to tell you I can't make it. But I've
got some business to take care of first. Let me talk to
Spieler."

"I need to talk to you, Arnold. I'm very worried about
something. I want to discuss something very important
with you. You will be here soon?"

"I'll be there as soon as I can. Please, Ma, let me talk to
Spieler."

He came on the line. "Hey, kid, you really pulled off a
beaut. Murray Grimes called and told me how you and
Elmo really put it to Wentworth. I'm real proud of you,
Arnie. Words can't express it."

"I'm glad you're going back."

"I'm glad the guys were smart enough to want me back."

"Spieler, you remember this morning you asked if you could help me out? I've been thinking about it and maybe you can."

"Name it, Arnie."

"Remember how you made contact with Uncle Pietro at the Villa Georgio for me? Well, I need to see him about something else. Can you set up another meeting for me as soon as possible? Could you do that for me?"

He was silent, thinking. "That's some request, Arnie. Are you in trouble?"

"Not me. Someone else. Tell Pietro I've got information about Johnny Salerno."

"Oh, shit! *Him* again! You sure you don't want me to see Pietro for you?"

"I want to see him myself. You take care of Myrna. I know how impossible she is when she starts to panic."

Spieler thought a bit. "Give me your number," he said. "I'll call you back in fifteen minutes, let you know if I've made contact. She sure ain't easy, I'll tell you that."

Spieler came through. He called ten minutes later and said he'd set up a meeting for me with Pietro an hour from now, at Battaglia's, a restaurant in Cicero, a southwest suburb. "Let me hear from you as soon as it's over," Spieler said.

Kim and I were at Diversey and Ashland, 1600 west, 2800 north. We had to go completely across the city to 4800 west and 2200 south. We started out across that vast blue sky with this strange feeling between us.

"You go see Pietro?" she asked.

"It's scary how you read my mind."

"Why you do this thing for me?"

"I've been asking myself the same thing. I honestly don't know."

"You damn fool for loving me."

"Maybe loving you is the only thing I've got."

Kim didn't try to stop me the rest of the drive. Maybe she knew she couldn't. Maybe she thought I could pull it off. She knew without my telling her what I was going to tell Pietro.

Right on time, I pulled into Battaglia's parking lot. I parked and put one foot out the door and looked back at her.

"The airport's not far away," I said. "Don't be tempted by it. Be here when I get out, okay?"

She stared thoughtfully at me, as though I'd made a mistake in putting the idea in her mind. She shook her head. "I be here, Arnie."

Uncle Pietro met me in a pine-paneled private room at the back of the restaurant. There were plaster statues and pictures of saints and virgins on the walls. We sat across from each other at a small round table. Two of his boys in sharp suits and fedora hats sat at separate tables on each side of him. Their suspicious eyes were glued on me.

Pietro also wore a sharp suit. He was an old hairless bird, with a sharp nose in a thin face, and he kept his eyes down as he stared grimly at the red wine in a wine glass he kept twisting the stem of. I think the reason I wasn't scared shitless in his presence was because he didn't seem too excited about my story. Maybe he'd reached the point where the same old shit — fixes, double-crosses, murder — didn't give him a kick anymore. It was no fun being head of the mob. Even the fact that he could recover his money from the Chinese guys didn't give him any satisfaction. When I finished, he looked up and said raspily, "You're *sure* the Chinese boys rubbed Johnny out?"

"My girl saw them do it."

Pietro frowned.

"Where's Salerno's body now?"

"I can show it to you, but first I'd like to ask a favor."

His eyes drilled into me, waiting. So did those of his two

associates. Favors weren't something they gave lightly.

"The girl who told me about Salerno is in trouble with the Chinese organization. I wonder . . . would it be possible . . . in return for telling you all this . . . for you to make sure that the Chinese organization will never turn her over to the FBI?"

Pietro looked hard at me. He frowned again. He began to study the wine again and twist the stem of the glass.

"Where's the girl?"

"Outside in my car."

"What do they have on her?"

"She's an illegal alien."

"Where's the body?"

"In the trunk of my car."

"Give me the keys."

I gave them to him. He gave them to one of his boys.

"Check it out," he said. "Make a switch if everything's okay. Bring the girl back with you." The two guys left.

Pietro looked up at me. He eyed me sternly.

"John Salerno was an asshole," he said. "He got what he deserved. Do you know why he got what he deserved?"

"Why, Mr. Celli?"

"Because he trusted a woman. I'm an asshole because I gave him money for that woman. I give him money a second time and what does he do? Goes out and gets involved with another broad! Are you *sure* you're not an asshole too?"

The question took me off guard. I thought a moment. Maybe I was, but I wasn't going to say so. "No sir, Mr. Celli. I don't think so. I wouldn't be here otherwise."

He nodded grimly. We waited in silence.

One of the boys came back with Kim. He gave the keys to Pietro. He said everything checked out.

Pietro looked coldly at Kim. "You got anything to add?" he asked.

She looked coldly back at him, shook her head.

Pietro looked at me. "Okay, you got a deal. This broad's secret is safe. I guarantee it." He handed me the keys. "Your car is a little lighter now. Forget this meeting. Forget we talked."

Kim and I turned to go.

"One more thing," Pietro said. "You should be grateful for a friend like Spieler La Chance. He gave his word you were on the level. Spieler is a good boy. Not an asshole like John Salerno, who fucked me twice." He stared grimly at his glass of wine.

I pulled the car out of the parking lot and started north on Cicero Avenue. We drove for a lot of stoplights without talking. The scariness of the meeting was finally hitting me.

Kim had been thinking hard all the way.

"What's on your mind, Kim?"

"That some fine thing you do for me."

"You don't seem too happy about it."

"No way I can repay you."

"You'll find a way."

We drove another mile or so.

"What's wrong, Kim? You can tell me."

"I guess I got to."

"Okay."

"You turn car 'round and go toward Midway."

"For Christ sake, are you gonna start *that* again?"

"Do it, Arnie. I gotta tell you something important."

I swung the car around in a gas station and headed the other way, toward the airport.

"Well?"

"I tell you lie, Arnie."

"Okay . . . What's the truth?"

"Chinese guys no take Pietro's money."

I was silent. We drove a little way. I didn't want to know who did.

"When I find money in Salerno's room, all sudden I see way to be free. No more Chinese guys know about me. No more be illegal alien."

It was hard to swallow. What could I say? I looked at Kim in amazement. "That was one incredible lie. You shouldn't have done it."

"I know how you feel."

"You could've told me."

"I no think so."

I had this awful feeling. Like the world around me was spinning. I didn't know what to do. Didn't know what to say.

A plane swooped down for a landing right in front of us.

"Where's the money?" I asked.

"In my suitcase." She glanced at the back seat.

"Where'd you keep it last night?"

"In your glove compartment."

"How much is it?"

"A hundred thousand."

I whistled between my teeth. The entrance to Midway was approaching. I drove right past it. Kim didn't say a word.

I stepped on the gas. The factories and gas stations and fields flew past.

"Where you going?" Kim asked.

"Going nowhere obviously."

"You keep it up, we get stopped by cop."

I drove faster. "You shouldn't have lied about the money."

"No choice, Arnie. No other way."

"You don't need that dough. I'll get you all the dough you want."

"You do too much already. I no want any more from you."

"I love you, Kim. Why *don't* you want what I want to give you?"

She was silent; wrestled with what to say. "Because you think me better person than I am."

I didn't know what she meant. It scared me. We were into farm country now. I drove faster on the open road.

"You only think you love me, Arnie. Years from now you be awful glad you don't."

She was scaring the hell out of me. "What is it you're trying to say, Kim?"

She wouldn't answer.

"Is there something else you're not telling me?"

She hesitated, chewed her lip.

"What is it, goddammit? Tell me!" I sent the car over a hundred.

"I can't be person you want me to. I not worth saving, Arnie."

And then I knew. I don't know how I knew. It just came to me. I floored the car.

Kim knew I knew. "For God's sake, Arnie, slow down. Don't be fool. I tell you when you stop the car."

I slowed and pulled onto the side of the road. I looked at Kim. "There *were* no Chinese guys at Salerno's."

"No Chinese guys," she said. "I kill Salerno."

I didn't say a word. Got out of the car and walked up the road. Stopped to look at night falling over the land. "What a bag of shit," I said.

Kim had followed me. I heard her voice right behind me. "I try to stop you every way going up there. I no want you get involved."

"You should've told me, Kim. Goddammit, you should've told me." I couldn't face her, was talking to the sky.

"Arnie, you gotta believe me. You-me, we never right for each other. Not in million years. We kid ourself, thinking otherwise. You too good for me. I kill Salerno, take money, to make you free."

I turned around and stared at her. Her mouth was firm as ever, but her eyes were finally close to tears.

I said bitterly, "I don't care that you killed Salerno. I don't care about the Chinese guys. They don't mean shit to me. But you shouldn't have lied to me the way you did. Somehow the lies killed everything. I can never trust you again. I'd never know when you'd run out on me. I couldn't live with that again. Goddammit, Kim, don't you see what you did?"

Her eyes were filled with pity, but her mouth was still firm. "You best guy I ever know. But some things can never be. I so sorry, Arnie."

"I hope you are, Kim. I hope you're half as sorry as me."

There was nothing more to say. We both knew it.

"C'mon, I'll drive you to the airport."

"I 'preciate, Arnie. We both got long way to go."

I left her off at Midway, then drove slowly north. I was shell-shocked but strangely relieved. One minute I wanted to get back in the nightmare, the next I was glad the dragon couldn't get me. My head was being ripped apart and I wondered how long it would go on.

I was sixty miles from Lake Geneva when I called Spieler from a gas station. They were there, I was told, but no one could find him or Myrna. I left word I'd be there in about an hour.

Cousin Selma's mansion was down a country road. It was right on the lake. I turned in on the gravel road leading to the house and parked at the end of a long line of cars running around the circular drive. I heard music from behind the house, near the lake. Vaughan Monroe was singing "Racing With the Moon."

I went around the side of the house and looked down the sloping lawn to where the music was coming from. Hundreds of people were eating at outdoor tables or dancing on a huge dance floor near the edge of the lake.

I walked out on a flagstone patio near the house. Under a lamplit tree, Myrna was sitting on a low marble bench.

With her chin against her fist, her legs stretched out, she
was brooding at the toes of her pretty shoes. She was totally still and seemed like she might've been sitting this
way for hours. I'd never seen her more lovely or more sad.

I went up to her. "Hello."

She looked up. "Oh, Arnold, you surprised me."

"I told you I'd make it."

"I'm really glad you're here. I've been waiting for you
every minute. Where are your friends?"

"Jamey wanted to be with Angie. Kim couldn't make it
at the last minute. I'm really happy about Spieler going
back with the Cubs. Where is he?"

"He decided to go back to Chicago early. Said he wanted
to get some things straightened out with Bobby Wentworth."

"How come you didn't go with him?"

She looked uncertainly at me. "Well, to tell you the
truth, I've had second thoughts about going away with
Seymour."

"Why, has he had second thoughts?"

"Not at all. I'm the one with cold feet. After the team
called him back, I got to thinking that maybe I'm not the
woman for him."

"Did you tell him that?"

"He said I was silly. He said how could we know if we
were right for each other until we'd been together."

"Well, I think you're silly too."

"But, Arnold, I've got this terrible feeling. Spieler is such
an important person. He's in the public eye. He's a ce-
lebrity. He knows all kinds of people who invite him to do
all kinds of things. He's very worldly. I worry that I won't
be the kind of woman he needs."

"What did he say to that?"

"He said I was crazy but didn't have time to argue. He
told me to get back to Chicago right after the bar mitzvah

is over. He wants me around for the final week of the season. He wants me to go to Florida with him."

"Sounds pretty good to me."

Myrna suddenly burst into tears. "Oh, Arnold, I'm so glad you're here. I'm glad you're alone without your friends. I need to tell you that I'm so afraid that Seymour and I aren't going to make it together. It's not going to last because I'm not good enough to have a relationship last. I just don't want to have another man leave me." She sobbed uncontrollably.

Oh, God! Just what I needed! Myrn needing *me* to reassure *her!* Weren't things bad enough without having to squeeze the bag even harder? I felt so bitter.

As she sobbed, I put my foot on the bench and stared away from her. I wouldn't say a word, I just wouldn't; I wasn't a goddamned savior.

Her sobs were getting hysterical but I didn't move. Let her suffer, I thought, let her suffer just like me. It would serve her right. Let her weep for both of us in our screwed-up lives.

So I'll never know why I did the next thing. I pulled out my handkerchief and knelt beside her and started to say soothing things as I dried her tears. I waited for her to calm down and then heard myself saying softly, "What you just said is crap, Myrn. You should never think bad about yourself. You look great. You talk great. You dress great. You cook great. You can do all kinds of things that make a guy proud to be with you. I don't want to hear this stuff anymore that you're not good enough. I got a hunch that one of the reasons Spieler goes for you most is because you're *not* part of the world he's always known. He wants something different, he's told me so. You can cut it in his world, but you're also down to earth, and that's what he really needs."

Myrna looked at me in surprise. Her face brightened.

"You really mean that, Arnold? You're not just saying that to make me feel better? You think I've got a chance to make it with Seymour La Chance?"

"He's got a chance to make it with you. *If* he measures up to your standards."

She nodded, reassured. Her eyes shone through her tears. "But if it doesn't work out...if...you know...it just doesn't work out...you will be here in Chicago waiting for me, won't you, Arnold? It's very important to me that I have a sense of our still having a home together."

"I'll keep the home fires burning, Ma."

"Oh, Arnold, you give me such courage."

"I've got something else to tell you. I've given up gambling. Gambling is a risky business. I'll start school again as soon as possible."

"Oh, I can't believe I'm hearing all this. You're so different lately. You've grown up. You feel responsible for other people. Believe me, you'll never be alone with your kind of love."

What could I say? The band was playing "The Tennessee Waltz." I asked Myrna if she wanted to dance. She was overjoyed. Hand in hand we walked down the sloping grass and onto the dance floor.

We danced without talking for a while. Myrna was deeply touched. Tears were in her eyes. "Will you do me a favor?" she asked.

"Anything you want, Ma."

"I knew you'd be willing. Spieler said I shouldn't ask you tonight, but I knew better. I knew the new grown-up Arnold Barzov wouldn't embarrass me by refusing."

"What is it, Myrna?"

"There's a girl here I want you to meet. Verna Simon's daughter Millie. So pretty and smart. All A's at Wisconsin. It won't hurt you to meet a nice girl for a change."

What could I say? Nothing that Myrn would understand. "You're right, Ma. It won't hurt to meet a nice girl for a change."

Oh, yeah. The Cubs didn't win the pennant. They *played* great, winning six of their last nine, losing three one-run heartbreakers, but the Dodgers were unstoppable, winning their last nine. Of course, if the Cubs hadn't screwed around so much, they would've won in a breeze. But I don't like to think about what might've been. And who's to say things would've been better if they'd been different? At least the fix was never exposed and none of the guys got in trouble.

The Cubs might not win a pennant for forty years but I'll learn to live with it. A diehard Cub fan can wait forever.

As for Myrna and Spieler, it's been a stormy affair but they've managed to stick together for over a year. Something in their chemistry is right for them, I guess. And there's no reason to think Uncle Pietro will ever know he rubbed out a couple of guys who didn't steal his money. Not as long as Kim's not around to tell him.

Kim. Did she really love me? I hope she did. I think she did. I want to believe everything she said and did was on account of it. It makes me think a lot of the time that maybe she was right when she said we could never make it together. If so — though I loved her so much — maybe things did work out best in the end.

It's something else I'll learn to live with.